PUNGO RIVER PASSAGE
AND OTHER STORIES

PUNGO RIVER PASSAGE AND OTHER STORIES

BYRON SHUTZ

To order additional copies of this book, contact:
Xlibris Corporation
1-888-795-4274
www.Xlibris.com
Orders@Xlibris.com
81664

Contents

Pungo River Passage 9

The Quarter-Mile 27

The Writing Workshop 41

Siblings 51

The Board Member 62

The Late Arrival 76

Going Back 81

Family 85

The Walnut Desk 101

Terror at the Door 122

Epilogue 187

Index of References Used in the Writing of Terror at the Door 195

Author's Notes 199

To my Children . . . .

Eleanor, Byron, Jr., Collin, Allison, and Lindley
and to my Grandchildren:

Tweedie
Ebby
Benton
Risa
Zac
Jake
Ava
Katherine
Ellie
Charlie
Christopher

Special thanks to my son, Collin Shutz, who designed the book covers and participated significantly in the final production of the book.

And most of all, I dedicate these stories to Marilyn, my wife and best friend. Her insightful suggestions and skillful editing contributed greatly to the final product.

Byron Shutz—2010

Pungo River Passage

Sam Johnson felt the old fear ignite in his gut, clawing at his self-respect, eroding his confidence. The closer he got to Bellevista, the more wary he became of going back.

Up ahead, the interstate glittered white-hot in the summer blaze. Almost five years now, since he'd last gone back, and that was when he'd laid his mother in the grave next to his father in a patch of ground set aside years ago for coloreds out east of town. Four generations of Johnsons rested there, the tops of their headstones poking above the straggly grass. The small burial place lay hunkered in against the shadowy-green backdrop of tall pines crowding the banks of the Pungo River.

Sam took a deep breath, and tried to relax. He'd always liked his younger cousin in Bellevista, Emma Mae Johnson, and looked after her, the best he could. The night of the assault, she'd called him, frantic and scared. Sam comforted her, saying he'd be there to help. But the fact is, he was enraged that she could be hurt that way. In the pocket of Sam's jacket on the car's back seat was a copy of the complaint report Emma Mae had signed. Sam knew the man she named, Billy Callison.

When the form arrived at the Division of Compliance—Department of Labor in Raleigh, where Sam was an inspector, his supervisor had called him into his office.

"Okay, Sam," his boss had said, after questioning him. "Go on down there, see what you can find out. Do it quietly, though. Just get the facts."

"That's all?" Sam asked. "But she's family. I got to do more than that. She doesn't have anyone else."

"If it happened the way she says it did, rape not harassment, then we've got no choice. I can understand her being frightened, the man being white. But even if she is too scared to file charges there, we'll still have to turn the case over to local authorities."

Sam ran the car windows down and turned off the air conditioner. He liked the way the dense summer air wrapped around his body, even though sweat was creeping down his back. The strong on-shore wind blustered flat against his face, buffeting the side of the car when he turned southward. The wind was shifting to the northeast, and farther out over the sound, the sky was darkening. That meant a storm was coming, maybe a gale, the kind that bends trees and floods the roads.

Thinking about Bellevista, Sam saw in his mind his old school for coloreds, a one-story frame building turned gray as a goat's whiskers, five rooms inside, privies on the outside, standing two blocks down the road beyond the red-brick building for whites. Each day, Sam had to walk past that school, looking straight ahead, hoping no one on the playground would pay him any attention.

That day as he headed home, there'd been no warning when the fragment of brick struck the side of his head. He'd cried out in pain. Heart pumping wildly as if he'd just clambered up a hill, Sam had turned to face the white boys bunched together, staring at him. One of them called out, "Hey, what's wrong, colored boy? That brick just fall out of the sky?" They laughed, and turned their backs, kicking a ball back and forth across the playground.

One boy, maybe two years older, chunky, wearing a cap pulled low over his eyes, left the playground and slowly walked toward Sam. His face had a surprised look. He stopped. It was Billy Callison, whose father worked on the shrimp boats. Billy's father wouldn't go out on the same boat with coloreds. Most everyone knew that.

"You're Sam Johnson, ain't you." Billy seemed more curious than threatening.

Sam nodded.

"You hurt bad?" Billy tilted his head back, as if to see Sam better from under the visor of his cap. Curious, he stared at the wound, the blood edging down onto Sam's forehead.

Sam let his books drop, and sat down on the ground. He leaned over, dizzy.

"Come on," Billy said. "I'll take you home. To your house. I'll go with you. In case you get sick, or something.

Sam didn't reply.

"I know where you live."

Sam looked up.

"Come on, I won't hurt you. You need to put some cold water on that. And a bandage."

Sam didn't move.

"My old man knows your old man. Leastwise, knows who he is."

After a moment, Sam stood up. He fished a cloth out of his pocket and held it against the bleeding.

"Come on," Billy said again, and started off. Sam followed, dragging along behind.

Looking back over his shoulder, Billy said, puzzled, "Your daddy owns his own boat. Hires other men to go shrimping with him. How'd he get to do that? Being colored."

"Don't know." Sam had never thought about it, but now he worried. What was it that his father did that was different?

When they reached Sam's house, Billy went inside with him, as if curious to see what Sam's mother would do. He watched while she doused Sam's head with cold tap water and fastened a kitchen towel around his head. When she asked Billy who'd done it, Billy just shrugged, and said, "Didn't see." She looked at him sharply, but said nothing further.

Not long after, someone snitched. Sam learned that it was Billy who had thrown the brick. Sam puzzled over that. Why would Billy throw the brick, then take him home to his mother? He never trusted Billy after that.

Mid-afternoon, feeling cramped from the long drive, legs aching to be stretched, Sam reached Bellevista. Along Jackson Avenue, bedraggled mansions broken up into apartments rose up above lawns weedy and disheveled, their verandas and pillared facades reminders of the old wealth that had fled Bellevista or been dissipated in later generations.

Sam took the river road past the boat repair yard. Shrimp boats, high and dry on wood blocks, squatted awkwardly, propped upright by timbers wedged against their hulls. Just beyond the boatyard stood the corrugated metal sides and flat tin roof of the seafood processing plant, cantilevered over the tidal waters of the river on massive wood pilings sunk in mud. A sun-bleached sign above the roof gutter along the front of the building spelled out "Seafari Crab & Shrimp" in mustard-yellow letters edged in peeling crimson. Inside the building, a dozen black women sat five days a week plus half-days on Saturday in season, picking white meat out of crabs delivered on one tray after another, until nothing was left but empty shells littering the table. The stink of dead sea-life fouled the air.

Sam turned his car into the processing plant parking lot. The wheels crackled over crushed oyster shells put down as gravel. A husky-throated whistle blasted the air. Break time. Women wearing bright-colored bandannas and stained cotton dresses sauntered out of the building two or three at a time.

Opening the car door, Sam swung his large frame out from under the wheel and took off his tie, already loosened. Standing next to the car, he looked around cautiously for Billy Callison, the plant foreman, but didn't see him.

Then he spotted his cousin, Emma Mae Johnson, standing off a little to one side, smoking a cigarette. She saw him, and her face said she was glad he was there, then her expression quickly clouded.

She dropped the cigarette and started toward him. Emma Mae moved in long, smooth strides, unhurried and loose. As tall as Sam, with a slim, fluid body, she removed the blue scarf wrapped about her head and tucked it, out of sight, into a pocket of the apron. Her hair, curled close to her head, glistened black, and the sun burnished her skin.

"Hey, Junior, what you know?" she asked in a slow, easy cadence, using his childhood name. Her arms and hands stayed loose at her side. "I've been waitin' for you, hoping you'd be comin' all right."

Sam stepped forward as she reached him and hugged her, wrapping his arms around her thin, hard body. She clung to him for a moment before letting go.

"How you gettin' along, Emma Mae? Holding up okay? Billy let you alone?"

"I just stay out of his way, make sure I got somebody with me. I'd quit, but don't hardly know where else I'd get a job. Things pretty slow 'round here." She paused. "Yeah, I'm going to make it, but I got to see he don't—"

"Big question is, Emma Mae, are you willing to testify?" Sam watched her face. "You got to tell what Billy did, tell it in court, tell it in front of other people. Because that's what it comes down to. That's what's got to be done."

Emma Mae drew a quick breath, closed her eyes tight. Then she looked back at Sam, her arms stiffening at her side. "Time comes, I'll tell. You just have to know I'll tell."

"That's good, that's good," Sam said, and with both hands reached out and clasped her shoulders. Suddenly his eyes were moist, and his voice caught in his throat. He struggled to get a wadded-up handkerchief out of his pocket.

Emma Mae lightly touched his arm. "Sure glad you're here, Sam. Sure glad to see you," she said, her inflection soft as a fresh breeze off the river.

After a moment, his voice steady, Sam said, "I want Billy to think this is routine, just a routine inspection. Safety compliance, health compliance, payroll records, things like that. You haven't told Tom Barber, have you? Tom still police chief?"

Emma Mae shook her head. "Don't you remember, Sam? Tom Barber's grandmother and Billy's grandmother were sisters. Tom and Billy are kin. No way I can tell Tom Barber about Billy."

Sam nodded. "I remember, now. That Tom, he always was mean. Just plain mean."

Emma Mae nodded, then glanced toward the door to Billy's office. "That's why I called you, filed that complaint, like you told me to, 'cause I figured I'd have no chance, no chance a all against Billy, against Tom Barber." She frowned. "You still think I did right? Think they'll put Billy in jail?"

"It isn't easy, proving something like this. It's your word, then his word. We need to find out whether he's assaulted anyone else in the plant, or maybe someplace else. It'll be rough, Emma Mae, things they'll say, and—"

"But Sam, what if no one—"

"Speaks up? I don't know. I'm not a lawyer. Whatever happens, my department will have to turn the case over to the locals when I get back." Sam thought a moment. "You'll have to file criminal charges. I'll help, if you want."

Emma Mae made no sign. "Did you know that?" Sam asked. "Criminal charges. Understand that?" Looking away, as if distracted, Emma Mae nodded.

"Oh, Sam, I'm—" Then suddenly her eyes widened, her face tensed, and under her breath she said, "Better be get'n back. Come to my house after dark, so we can talk some more." She walked away.

Sam turned around and saw Billy Callison standing at the top of the steps outside his office door. A puzzled expression on Billy's face leaped the distance between them. His lips moved, but nothing came out, and he squinted as if looking into the sun. Then, surfacing from whatever dark depths he had plummeted into, Billy replaced his normal scowl with a forced grin, waved, and called out, "Sam Johnson! Whatever brings you to town? Come on in, come on in."

Following Billy into the cramped office, Sam sat down on a folding chair across from Billy's battered desk. Sam smelled the sweet, elusive odor of raw crabmeat and shrimp, not yet iced.

Billy leaned his hefty body back in the chair, springs squealing from the weight, and plopped his feet onto the top of the desk. He had the makings of a big belly from too much beer and fried food. The sleeves of his red-plaid shirt were rolled up above the elbows, and his muscular forearms were glazed with rust-red hair, the skin reddened from the sun.

"Well, Sam, you here checking up on us again?"

"You know how the government works, Billy." Sam smiled slightly, looking relaxed, and clasped his hands in his lap as innocently as if he were sitting in a pew at church. "Got to be sure all the rules are being followed."

He felt himself slipping into the old self-deprecating way of talking to a white man, the way blacks had always protected themselves, letting whites feel superior. He detested this lapse, and fought to overcome it.

"Yep. Guess that's the way it is." Billy gazed at Sam, his expression flat, then said, "Well, how 'bout a touch of bourbon, 'fore you get to work?"

Sam disliked drinking whiskey. It made him drowsy, and he needed to stay alert. But accepting might dilute any suspicions in Billy's mind.

"Can't hardly say no to that, Billy."

Billy reached down alongside the desk, pulled out a bottom drawer, metal screeching on harsh metal, and swept up in one big hand a bottle and two shot glasses.

After pouring the drinks, Billy looked at Sam as if for the first time.

Sam was dressed in a white shirt, the wrinkled collar held down with tiny buttons at the corners. His sleeves were rolled back to just below his elbows. The large wristwatch he wore on a gold expansion bracelet glinted yellow against his dark skin. Sam's trousers were creased, his black socks straight, and his shoes polished beneath the dust.

Feeling Billy's gaze taking him in, Sam tried to guess what Billy might be thinking. Was he envious? Did he resent that Sam must be making a lot more money than Billy made? Sam had left town, gone to college, gotten a good job with the government. After twenty years, he had status, security, and recognition as a man who did his job well.

Sam was an officer of the government of North Carolina. He had the power of the state behind him. Billy must resent that power, Sam figured. Billy must be angry that Sam Johnson, that colored boy whose daddy once owned a shrimp boat, could threaten Billy Callison, could make him comply with state laws for food processing, could make life bad for Billy.

But whatever Billy was thinking, he kept quiet and finished his drink.

"You know, Billy," Sam said, breaking the silence, "On the way into town I was thinking about that time once when you helped me out, long time ago."

It was a moment before Billy said, "Yeah, I remember," his voice flat.

"Well, I appreciate that, what you did." Sam looked down at the floor, then raised his eyes to Billy's. "What I don't understand, exactly, is why you never owned up to me that you were the one who threw that piece of brick."

Billy picked up the whiskey bottle and the two shot glasses in one hand, leaned down, and opened the desk's bottom drawer. Speaking with his face averted, he said, "I don't rightly remember everything that happened back then." The bottle and glasses rattled as he dropped them into the drawer, then he sat back up again. "Guess you ought to get on with your work, Sam. I've got things I need to be doing, too." Billy stood up, shoved his chair aside, and stepped around the end of the desk.

Then, Billy seemed to raise himself up high, straightening his shoulders, tilting his head back. Even though he was no taller, Sam felt that Billy was looking down on him, as if Sam was nobody.

After he'd finished inspecting the plant for any violations, Sam checked into the musty, two-story brick hotel downtown, ignoring the desk clerk's air of insolence. He went up to the room, clicked on the ceiling fan, took a shower, changed clothes, and sat in a chair where he could look out the window and do some thinking before time for supper.

His father had worked a shrimp boat almost to his last days. That's how he'd sent Sam to college. His father had once told him that the sea grapples with a man when it gets angry, like two men wrestling, tugging and straining until one or the other is whipped.

With its great strength, the sea tosses a boat fore and aft, the blunt-edged bow plunging into the waves, spraying white water to either side. Then the sea sends another wave, catching the vessel unaware on its flank and sweeping under its hull, so that the fisherman struggles to keep his balance against the fast-rising deck. Like a dog shaking a rat in its mouth, the sea knows the force of its grasp, and won't let go.

When Sam was about seven years old, they had sat one evening, silent, on the top step of the front porch of the pine-boarded house where they lived, listening to the cicadas chirping in the twilight. Sam's father had told him he'd show his son, right there on the porch, how to ride the deck of a shrimp boat. So he stood up, and bent his knees as if he was absorbing the upward roll of the deck, then straightened his legs, locking the knees momentarily to match the deck falling away beneath him as the boat rolled again. Sam got up, too, and standing next to his father, tried to imitate his father's movements. Next, they pretended it was a really big wave sweeping toward them. They bent their knees almost to the floor, and rocked back and forth to meet the ceaseless motion of the seas rolling under the porch. The wood floor creaked beneath them with the shifting weight of their bodies.

Suddenly, his father had reached down and lifted Sam up, setting him high on his shoulder. Sam and his father busted out laughing, laughing so loud that Sam's sides hurt.

Whenever Sam thought about that time on the porch, he remembered all those years he'd gone out on the shrimp boat with his father, and he was proud of what his father had made of himself.

By nightfall, the wind was straight out of the northeast, moaning through the pines. Sam left the hotel and drove the blacktop east out of town until he reached the red-clay county road that parallels the river. He sensed rather than saw the low-lying clouds rushing past overhead through the dark sky. When he turned off the road, shallow ruts led him through the grove of trees to Emma Mae's house.

Emma Mae lived alone in the small house she had grown up in, five miles down river on the north bank, out where the pines grew straight and tall and softened the ground with sweet-scented needles.

A shabby dock used by commercial fishermen lay just beyond Emma Mae's place. Three or four shrimp boats were tied up alongside, bows into the ebbing tide, sterns into the flood, spring lines taut against the pull.

Sam's car moved like a whisper over the pine needles. He parked next to Emma Mae's battered two-door Chevy, and saw the light yellowing the window curtains. He walked toward the door. Out on the river, where the wind had a broad, unchecked sweep, white caps danced like demons.

"Who is it?" Emma Mae called out when he knocked, not a friendly, "Come on in, Junior," like he'd expected.

Emma Mae was sitting in a chair at the bare kitchen table as he opened the door, no glass or coffee mug in front of her. The only light in the room was a shaded lamp behind her, leaving her face in shadows. Sam closed the door, stepped closer and started to speak when the look on her face hit him as if he'd been punched in the stomach.

Then a man's low voice said, "Sit down at the table, Sam," and Billy Callison stepped out from behind the drop cloth concealing Emma Mae's walk-in closet. A double-barreled shotgun, the barrels sawed off short, came out first, held low in his hands, at waist level. Sam stared at Billy's thick forearms, the rolled-up sleeves of the red plaid shirt, the curly chest hairs visible where the shirt gaped open at the top, and his gaze rose to Billy's face. Sam couldn't see Billy's eyes, the lids had closed down so, and sweat gleamed on his forehead. The smell of whiskey was strong. His hands gripped the shotgun hard, as if it might suddenly buck on him.

Billy motioned with the barrel of the shotgun toward the other chair across the table from Emma Mae. "Sit down, Sam," he said again, more forcefully.

"Got a situation here, ain't we," Billy added accusingly, "which you done made. You think you know what's going on, but you don't." He stared at Emma Mae. "He don't know, does he, Emma Mae."

"No, Billy, no. Don't, Billy. Leave it alone."

"But you're the one brought him to town. You said things that weren't true. You got everything all mixed up."

Emma Mae covered her face, and began to weep.

"Let her alone, Billy," Sam said. "She hasn't done anything."

Billy sneered. "That's what you think. How 'bout it, Emma Mae? He don't know, does he?"

"But you wouldn't let me be, Billy. I told you I couldn't be with you no more, but you wouldn't—"

"I said it weren't just your choice to make. I got rights, too. You can't just change your mind one day, and say that's it, no more, you want to end it. You can't just put me out the door like takin' the trash out, and—"

"But I couldn't go on, Billy, all that sneaking around, folks watching, maybe suspecting."

As her voice rose in anguish, Sam stood up and started toward Emma Mae. He needed to help her, protect her. Billy saw the movement, turned quickly, and swung the shotgun around toward Sam. Emma Mae rose out of her chair. Sam stopped, facing Billy, who was swaying on his feet. The blast reverberated, violating the small room, and pellets tore into the wall to one side at Sam's back. Billy looked startled, then frightened.

"Oh, Sam," Emma Mae sobbed, and sank back into her chair at the table.

"See what you done, Sam, see what you done?" Billy's voice rose, frenzied. "You come all the way from Raleigh, Sam, pokin' your head into somethin' private between Emma Mae and me, somethin' that don't concern you." He sucked for air. "You and those nosy government people takin' it onto yourself to change things around here." His hands holding the shotgun shook with anger and frustration, his face distorted. "Why should I put up with all that shit?" he shouted at Sam. "Why should I be takin' that shit all the time?"

'Way in the back of his mind, where it was very quiet, Sam was trying to make sense out of what was happening. He'd lived for years with feelings just like those Billy was describing. But right now he tasted how bad that thinking was, and he was scared.

"Now slow up, Billy, slow up a little," Sam began. "I don't think—"

"I don't give a shit what you think. I'm fed up with all the crap I put up with. I'm through talkin' and givin' in and makin' changes—adjustments, ain't that what you people call it? Adjustments? Well, I've had it, all the way up to here!" With his free hand, Billy slashed across his throat.

"Come on now, Billy, you don't mean no harm to Emma Mae and me." Sam fought for time, trying to penetrate to wherever Billy's sensibilities might lie. "We've known each other a long time, since we were kids, and I—"

"B-u-l-l shit!" Billy spat out, his body trembling, and glared at Sam. "Get up!" he shouted. "Let's go!"

He pointed the shotgun's barrel toward the door. Emma Mae, startled, only half rose, and Billy kicked the chair out from under her so vehemently it clattered against the wall opposite. He fumbled in his pants pocket, pulled out a new shell, broke open the breech, and replaced the spent shell. He snapped the gun closed, and cocked one of the hammers. It was an old-model 10-gauge, built for bird shooting, but at close range the pellets would tear a hole in a man.

As they stumbled out the door into the shriek of the wind, Sam kept thinking of that cocked hammer. Particles of grit swept up by the wind from pine needles on the ground grated against his teeth, and he tried to spit them out.

"Go to the docks!" Billy shouted, and poked the end of the steel barrel into Sam's back. Emma Mae gasped, and groped for Sam's arm, clutching tight when she found it.

The sound of the waves smacking against the dock pilings came from just ahead. Sam could barely make out the looming shapes of the shrimp boats tied alongside, moving fitfully on stretched dock lines. Waves bludgeoned the windward sides of the hulls, and the outgoing tide sweeping along the shore exerted a constant pull.

"Over there!" Billy hollered, pointing with his free hand toward the shrimp boat tied up last in line, down river.

"Billy," Sam called out against the fury of the wind, "this isn't going to do any good. Can't you see that?" He gulped for air. "Let's go back to the house, sit down, talk about it."

Angrily, Billy kicked Sam from behind, his boot striking Sam in the buttocks. Sam arched backward as he fell forward, legs thrashing to keep him on his feet. Emma Mae's cry was gagged by the wind.

"Keep movin', Sam," Billy lashed out.

Within steps they reached the boat. High above, the steel outriggers holding the nets towered skyward, locked in place, swaying dizzily with the boat's motion. The hauling lines, fastened at both ends, were plucked madly by the wind, slapping against the outrigger poles. The boat groaned as the waves shoved the hull against the dock. The strong odor of dead fish and seawater, damp wood and diesel fuel, choked the air.

Sam helped Emma Mae struggle over the side and onto the deck.

"Back there," Billy commanded, nodding toward the stern. Sam put his arm around Emma Mae, and together they stumbled over the clutter on the deck, groping their way to the aft deck. It was open on three sides, the deck rail set low so nets could be hauled over the sides.

Billy stepped up to the ship's wheel, and turned the ignition switch. The diesel responded eagerly, rumbling deep in the boat's vitals. Cooling water from the engine belched out the exhaust pipe at the stern into the face of the current. Emma Mae faced Sam, fear in her eyes, and clutched her hands to her mouth to keep back a cry of panic. Sam felt cornered, but he was determined they'd find a way out.

"Sam, go forward," Billy bellowed over his shoulder. "Let go the bow line and the after spring. Then come back".

Because the tide was pushing the bow hard against the dock, both lines slipped easily off the piling. Billy put the engine in reverse, spun the wheel to port, and stepped back to the stern.

The he bowline free, he slipped the stern line and then the forward spring. The current caught the boat's stern like a starving dog catches a tossed scrap of meat, and the vessel swung out and away from dock. Billy shifted into forward, shoved the throttle as far as it would go, and spun the wheel to starboard. The boat moved out into the channel, headed toward the open Sound. The noise of the wind and the seas smashing against the hull all but drowned the pounding of the diesel.

Pellets of spray struck their faces. It was no good jumping overboard. They couldn't make shore. Sam was certain that Billy would shoot them and dump them over the side for the tide to carry their bodies out to sea. He struggled against a mounting feeling of defeat.

At wide-open throttle the boat plunged ahead toward the deep waters of the Sound a quarter-mile ahead. The deck beneath their feet trembled from the vibration of the hull forcing its way through the water. The seas were steep, tossed into confusion up, back, and sideways by the outgoing tide running against the wind's ferocity.

Desperately, Sam looked around for something, anything, to use as a weapon. Lengths of line, crumpled dock fenders, and piles of strangled nets sprawled in a jumble on the deck at the stern, but they were limp, useless.

Spray came in sudden sheets as Sam and Emma Mae crouched against the starboard side of the boat, clinging to the gunwale to keep from being tossed around.

"Don't give up," Sam called into her ear, and pulled her up against him. "Watch for anything. Anything that might happen. To give us a chance."

Grasping for a handhold, Sam felt instead a long-handled iron gaff hook mounted on the underside of the deck rail. Billy peered over the cabin roof, squinting against the blinding rain. He still gripped the shotgun in his left hand; his right hand clutched the straining ship's wheel.

Sam fumbled to unsnap the gaff hook, finally freed it, but didn't remove it. Emma Mae felt the movement of his arm, sensed what he was doing. Her body tightened, as if coiled like a spring.

Suddenly, the boat shuddered and canted sharply to starboard. Solid cold water crashed over Sam and Emma Mae. A bell clanged violently as the boat careened off a monstrous red buoy, looming like a tower higher than the cabin roof, grinding against the port side along the entire length of the boat before disappearing off the stern into blackness.

The steel shaft of the outrigger wrenched loose and crashed to the deck, the top dragging alongside in a tangle of nets. When the boat pitched forward again, the stern lifted high in the air and the propeller rose clear of water. Momentarily freed of its burden, spinning wild, it gave off a high-pitched shriek.

Sam leaped up, the gaff hook gripped in both hands. He spread his legs wide, knees bent to absorb the wild pitching of the deck. Billy, trying to keep the bow head-on, did not look back.

Sam watched the oncoming seas for the next valley between cresting waves that would give him an instant of steadier decks. When the valley formed, he staggered forward the few steps to where Billy stood and swung the gaff hook with all his strength. The blow struck Billy on the side of his head with a solid whack that Sam could not hear but felt in tremors traveling through the shaft into the palms of his hands.

The boat veered and was caught broadside by an oncoming wave. Like hoisting a bucket to toss the contents overboard, the deck of the boat lifted and catapulted Billy over the low deck rail. He was gone.

Sam threw himself against the wheel, struggling to force the ship's rudder against the next wall of water rising against them. For one terrible moment, they lay broadside to the towering wave. Then the propeller dug deep into the trough where the boat hovered. As if summoning its strength, the boat quivered, its beam-ends straining against each other as the bow rose against the massive oncoming wave.

Struggling to turn the boat toward shore, Sam swung the rudder hard over to port. With the diesel thundering, the shrimp boat grudgingly came about and put her stern into the next big wave. Abruptly they found themselves on the downward sloping face of the great mass of water rushing beneath them. Sam spun the wheel back to center, and the boat glided swiftly forward, seas tumbling under it from astern.

Emma Mae lay on her stomach on the deck near the helm, welding her body to the wood decking by clinging to the hatch cover, her feet braced against the gunwale while sea water swirled on the deck around her.

Sam fought to maintain their stern to the oncoming seas, and searched the darkness for a landmark that would identify the river entrance. He had lost all sense of time.

The ragged stone parapet of the breakwater at the channel entrance gradually emerged from the slanting rain and haze, as if pulled back from oblivion. Sam then pointed the trawler's bow toward the surge flowing out through the channel.

A powerful ocean swell from astern overtook them, lifting the hull of the boat like a father hoisting his small child onto his shoulder, and carried them with a sweeping rush into the channel waters.

Once inside the river entrance, the terrible force of the seas subsided. Time reasserted itself once more. The wind, unabated at gale strength, churned up the water about them, but the landmass to either side crippled its force. Through the blackness, the rain gradually slackened.

Emma Mae struggled to her feet, and went below. She came back, still shivering, with a blanket wrapped around her shoulders. Standing next to Sam at the wheel, she grasped the binnacle with one hand for support.

Sam was the first to speak, his voice raspy from strain and his emotions drained. "Why, Emma Mae? Why? That's what I don't understand."

"Why Billy? Is that what you want to know?"

"And what really happened."

Keeping her eyes directed into the darkness ahead, rather than look at Sam, Emma Mae said, "I know. I know it don't seem right. I went to see him 'bout a job, maybe a year ago. Hadn't been able to find much of anything, what with the town dying and so many out of work. Figured he'd know me, 'cause I'd seen him couple of times noticing me, when I was at the town docks, buying catch off the boats."

Sam turned his head, and scanned Emma Mae's face, as if hoping to learn more than her words told him.

"Billy hired me, ahead of some others, I guess, and taught me how to pick out the crab meat, working fast, the way they want it done." Then she added, "He was nice to me, Sam. He was, that's for sure. I got so I wasn't afraid of him any more."

"But he—"

"He got to bringing me things out to my house, thoughtful things like, oh, I don't know, a cured ham once, fresh-cut beans, things like that."

"But, Emma Mae, you—"

"I asked him in once for coffee. He was my boss, so seemed like it was okay to do that. I was careful, no doubt of that. But we got to talking, you know, 'bout different folks in town, what it was like when we were kids growing up. Billy seemed to like talking about that."

Sam heard the warmth in her voice.

"After a time," Emma Mae continued, "Billy looked to have changed a little, like maybe he wasn't the Billy I once thought he was. Feelings grew between us, not enough to notice right off, but I can't say it wasn't so."

Then, as if answering a question Sam hadn't asked, she said, "I didn't do anything I didn't want to do, Sam. I got to accept that. My fault, much as his."

"What happened next? Between you. To make things go bad."

"One morning, I woke up after Billy had left, and realized we was headed for nothing but trouble. He was coming to my house only after dark. There was no place we could go together without being seen. Not around here. At the plant, when I was working, he tried not to let on how he felt, but I think that sometimes, the way he looked at me—well, I worried it might—"

Pointing ahead, Sam called out, "Look, that's your place, off to the right, there, see it?"

Emma Mae nodded. After a moment, she continued, as if determined to purge herself of what she knew. "So, last time he came to see me, I told him. Told him we had to stop. Told him it was no good for both of us." Emma Mae trembled, pulling the blanket tighter around her shoulders.

"What did he say?"

"Billy got real angry. Said I couldn't do that. Said he liked me a lot. Said he didn't want to stop seein' me." She stared into the gloom, silent, as if that was all of it.

Then, still not looking at Sam, she said, "About two weeks passed. I just paid him no attention at work, and he let me alone. Then, end of the afternoon one day, he told me to come into his office. Said he wanted to talk to me. We argued. Billy just got madder. He finally wasn't listening. By the time I'd said all I could say, and started to leave, there wasn't no one else left at the plant except him and me." Emma Mae stopped, and was silent. "You know the rest," she finally said. "It was mostly like I told you, that night I called."

The boat was approaching shore. Sam sent Emma Mae forward to handle the bow line as they edged in toward the dock, against the still-ebbing tide. Line secured, the boat dropped back with the current. Sam put a spring line in place while Emma Mae went aft to secure the stern.

Suddenly, she cried out and turned away from the deck rail. Sam ran to the rail and looked down into the water alongside. Trailing along the port side was a long tangle of net still fastened at one end to the outrigger pole, torn loose when the bell buoy scraped along the boat's hull. Clearly visible through the webbing near the stern was the pale, luminous face of Billy Callison, hair matted, eyes staring. His body was shrouded in the snarled fishing net, his arms reaching above his head as if still grabbing for something solid when the harsh saltwater invaded his lungs.

Emma Mae and Sam looked at each other. She grabbed both of his arms, her voice trembling. "What are we goin' to do, Sam? What are we goin' to do?"

Sam stood motionless, looking off, as if to some other place.

Emma Mae's words, low and urgent, barely reached him. "Sam, let's go—let's go to Florence County, down to Florence County, below the state line." Her grip on his arms tightened. "There's Johnsons down there. Johnsons like us, out in the country. They'd hide us, I know for sure they'd hide us." Her voice rose, beseeching. "We'd have time, Sam, have time to—"

Sam turned and stared at her, then shook his head, slowly. "No good, Emma Mae. It'd be no good." He stepped back from her. "Come too far. I'm not going back, not starting over."

"Not going back? Not going back? Sam, you can't ever, ever leave that behind. You can't ever get rid of it." She turned, looking out past the side of the boat, back toward her house, concealed in shadows. "They're going to say we killed Billy. Killed Billy. Can't you see that, Sam? Don't you just know that?"

"I can't think, Emma Mae. I can't think. There's got to be a way." Sam smothered his face with his hands, rubbing his eyes, trying to push away dismay, so he could face what needed to be done.

As if talking to himself, Sam said, "Can't call Tom Barber, not Tom Barber, not with Billy dead down there in the water, Billy his kin. No telling what Tom Barber might do, policeman or no policeman."

"But where're you going to turn, Sam?" Her voice was flat. "We got to do something. Billy won't just go away. Who else can help us? Who else, Sam?"

Sam's face brightened. "I know, I know who. Eddie Lee. Eddie Lee. He's State Highway Patrol. Eddie Lee, he's black. Met him in Raleigh, a seminar, last year."

"But how's he going to help, Sam? What can he do?"

"Eddie's at the District Station in Calhoun, maybe twenty miles from here. I can call him."

"But what if he's not there, what if he's gone?"

"We'll find out. We first got to find out. Let's get back to your house, call him, see what he can do."

Sam found the number in the directory, and dialed.

"Off duty?" he repeated into the phone. "I'll wait, I'll wait." Excited, and turning to Emma Mae, Sam said, "He was just walking out the door, going home. They said they'd catch him."

When Eddie Lee came to the phone, Sam told him who he was, where they were calling from, why they needed help. When he set the phone back in its cradle, the hand piece was wet with sweat stains.

"Less than half an hour. They'll be here. Eddie and his partner." Sam seemed unable to get his breath. "They won't call Tom Barber on the car radio until just before they get to town. That way they'll get here before Tom." Sam dropped into a chair at the kitchen table, his body drained of energy, his legs without feeling. "Said for us to stay right here. Don't do nothing." He laughed, a little out of control "What else we'd do? Where else we got to go? I don't know, I just don't know."

Emma Mae went to the cabinet, got out coffee mugs, ran water into the coffee maker, scooped coffee out of a can, turned on the butane stove, and set the pot on the burner. They waited, not talking, thinking about what might happen.

When Eddie Lee turned off the clay road and pulled up quietly next to the house, the white muslin curtains at the window turned crimson, then paled to white, then red again as the revolving red light on the patrol car caught the house in its gyrations.

Sam stepped outside to meet them. Eddie's partner was white, but Sam guessed that would be okay. They walked down to the docks, Emma Mae with them, and Sam pointed to where Billy lay in the water, wrapped in the nets. Tom Barber arrived not long after. Eddie and his partner were very professional, even though they coolly deferred to Tom Barber, letting him take the lead, since this was Tom's jurisdiction. Sam told again what had happened, starting with when he got to Emma Mae's house after supper.

Eddy then walked out onto the dock to show Tom where Billy was. Tom stayed there awhile. He took pictures, the flash bulbs exploding in the black night with fleeting brilliance. When he came back, he asked more questions.

Eddie Lee then helped Tom Barber untangle Billy, cutting the net with a knife to set him free. Tom put his hands under Billy's arms at the shoulders, lifting him up so Eddie could reach down and grab Billy's legs. They hauled Billy out of the water onto the dock. The back of Billy's head was hard against Tom's stomach, forcing Billy's chin down against his chest, the red plaid shirt stained dark with seawater. Then they laid him on the dock. Billy looked like a stranger in Billy's clothes, oddly forlorn, Sam thought, stretched out on his back, legs close together.

Tom Barber told them there'd be a coroner's inquest. Sam and Emma Mae ought to get a lawyer, not leave the county, and they must call his office each day to check in.

Some weeks later, the coroner's jury acquitted Sam and Emma Mae of responsibility for Billy's death. Soon after, Emma Mae sold her house and left Bellevista. She didn't get a whole lot for it, but maybe enough to begin a new life in Carthage, a long way from Bellevista.

Sam goes back to Bellevista now and then, to visit the cemetery on the bank of the Pungo River. His father's house, with the wide front porch, is still there. Couple of years after Billy's death, when he learned the house was up for sale, Sam bought the old place. It sits there empty, and Sam can't tell you for sure what he's going to do with it.

The Quarter-Mile

Gasping from a practice run, Danny stumbled off the indoor track. His lungs heaved, desperate for air. Leg muscles cried out in spasms of pain. He bent over, to ease the pain, and wiped sweat from his eyes with his T-shirt. He checked the stopwatch on his wrist. Better, but not great. A long way yet to go.

Located in a subterranean area beneath the gym at Selby Hall, a boarding school for boys, the track bed was dirt, banked steeply on the turns against the stone foundation. The track was dry, but the air smelled of earth, as if damp and newly dug, and of sweat from the runners. Sallow light from naked bulbs suspended from the low ceiling dwindled away before reaching the ground.

Danny, fourteen, paced back and forth, swinging his arms, his mouth slack, face strained and pale, then flopped onto a wood bench. His older brother, Ted, now dead, had set a new quarter-mile record in high school back home. Danny had seen the taut cord snap when his brother's chest broke through it at the finish line. Ted excelled at everything. But Danny was not a natural athlete. If he could do this one thing, at least match Ted's record, he could show what he was worth. Maybe his father would look at him differently.

Stretching his legs out in front of him, Danny leaned back, and raised his arms above his head. Then he reached forward to touch the toes of his track shoes. For a moment, he held that position, his eyes closed, as normal breathing began to return.

When he opened his eyes and sat up, Ferris, a senior, was standing close in front of him. Hands on hips, feet apart, Ferris smiled, scornfully. He wore blue running shorts and a sleeveless undershirt, clammy with perspiration. Taller than Danny, Ferris had the legs of a runner, long and muscular. As he played with the towel around his neck, pulling the ends back and forth, the biceps in his arms rippled.

"Danny boy, I want you to do something for me. Tomorrow, after class." A senior, Ferris could order freshmen to do whatever he wanted. Hazing was a school tradition. Faculty looked the other way. Other acts violated published rules, but went unreported, undetected.

Tucked into the waistband of Ferris's shorts, hidden by his undershirt, was a small plastic case. Glancing around, but seeing none of the coaching staff, Ferris took out a hand-rolled cigarette, lit it, and furtively dropped the blackened match inside the case. Taking a deep drag, he cupped his hand around the cigarette, hiding it.

A sweet aroma drifted toward Danny, as if to ensnare him. He quickly stood up, and stepped to one side, away from the haze.

But Ferris moved with him, standing in his way, his chest inches from Danny. "I want you to make a run into town for me," he said. His eyes searched Danny's, as if deciding whether he could trust him with such a mission.

Two years older, Ferris was known for his sarcasm, his cockiness. Sycophants latched onto his self-assured, aggressive style, hoping to gain a step up in the inevitable hierarchy among students.

But Danny feared Ferris. Soon after he arrived at Selby, Ferris had summoned Danny and his roommate, Nicholas, to Ferris's room on the top floor of the dorm. Ferris and two other seniors were waiting for them. Ferris held a polished, black leather belt, the length of his arm. He told the boys to face the wall, lean over, place their hands on their knees, and keep quiet. Just a little introduction, Ferris said.

With each blow, there was a whoosh, then a whack as the leather struck, sounding like the flat of a hand slapping the surface of water. Danny held his breath before each stroke, and winced when the blow landed, but did not cry out. No one spoke after the beating began. To Danny, the air in the room was stifling, dense with the injustice of the act. When the ordeal ended, Danny and Nicholas returned to their room, walking stiff-legged, their faces rigid.

Now, at the track, looking up at Ferris's expression, Danny was scared. He felt helpless against Ferris's physical strength and authority.

Suddenly, the shrill ring of the school bell exploded in the air.

"Gotta go, Danny boy," Ferris said, "but tell you what, I'll catch you tomorrow." He grinned, as if savoring the power he held. "You can count on it."

Not long after Danny arrived at Selby Hall, Nicholas, his roommate, told him about an upcoming fight. From a stall in the dorm washroom, unobserved by two boys whispering together, Nicholas had learned about it. Ferris and another senior had agreed to settle their argument at the end of athletic period that same day. The fight was to take place in the shooting range, a long, narrow room secluded in a basement area beneath empty classrooms. Stone walls would muffle the sounds. Fights, against school rules, were kept secret, yet word leaked out.

Danny and Nicholas decided to risk it. Still in their sweats, they drifted unnoticed by any of the teachers down the basement steps and through the dank passage leading to the rifle range. Others were already there, talking quietly but nervously, waiting for Ferris and his opponent to show up.

Windowless, with a low ceiling, the room was musty, claustrophobic. Thick, gray canvas padding covered the floor from wall to wall where the riflemen lay, knelt, or stood when firing at paper targets at the far end of the range, now black. Nicholas nudged Danny toward one wall where they would be on the outside of the circle.

Ferris appeared at the door. Students nearby fell back to make way. Supporters gave a muted cheer. Ferris grinned and stripped to tennis shorts and jogging shoes. Self-assured, he did deep knee bends, arms outstretched for balance. His lean body was muscular, pale-white in the dim light.

There was a stir at the door. His opponent, a senior nicknamed Buck, strode into the room. He was also wearing shorts and jogging shoes. Slightly shorter than Ferris, he was heavier, solid, a scrappy hockey player. Buck ignored Ferris's showing off and leaned against a metal column, waiting for the fight to begin.

A senior named Price agreed to referee. He'd end the fight when it had gone far enough, he said. There were no rounds. The fight lasted until one of them quit.

Price looked around, then said "Okay, let's go!".

Ferris and Buck approached each other, arms bent in the boxer's stance, bare fists clenched, bodies turned a little to one side, heads down, eyes watchful. The other boys backed off just enough to give them room.

Ferris, the aggressor took a sharp jab at his opponent's face, struck instead the defensive arm quickly raised, but followed with a left blow, low, into the gut that landed solidly. Shouts of "Atta boy, get him!" came from those backing him. Buck recoiled, but immediately charged forward, his head low, and struck Ferris on the side of the head with a strong blow. Ferris's head jerked. He came back with a vicious right-handed jab striking Buck on the nose and cheek, opening a cut below the eye. Dark blood ran from his nose, down onto his upper lip. Buck licked it away.

Back and forth they fought, grunting, panting, sweat glistening on their chests and backs, pummeling each other with spurts of fury and strength. Price did not interfere. Danny and Nicholas watched, fascinated by the raw spectacle so close at hand, uneasy with the ferocity of the fight, thankful it wasn't happening to them.

Both Ferris and Buck gasped for breath, inhaling gulps of air. Rivulets of sweat were inflamed with blood. Faces bore ugly blue stains and cuts above the eyes and on the cheekbones. Ferris pulled back, as if to turn away. Buck, weakened, his vision blurred by swelling around both eyes, lowered his guard a few inches. Ferris suddenly aimed a straight right with all his remaining strength at Buck's head, which jerked back. His arms fell, he leaned forward, dropped to his knees, and toppled slowly forward onto forearms and elbows, where he remained bent over, gasping, beaten.

"Okay, that's enough," Price said evenly.

Staggering, Ferris raised his arms over his head, clenched his hands together in victory, walked a few steps, dazed, and sat heavily against one wall. Someone handed him a towel. He draped it over his shoulders, head lowered onto his chest, still breathing with difficulty.

Buck's friends helped him up and into a sweatshirt. They led him into the nearby washroom. When he was able to walk, they would take him to his room by a back way where they'd not be seen. Tomorrow, when his face would have begun to heal, he would not talk about the fight. He'd just reply that a few knocks he'd taken at hockey practice had been rougher than usual. If the administration learned about the fight, both he and Ferris would be kicked out. After four years at Selby Hall, graduation at the end of the year was too close to let that happen.

The raw violence of the fight stuck with Danny.

At 11:30 on Friday the bell rang shrill through the halls, liberating students from their last morning class. Corridors filled. Books under his arms, Danny sauntered in the direction of the mail room, and peered through the miniature window in the brass mail box bearing his number.

Seeing a white envelope inside, he twirled the dial until the combination clicked. Last week his father had written, only a brief note, but warm, saying that he missed Danny. He pulled from the box a thick envelope, in his mother's handwriting, smelling distantly of sage. He guessed that newspaper clippings were enclosed, conveying local news she thought would interest him. He put the envelope, unopened, in a side pocket of his trousers, where he kept loose coins.

Only a few students were visible in the coat room. Danny scanned the bulletin board until they left, then stepped inside, looking for Ferris in the weak light. Ferris had told Danny to meet him there at class break. He walked tentatively toward the far end of the room that turned into an ell, with additional coat racks. The dank smell of wool coats and body odor pervaded the air.

Danny sensed a presence behind him. Turning, he confronted a grinning Ferris within arm's reach.

"Surprised you, huh?" Ferris chortled at his own craftiness. "Glad to see you showed up, ol' buddy!" Hands on hips, he leered at Danny, transfixing the younger boy.

Danny's heart pulsated. He could barely think.

Ferris reached into his inside coat pocket and pulled something out, hidden in his hand. "Here, stupid," he said, and stretched out his hand toward Danny, palm down, fingers closed around the object.

Danny slowly advanced his hand and took the roll of bills from Ferris.

"There's fifty-five bucks there. I'm getting some stuff for other guys, too. See that you don't lose it. I'll meet you here after supper tonight. Understand?"

Danny nodded, crammed the money into his back pocket and buttoned the flap.

In a low voice, Ferris gave instructions where to go. "Be careful! I've told you exactly what to say. Don't screw up!"

Danny was unable to reply. Ferris's lean face was ominous. "If you get caught," he added derisively, "don't rat on me, scum bag. I'll deny it. So will the other guys. Understand?" With that, Ferris turned and walked out. Danny remained frozen until he could pull himself together and leave the coat room.

That afternoon, no classes or required activities were scheduled. Students could walk into town if they signed out in the headmaster's office. Danny asked Nicholas to go with him, but said nothing more.

The snow-packed trail into town dropped off the edge of campus down a steep hill through new growths of timber, along the railroad tracks and across the bridge over Stone Mill Creek. The two boys talked about the upcoming hockey game and girls they had met at social functions with Selby Hall's sister school nearby. Nicholas was also a new boy. The two boys backed each other up, toughed out the hazing. They learned to stay out-of-sight, follow the rules, and take what came without bitching. Next year, as "old boys", they would be free.

Once across the bridge, the road into town stumbled through an industrial area and past shanties where the town's few black families lived. No one was in sight. On a corner near the railroad tracks stood Mike's Lunch, a battered two-story frame building next to an empty lot. Dry fragments of white paint, edges curled back like birch bark, clung to the scabrous siding. Shoveled mounds of snow on either side of the cinder path to the door were blackened by coal dust from trains rumbling by.

Mike lived in an apartment above the restaurant with his only waitress, who might have been his wife, no one knew for sure. Inside was a counter, with back-less stools, running the length of the room. Mike's hamburgers and shakes were known to students at Selby Hall largely because the place was off limits. So, too, were the town's pool hall, liquor store, and hotel.

Two railroad workers in scraggly coveralls, dreary flannel shirts, and caps stained with oil, sat silently at one end of the counter. They wolfed fried egg sandwiches and French fries, cherry pie and coffee. The waitress was not in sight. The room, too warm, poorly lit, smelled of grease and stale air.

Danny and Nicholas walked halfway down the counter and took stools across from the black iron gas range where Mike was frying a hamburger. He flipped the patty, raw-meat red on one side, and tossed a slice of cheese on top. He emptied a saucer of sliced onions onto the sizzling grill, spreading them out with a spatula before he turned to look at his customers. Mid-fifties, sturdy, curly red hair on his arms, red fringe on his head and pale, flaccid face, Mike wore a soiled apron, covering him from neck to his knees.

"What'll it be, boys?" he asked, his face distorted into a smile. He guessed they were from Selby Hall.

"We'd like two shakes, chocolate please," Danny said.

Mike grunted. He took aluminum containers off a shelf, flipped open the top of the freezer, and reached deep inside to scoop out vanilla ice cream. When he opened the refrigerator door, the rubber insulation hung loosely across the top. He took out a carton of milk, poured some into the shaker and added skimpy quantities of chocolate syrup from a restaurant-size Hershey canister. In a single movement he inserted both aluminum containers into the electric mixers, turned them on, and went back to the hamburger patty and onions frying on the grill.

The two railroad workers, draining their coffee cups, pushed back their plates, and picked up the checks. Mike walked over to them and rang open the cash register. Muttering, he gave change back. The men walked out, letting the coiled spring slam the door shut behind them.

Mike glanced at Danny and Nicholas, but said nothing. He checked the mixers, removed the containers and poured the thick, coffee-colored shakes into two tall glasses and sat them down on the counter in front of the boys.

"Want a spoon?" he asked.

"Sure," they said together. Mike got out spoons, wiping them with a corner of his apron, and turned his back to give the onion rings a stir with the spatula. The compressor for the refrigerator cycled on, wheezed, then ran raggedly. Fat from the hamburger sputtered on the grill.

"It's a great day for having a good time!" Danny blurted.

The movement of Mike's arm hesitated, then resumed. Picking up the hamburger with the spatula, he deftly laid the cooked patty he'd prepared for himself on a slice of plain white sandwich bread, poured ketchup from a bottle, scooped up the onion rings and spread them across the hamburger, slapping on a second slice of bread. He turned to face the boys.

"Which one of you said that?"

"I did," Danny answered. Mike stared at him, his face blank. Nicholas looked at Danny.

"Come on," Mike said. "I've got something out back I want to show you."

Danny got up, walked around the corner of the counter, and followed Mike into a back room.

In less than a minute, Danny returned, followed by Mike, who stayed behind the counter, chomping on his hamburger, ignoring them. The two boys finished their shakes. Danny put some coins on the table and they got up to leave.

"See you," Mike called after them.

"Yeah, thanks," Danny said, and closed the door carefully behind.

Empty storefronts in the red brick buildings mocked the optimism that built the town in the first years of the century. A brewery, a cheese factory that stored yellow rounds to age and ripen in the limestone caves in the bluff along the river, the repair yards and turnaround sheds constructed by the railroad, even a woolen mill, all prosperity that didn't last. The dark winter afternoon made the town's future seem forever abandoned.

Nicholas guessed what had happened in the back room. "Danny, are you crazy? You don't even use the stuff!"

"But Ferris, he said he'd wipe me out if I didn't!" Danny's voice broke and his face worked with emotion. As they trudged along the deserted street, Danny told Nicholas about Ferris accosting him in track and the meeting in the coat room.

"You saw what Ferris did to Buck at the shooting range!"

"I understand. He's a son of a bitch, all right! But Danny, we'll figure something out." They were silent all the way back to school.

Following supper in the refectory, Danny hung around in Milton Hall until students required to attend study hall had left. Others drifted off to their rooms for study period at seven. The few students remaining checked for messages on the bulletin board or waited to use the public phone. Unnoticed, Danny slipped into the coat room and moved through it to the ell at the rear. Startled, he saw Ferris standing just inside the ell, slouched against a wall.

"Well, have you got it?"

Danny nodded, reached into his back pocket, and took out a plastic freezer bag wrapped with twine. He handed it to Ferris.

Ferris held up the bag, examining the contents through the plastic, and slipped it inside his jacket. He reached out with both hands and gripped the upper part of Danny's arms, squeezing until Danny winced. "You don't know anything about this, understand? Understand?" Danny nodded. "Wait here and count to ten, slowly. Then go to your room." Ferris turned and was gone.

Danny and Nicholas were at study desks in their room, bent over their books, when someone knocked on the door. Thinking it was the senior floor monitor checking to be sure they were in their room, they called out "Here!" But the door opened and Mr. Eberhard was standing there.

"May I come in?" Danny and Nicholas stood up. "I'd like to talk with you a few minutes. No, no, sit down, sit down."

Mr. Eberhard in his long black topcoat pervaded the room. Nicholas gestured toward his chair at the desk, and sat on the edge of the bed. Mr. Eberhard did not remove his coat, but eased himself into the chair offered by Nicholas and gazed at them, his face unreadable.

It seemed like Mr. Eberhard would never speak, then "I understand the two of you went into town today." They nodded. "Can you tell me about it?" His voice gave nothing away. Danny and Nicholas looked at each other. Nicholas spoke first, hoping to direct attention away from Danny.

"I had to get some stuff at the drug store. Danny went along with me."

"Did you go anywhere else?"

"We fooled around for a while."

Mr. Eberhard stared.

"Then we came back to school. That's all."

"Are you sure?" Both boys nodded.

Mr. Eberhard reached into a side pocket of his overcoat. His hand withdrew a white envelope. Startled, Danny recognized his mother's handwriting. Instead of offering the envelope to him, Mr. Eberhard continued holding it in the fingers of his large, basketball hands.

"One of my responsibilities as a senior master," he explained, "is to check the few places in town off limits to our students." His eyes caught and held Danny's with a look of mild reproach. "It so happens that I decided to make the run late this afternoon, before returning to school for supper. I stopped at Mike's Lunch. Thought I'd have a cup of coffee, give me a chance to visit a little with Mike." He smiled slightly. "Having been around as long as I have, it seems like I know a lot of townspeople. Mike and I aren't friends, and I don't like what I suspect he does on the side, but I thought I might learn something."

Mr. Eberhard shifted position in the straight-backed chair, stretching out his long legs for relief. He seemed in no hurry. "Well, as I was sitting there at the counter, I noticed an envelope, this envelope, on the floor, up against the base of the counter. It's addressed to you, Danny." He stretched out his arm and handed over the envelope.

Heart racing, Danny took the letter, stammering out a thank-you.

"That's not quite all of it."

The two boys looked quickly at each other, then back at Mr. Eberhard.

"One of our senior students is suspected of selling pot to other students." He watched them closely. "Some think he sends 'new boys' into town to pick it up for him." He cleared his throat. "Either of you know anything about that?"

Danny blanched, shaking his head. Nicholas said, "No, sir."

Mr. Eberhard looked around the room. "That's a very handsome rug you have there. Navajo, I would think. Assume you brought it from home. Belong to you, Danny?" Danny nodded. "Good people, the Navajos. Honest, hard working. We can learn a lot from them."

Mr. Eberhard's big hands, clasped loosely together, rested in his lap, the thumbs circling each other. He had plenty of time.

"Were you at Mike's this afternoon?" he finally asked.

Danny paled. "We stopped in for a shake."

Eberhard looked at him thoughtfully.

"That's what I thought." He looked in pain. "I'm sorry, boys, but each of you will be restricted to campus until Thanksgiving break, for going off limits. You'll also be on required study hall. That's the penalty." Lowering his voice, he added: "I figured you'd have a little more to tell me." Neither boy spoke. "Well, think about it. If you want to see me, leave a note in my message box." He stood up.

Danny and Nicholas rose to their feet. As if he were about to say something more, Mr. Eberhard hesitated, but turned away, opened the door into the hall and left.

Attendance at Sunday evening chapel was required at Selby Hall. Danny liked going, not for the service, but because he felt secure there.

Rows of golden-hued oak benches faced each other on either side of the single aisle, wide enough for the choir, two abreast, to pass by, preceded by the priest and bearers of the brass cross and the silken white flag of the church. The remaining sunlight softly illuminated the red, yellow, and blue panes of the stained glass windows. Standing guard in the chancel, wax candles mounted on bronze candelabra as tall as a man cast a softening light on the robed figures nearby.

Only half-listening to the liturgy, Danny thought about his older brother, his violent death. Danny felt that something undefined yet essential had been ripped from the core of his own body. He struggled to sort out the feeling. He was also troubled by an unaccountable ambivalence over his older brother's death. Why this sense of release?

For a time Danny had hoped his father would open up to him, take him in, but that had not happened, and he did not understand why. Puzzled, Danny felt a sense of freedom, yet thought he might have been responsible in some way. He reasoned that he should assume the mantle Ted had worn, yet he did not know how nor did he know what he must do.

Several weeks passed. Danny saw Ferris at the track and in the wash room, sometimes across the refectory at meals, but Ferris was oblivious to him. They never spoke, yet Danny could not forget the threats. One night he dreamed that Ferris backed him against the hard, cold wall in the shooting range, Ferris's face close to his, the oval mouth shouting obscenities. He awoke abruptly.

Danny's mother wrote him regularly. One morning, Danny stopped by the mail room, expecting a letter. He saw Ferris come out of the coat room, carrying his books, and walk nonchalantly away. Fear gripped Danny. Pretending to look at the bulletin board, he watched the entrance to the coat room. A moment later a "new boy" came out, looked nervously about him, and proceeded toward the outside exit.

The scene he witnessed replayed the terror of his nightmare. The image haunted Danny, arousing fear.

Studying in his room that night, he told Nicholas about what he had seen.

"What do you want to do about it?" Nicholas asked.

"I've got to tell."

"What about Ferris? He'll beat the shit out of you. Maybe out of both of us."

"Won't the school protect us?"

"Maybe. I don't know." Nicholas looked worried. "What about the new kid. Maybe he'll tell, or not go through with it."

"I don't know."

"Just because you tell doesn't mean you won't be expelled. You're still guilty, you know. Buying the stuff. Delivering it to Ferris."

Danny didn't answer.

"They could kick me out, too. After all, I was with you. I knew what was going on. And I didn't report it. Eberhard gave us a chance to tell him, but we didn't."

"I think they know about my brother," Danny said flatly. "That he was into drugs. They think I am, too."

"But they can't hold your brother against you, Danny."

"Yeah, but they don't understand. He just got in over his head, trying to be the big man at college, like he was at home."

Nicholas was silent.

Struggling, Danny said: "I can't do it. I can't keep it a secret." He stood up, his body tense. "I've got to make it right, Nick. I've got to find a way out."

Danny's outburst was a specter in the room. After a moment, Nicholas asked quietly, "Who would you tell?" Shaking his head in distraction, Danny flung himself onto his bed, face down, burying his head in the pillow.

"Maybe you could write a note. Put it under the headmaster's door when no one's looking. Not sign your name."

"But would they believe it?" Danny's voice was muffled. Agitated, he flipped over onto his back, gazing at the ceiling. "How could they get Ferris if they don't know who wrote the note? Ferris would just deny it. How could they prove it?"

Nicholas shook his head, stumped.

"I need to tell them you weren't in on it, Nick. Because I think Mr. Eberhard knows what I did. He's just waiting for me to admit it. But you didn't know why we went to Mike's until after I'd bought the stuff."

Nicholas nodded.

"I'm sorry I got you into this, Nick. It's all my fault." Danny got up from the bed, and flopped into his chair, slumped over, eyes fixed on the Navajo rug. "What will my parents think?" he moaned. "Ted, and now me! What will this do to them?"

Outside, the chimes in the bell tower struck the hour and began the slow, deliberate count to nine. A bell clanged harshly in the dormitory hallway, ending the study period.

Nicholas stood up, stretched his arms out to the side, and looked at Danny. "Think about it tonight. We can decide in the morning."

There was no chance to talk the next morning. The boys dressed hastily and rushed to get to breakfast. But as they left the room, Nicholas turned to Danny. "So what have you decided?"

"I'm going to do it. There's no other way."

"Then let's do it!" He gave Danny a gentle whack on the arm.

At breakfast Danny asked Mr. Eberhard if he and Nicholas could talk with him. Mr. Eberhard's dark eyes gave no hint of what he was thinking.

"Certainly," he said. "Come to my house at seven. When study period starts. I'll tell the hall monitor I've asked you to come by to work on math skills."

Danny nodded.

John Eberhard lived on the edge of campus in one of half a dozen frame two-story duplexes for faculty. At seven Danny and Nicholas rang the doorbell, their breath suspended in the bitter, motionless air.

Mr. Eberhard, a dark gray cardigan hanging loosely from his bony shoulders, opened the door. Tall, forbidding, he crowded the doorway with authority. Motioning the boys to stiff-backed chairs close to the wood fire, Mr. Eberhard tossed on a new log, momentarily watching the sparks scatter wildly and then rush upwards, swept away by the draft. Carefully, he settled into a reading chair across from them, next to a floor lamp with dangling pull chains and a dull shade discolored by the years.

A clock on the mantle, its brass key protruding from the center, tapped in a deep metallic voice each slight edging forward of the minute hand. "Well, boys," Mr. Eberhard at last said, "What's on your mind?"

Nicholas looked at Danny, who began haltingly, awkwardly, telling about the encounter with Ferris at the indoor track, Ferris's threats, the meeting in the coat room, the fear of being beaten. Mr. Eberhard remained silent, his face immobile, until Danny related going into the back room at Mike's, at which Mr. Eberhard's eyes perceptibly narrowed.

"Why didn't you tell me about this when I came to your room?" he asked when Danny finished.

"I don't know, sir, except I knew I'd be kicked out." Danny's voice cracked, and his face tightened. "I just can't do that, not to my parents. Not after all they've gone through."

"And what about you, Nicholas?"

"Danny's my friend. I couldn't let him down."

Mr. Eberhard's big hands clasped one knee, which he lifted up as if to ameliorate persistent pain, his thumbs rotating in a circle. "You've done the right thing, coming to talk with me," he said. "Tomorrow morning I'll see the headmaster. You'll have a chance to tell him what you've told me. We've had suspicions, as I said. Your coming forward will help us get to the facts."

"But what about Ferris, sir? When will he find out?" Danny asked.

"Well, I suspect the Headmaster will ask Ferris to come to his office. He'll then call Ferris's parents. My guess is he'll tell them it might be best if Ferris left school during the investigation. Law enforcement people from town will need to be involved."

Nicholas looked worried. "What's going to happen to Danny and me?"

"Probably no additional punishment for you, Nicholas. But Danny, you could be expelled, I have to say that, although I'll recommend probation instead. You did come forward. The Headmaster will have the final word."

Apprehensive, Danny asked "What about my parents?"

"I think they need to know, but I'll tell them what you've done to make things right." He smiled slightly. "I know your brother would have thought you did the right thing."

Mr. Eberhard started to get up, but paused. "Danny, would you like to call your parents? Call them now?"

Danny nodded.

"The phone's in the kitchen."

Muffled by the door between them, Danny's voice was low, his words indistinct. The murmuring ebbed and flowed, with long pauses in-between, over what seemed to Nicholas a long time. Abruptly, his voice ended ended, and Danny came back into the room.

Hesitantly, he said "My mother was at a meeting . . . but I talked with my dad." His face flushed with emotion. "My dad says he understands. He said that everything will work out okay." Danny's eyes brightened. "My dad says he's proud of me."

Mr. Eberhard was silent, but looked satisfied. He walked with the boys to the door, said goodnight, and shook hands with each of them somewhat formally. He watched as they walked across the porch, down the steps and started back across the campus, a bold lithograph of white ground and sharply edged black buildings, towers, and beyond, a forest of trees.

The Writing Workshop

Howard looked distraught, so I asked if I could join him. When he nodded, I sat my coffee cup on the cafeteria table and plunked down my books and manuscripts.

"I can't believe it," he said. "What Kachur just told me. During my consultation."

Howard and I had met on Monday, the first day of the workshop. This was Wednesday.

Howard looked away, then leaned in over his coffee, hunching his shoulders, and toyed distractedly with a red-plastic stirrer. "Kachur said I shouldn't write short fiction. Thinks I have the voice of an essayist, not a storyteller."

I slit open the Coffee Mate and tapped the edge with my finger until enough powder slid into the cup, then added sugar. "What brought that on?"

"I asked him about dual interior monologues. I'd read a story where I thought it worked really well. 'The Stucco House.' Ellen Gilchrist."

He looked at me, questioning. I knew the story.

"I told him I'd like to know more about the connection between a character's voice and the authorial voice." Howard paused. "Kachur just said . . . well, what I told you he said. I think he'd been waiting. Waiting for the right time. I think my using the word 'voice' set him off." Howard shoved aside his coffee cup. "Hell, I like to write short fiction. I've always liked writing. I don't understand where he's coming from."

Over the top of his reading glasses, Howard looked around the room, beginning to fill with the lunch crowd. His face was pallid, strained, his dark hair jumbled.

Howard is a lawyer, a senior staff member with the Public Defenders Office in Toledo. Divorced, two grown children, neither of them living in Toledo. That's about all he'd told me, except that his wife remarried years ago. Earnest about writing, he'd been trying to get published in university quarterlies.

"Right out of the blue," he added. He forced a laugh. "Man, I never expected anything like that when I signed up. Some workshop."

I thought about it a lot, the next few days. What should I expect from a writing workshop?

We were twelve participants—four men, eight women taking advanced short fiction writing. Only one, a former journalist, could say he'd been published—but not his fiction. It was already late July. The upper-Midwest university, with splendid brick buildings and sun-drenched, spreading lawns, was renowned for its writing programs. Each of us came that summer with our own expectations and apprehensions, wanting to learn more about the craft we practiced. All hoped to find encouragement and validation.

George Kachur taught the workshop. A short, stocky man of muscular build, he juts his head forward in a boxer's stance. About 50, fair complexion, fringes of light-brown hair. He let us know he's Scandinavian, grew up in a small town of Danes and Norwegians not sixty miles distant. "Everyone knew what everybody was doing," Kachur declared with a grin. "If someone in town hadn't seen you in the last hour, they'd come find out what you were up to." Tough, funny, he entertained the class with anecdotes and opinions on writing, other writers, teaching, and life in academia. Trademark of a popular teacher, I decided.

He wore a tan canvas vest over a dark jersey with short sleeves, and cowboy boots, Georgia-clay red, with pointed toes. Plastic-rimmed glasses he took off, put back on, then took off again as he talked. Married, no mention of children. Wife went back to school in her early forties and got an MFA in writing at the university where he now teaches. She reads manuscripts submitted to the university's literary quarterly. George Kachur ridiculed submission letters seen by his wife that some writers sent with their manuscripts; irrelevant, a joke.

From the workshop catalogue I learned Kachur had taught creative writing and literature at two other colleges. His own short fiction had been published, mostly in university quarterlies, and he'd received a prestigious regional award. One day, he distributed copies of a story of his recently published in the literary magazine at a college where he'd once taught. Neither Howard nor I were impressed. We thought the story slick, self-absorbed with hip attitudes and language. Wouldn't Kachur have given us one of his best stories?

Later, when the workshop was over and I thought about Howard's quandary, I speculated about what Kachur might have told others in their one-on-one consultations. Was Howard the only one he discouraged from writing fiction?

Harriet, for example. Mid-40s, attractive, slender face and body, she wore sleeveless knitted jerseys and slacks. Black hair cropped close, dark complexion, good tan. Four earrings dangled from holes punctured in the right ear, a long silver pendant drooped from the left. Warm, likable, expressive personality. From Duluth.

Each of us had sent not more than two stories three weeks in advance. George Kachur critiqued the stories beforehand and, when the workshop met briefly on the Sunday evening we arrived, handed them back with his written evaluations. For me, his comments covered a full page, single-spaced. Not the kudos I had hoped for, had even thought I might get, but begrudgingly I recognized that most of his criticisms were justified.

That same evening, we passed out copies of our story to other workshop members. The next two days the class critiqued each other's work, cautiously at first, then more candidly, finally pulling no punches. Later in the week, after revising our stories, we again distributed copies for criticism.

"Think of the workshop as a conversation," said George Kachur class, *"not an argument. Don't say you liked or didn't like a story; say how to improve it, or what works and why."*

Harriet's writing improved during the week. Her story "Carrie" was about a wife/mother-of-teenage-children who, while in the basement doing the family laundry (a task told in detail), finds in a pocket of her husband's slacks a folded-up yellow post-it with a note from his younger lover and the imprint of a kiss in lipstick. Carrie's grief, anger, and ruminations go on and on, and not until too long does Carrie gain the courage to act. Someone commented that good detail makes the story real, but that Carrie should throw the bastard out sooner; the ending lacked punch.

Harriet accepted this and other criticism as constructive, asking one or two questions in reply. She wanted to improve her story; if she was stung by the criticism, it didn't show.

Harriet wears a wedding ring. Inevitably, one wonders how much such stories reflect the author's own life; and what did George Kachur say to Harriet in her one-on-one consultation? The considerable cost of the workshop, with room and meals and travel, may have meant sacrifice. Was she satisfied with what she got?

"Clarity is a skill, the first standard," Kachur told us. *"Character, action, clarity. That's what it's all about."*

Jason, another participant, challenged us with his skill and eccentricity. Late-30s, thin, shock of wavy black hair falling over his forehead; glasses with glistening steel frames, eyes fidgeting when he listens intently. My unconscious habit of snapping the pocket clip on my pencil when I wasn't taking notes bothered him. Twice, seated next to me, he looked my way, pointedly directing his eyes down toward the pencil I held in my right hand, dangling below the seat of my chair. I stopped, laying the pencil down on my tablet. During break, I apologized. "I have very sensitive hearing," Jason said, seeking to reassure me. Later, when I ran out of lead, and asked if anyone had some I could borrow, Jason dug into his backpack and found a ball-point pen.

Jason was the most perceptive reader in the workshop, articulate in analyzing our stories, by far the most experimental writer. He was also the most difficult stylist to accept or understand. Two pages of his story physically took the shape of inverted pyramids, as if clipped out of a conventional page of manuscript, so that words outside the triangle were missing, yet what remained inside was decipherable. George Kachur admired the work's originality, but questioned whether a publisher would accept a story in the format Jason had used, because of problems that would arise in printing. Yet as the discussion ended, he declared with finality, "Send it out and see what happens." Only one other time during the workshop did Kachur openly endorse a story one of us had written, signifying it was suitable for publication.

When Jason's turn came to read aloud the last afternoon, he read a short-short story about one's looking in the mirror and meeting one's self, getting to know one's self, not to be afraid. His voice and articulation were so exceptional that I was moved, and I sensed that others were, too.

He's a performer, I thought to myself, skillfully manipulating us with the rise and fall of his voice, massaging the words, pulling us in, capturing our emotions with the instrument of his voice.

I have no idea where Jason's from, or what he does, or where he's heading. That was true for others in the workshop. It was as if one's private life outside of writing was not to be asked about, not to be disclosed. During class breaks, the women split into groups of two or three or four; the men, perhaps more disparate in age or background, stood alone or wandered off.

In the class discussion of Howard's story, Jason said to him, as a gentle preamble, "You're a writer, no doubt about that," then incisively told Howard what was wrong with his story.

"Your writing must be crisp, vivid," Kachur urged us. *"Your characters must be made up of an accretion of detail inside the author's head. Penetrate to your character's inner life, to what guides him, and do this in a series of scenes. Think about, what choices does the character have?"*

Jenny was about seventy, a former editor for a publisher in New York, where she still lives. Gray-blonde hair hanging straight down, cut evenly all around, like a soft helmet; it looked nice. Refined features, clear white skin, small mouth. Her eyes narrow when she talks, as if concentrating. Looks like a fashionable street character, dressed in an oatmeal-colored short jacket over a blue-and-white striped jersey, once-crisp linen slacks, soiled running shoes, and a canvas hat pulled down low on her head. In conversation she pauses, searching for just what she wants to say, but talks sense. When she rolls her sleeves up, the skin sags on the upper arms, and her lower arms are mottled with brown age spots.

In class discussions, Jenny was informed, unpretentious, straight-forward. Elements of her stories were often good, and true to life. One of them, "Summer Rental," is about an older couple from Manhattan who rent a farm house in South Dakota. During the night they hear fruit jars, canned by the deceased mother of the man who owns the house, exploding randomly in the cellar, like popcorn in a microwave paper bag. Her story stayed with me.

The last day, Jenny read aloud a funny short-short story she wrote as a workshop assignment that had everyone laughing. A long-distance caller named Jimmy is on the phone with the narrator, has the wrong number but persists, as if he can't hear, in asking preposterous questions concerning people and events the person receiving the call knows nothing about.

Jennie told me that she hadn't signed up to meet with Kacher, implying that she didn't need to know what he might say about her work.

"Some efforts will end in failure. You wanted to be a writer. Learn what doesn't work. Keep going. There is much to do."

Carolyn had been out of college four years. A political science major, she'd done a lot of theater, she told me, and that was her bridge to writing fiction. Thin, good tan. Hair the color of dark honey, long and lots of curls, frizzy. Wore sleeveless cotton dresses, short skirt length. Blue-gray eyes, serious most of the time, and rather cool, as in distance. Thin features, with a small nose. Remarkably confident of herself and her writing.

Two of the stories Carolyn submitted were placed in Medieval times. There was lots of action, bloody, violent, highly descriptive, and explicit sex. Her stories soared, fleet-footed, chockfull of metaphors. I sensed the tales came easily to her, that they flowed as fast as she could get them down on the computer. Sitting next to her one afternoon, I asked, and she acknowledged they did.

During the class discussion of my own story, Carolyn sat next to me. "I don't know who your protagonist is in this story," she said, looking straight at me, "and I don't know what it is you want to say. What *is* it you want to say?" It was like a parent being admonished by another parent: "Why does your child act like that? Why on earth don't you do something about it?"

A generation older than Carolyn, I was stunned by the harshness of her criticism. Was she right? I thought I knew my protagonist; I thought I knew what I wanted the story to say. Had I failed so utterly?

After the last session of the week, I passed Carolyn sitting on a bench near the Lake Walk, in the sun of late afternoon, reading. We exchanged casual "Hi's" as I walked by, but her criticism still resonated shrilly.

"Take the advice you need, forget the rest." And: *Does the first paragraph crack the whip?*

Rick, mid-30s, must have been six-feet-one, slim, with an oblong head, dark complexion, and close-cut hair. He arrived with a week's growth of scraggly beard, but on the fourth day appeared in class with clean-shaven cheeks and a precise, black goatee. He wore small, round glasses with tinted lenses, rimmed in steel, and spoke in a baritone voice, hushed, as if in a library. Lives in Chicago, and teaches high school social studies.

I stopped to talk with Rick after lunch one day in the Student Union. He was working on a laptop computer, dark green with sleek, Gropius-inspired contours. I asked him about it.

"They're pretty expensive," he drawled, "about $3500 but that's what you have to pay to get one that will do everything this one will."

Rick's story was about a mom and the baseball bat that had belonged to her son's grandfather. The mom loved to play sandlot baseball, knew all the lingo, and was teaching her son, about 14, how to play the game. They were poor, the father was no longer around, and they moved from one tenement apartment to another whenever his mother began to disapprove of the neighbors.

Rick took in criticism with no expression, only occasionally asking for elaboration, his suppressed voice scarcely audible. The story gained clarity and purpose during the week. On each of three days in a row he returned to class with a reworked manuscript, distributing the new version for additional comment. By week's end, his story had received more input than any other. Kachur at last said, "Rick, make a few more changes, then send it off." He didn't suggest where, at least not in class, but Kachur's words told us the story was marketable.

Rick struck me as smart, persistent, and a good writer who used his opportunities. I suspect he went home to Chicago satisfied with what he'd gotten from the workshop.

"Fiction writers fail when they're too logical, too reasonable, too timid. Kick ass! That's the way to write good fiction."

Lila was the only African-American. Her blackness was a part of the appealing personality that walked in with her each time she entered the room. Divorced, she was a large person, but not tall. One afternoon Lila returned from break with a machine-vended yellow bag of M & Ms. She down next to me, took off her sandals to air her feet, opened the sack, offered it to me, then spilled out the contents onto a sheet of typing paper in front of her and proceeded to munch them one by one. Lila's round face was quite beautiful. Her black hair was short and curly, lying close to the head. When the class took turns reading, her voice ambled with rhythmic cadences, the south-Texas inflections gentle and lyrical.

Lila's story takes place in rural Texas outside Dallas. A young girl relates how her grandmother saves up money so that once each year her son can drive her into town to buy a new hat at Neiman-Marcus. The girl's grandmother is known for the stylish hats she wears to church on Sundays. The granddaughter goes with her on the shopping trip.

However, the sales person in the hat department who has sold the grandmother hats in the past has retired, and another salesperson, who is also the manager of the hat department, waits on her this time. When the grandmother selects a hat to try on, the manager brusquely says, No, you can't try the hat on, because of the oil in your hair, you should know that by now. So the grandmother, her dignity bruised but intact, returns home, chiding herself for being so prideful about the hats she wears to church. That evening, before she goes to bed, the grandmother takes her hats and the Neiman-Marcus boxes she keeps them in, and burns them with the trash.

Someone in the class questioned that a salesperson in a store would act in such a way today, or even twenty-five years ago. Lila replied that when she went to the airport to fly to the city where the workshop was held, and pulled up at the curb to unload her luggage, the skycaps, all of whom were black, were rushing around taking care of the white people, checking their luggage, and ignoring her. So she pulled several dollar bills from her purse and held them in her hand where the skycaps could see, just so they'd know she intended to tip, even though she was black.

Lila knows a lot about people.

Howard's Pungo River story was discussed the second day of the workshop. He'd written it in first person, but George Kachur told him he ought to re-write it in third person. He didn't say why, or what might be gained. Howard showed me Kachur's typed evaluation of his story.

It's too wordy at the beginning, Kachur wrote. *The story starts on page eight. The language brightens, the sentences become more active, the character begins to come into focus.*

The first-person narrator, as Howard had written the story, is Sam Johnson, a black man, forty-five years old, from a remote river town in North Carolina, whose family has been there four generations. All the men in the family had labored in the fields until Sam's father became the first black man to own a shrimp boat, and Sam the first black to go to college.

This story needs something special to be worth the effort. I'm convinced the characters are underplayed, underdeveloped – and perhaps the plot. I see an episode here, maybe not a whole story yet.

Sam returns to Bellevista from Raleigh where he's a compliance inspector with the State Fair Labor Practices Department. He's looking into a reported case of on-the-job rape. The alleged victim is his cousin, Emma Mae Johnson. The accused perpetrator, Billy Callison, is the foreman at the seafood processing plant where Emma Mae works. Although blacks in Bellevista went to segregated schools, Sam and Billy knew each other growing up. Billy once came to Sam's aid when they were children, yet they had an uneasy, distrusting relationship.

The plot is nothing new but you manage to get some tension up by writing energetic sentences. I don't know if that is enough to make a story but it is a good start. It's not an easy story to tell and you have a good start here as long as you realize it needs a good shaking.

Howard told me later that he thought the criticism from the class was good; he'd work on bringing his characters more to life, show what made them act as they did. After reading his story, I thought Howard had a true sense of place. The action was dramatic, and the characters believable, if maybe thin. Lila accepted Howard's characterization of a black protagonist, how he felt and reacted, but suggested that Howard heighten the tension by Emma Mae confessing that she had been Billy Callison's clandestine lover; when she tried to end the relationship, he raped her.

Outside of class, I seldom saw Howard. He ate dinner off-campus, alone. I suppose he read manuscripts for the next day's discussion, and further revised his own story.

When Howard distributed copies of his new draft, he had changed the point of view to third person, began the story farther along in the narrative, added more dialogue, and cut some descriptive sentences. But he later confided to Lila and me that he felt the texture of the writing he'd tried to create had been lost in the revision, that he must find a way to restore the story's aura as he saw it.

The class critiqued Howard's latest revision, acknowledging the improvements, but fell short of enthusiasm. Kachur remained silent, letting the class carry the discussion. By then he'd already met with Howard.

Phyllis announced she agreed with Howard: it was a Southern story as he'd written it, and the story shouldn't lose that quality; he must do what sounds right to him. One smart lady, I thought.

Following the final session of the workshop, Howard and I met for the last time for coffee. He still sagged under the weight of Kachur's proclamation.

"He didn't really say why, you know. I took a long walk after he'd told me, trying to understand what had happened. At first I said to myself he must know what he's talking about. After all, he's the teacher." Howard sat back in his chair and hitched his thumbs into his belt, trying to look relaxed. "But what the hell does he mean? Is being a storyteller so inexplicable? I wish he'd explained, been more specific. Maybe he thinks I can't weave a story, build tension, flesh out my characters, that sort of thing. But can't I learn?"

I didn't know the answer. If a teacher risks demolishing a student's confidence, shouldn't he find out the person's reasons for writing fiction, where he hopes to go with his writing, ask whether he's explored other kinds? Should he flatly say that the person shouldn't write fiction?

"Maybe he's wrong," Howard said, finishing the last of his coffee. "Wouldn't that be something, if he were wrong." He gathered up his notepad and manuscripts. "I think he is. Hell, I know he is."

Siblings

Catherine Orthwein Ridgeway died quietly at eighty-one, alone at night in the big house except for her housekeeper. Each of her children, in their quite individual ways, mourned their mother's death, yet were relieved that it may have come easily for her.

Not long after, the two sisters and their brother agreed to meet at the house in which they had grown up to begin dividing up the inherited family possessions. English and French furniture, a great aunt's collection of ivory figurines, family pictures in silver frames from table tops and dressers, fine china given as wedding gifts generations before, even everyday glassware from the pantry had to be disposed of. Every article was valued by estate appraisers, then tagged, stacked on tables, sorted into cardboard boxes, and set aside by categories in the now-lifeless Georgian house on the Connecticut shore.

While they worked at organizing the immense aggregation of possessions, the siblings shared occasional laughter reminiscing about events from childhood and exclaiming over long-forgotten mementos. Discovering an album of sepia photographs of the vacation trip to Yellowstone they had taken as children with their grandparents, now dead for many years, they silently considered their own mortality.

Before the task began, Peter and Ellen and Judy devised an elaborate procedure for taking turns in choosing the possessions each wanted. What none of them chose, however, either for themselves or for their own children, they expeditiously sold at auction or, as a last resort, gave to the Salvation Army.

Despite their veneer of affability, strong emotions revealed themselves in impatient replies, a glance surreptitiously exchanged between the two sisters, or a tightening in Peter's voice when one of his sisters selected their father's ornate desk from the library.

Innate good manners camouflaged an underlying distrust, the submerged yet fierce feelings from childhood. As if confronted by a shared threat, the sisters contrived in subtle ways to thwart a choice they thought their brother might make if it was an object one of them especially desired.

The last remaining item to be distributed, a decision postponed for some months after all else had been apportioned, was their grandmother Orthwein's antique silver collection, still locked away in a bank vault. By then, the siblings had resumed a semblance of their congenial, if guarded relationships. They agreed to gather on Friday afternoon at Ellen's house in Greenwich.

Ellen telephoned Judy the night before. "Let's have lunch tomorrow, before we go to the bank. Okay?"

"I'd really rather not, I have—."

"Oh, come on now, no excuses. We'll just go to the coffee shop, it won't take long. Besides, I think we need to talk before we see Peter—you know."

There was a pause. "Right, okay. I'll be there." Judy often resented Ellen's more obvious maneuverings, even yearned for more freedom than the relationship allowed, but the sisters saw each other or talked by phone almost every day.

Ellen was late. Judy watched her as she strode into the coffee shop, her natural elegance offsetting the seemingly careless, youthful way she wore her dark hair. She bought her clothes at the best shops, liked bright, exquisite scarves, ultra suede jackets, designer slacks, and gold jewelry. There was a touch of color in her cheeks, as if brushed by early frost.

Ellen smiled brightly, but complained about the noise clatter, and sat down at the small table.

They did not look like sisters. Judy had Ellen's clear skin, but she was smaller, more feminine. Her auburn hair was in a trim page boy. The baggy beige sweater she wore over an off-white blouse was too much like the color of the wool slacks in a gray and brown check to be smart. If not for the alligator bag suspended from its shoulder strap looped over the back of her chair, she might have been the headmaster's wife from a nearby prep school, or just another suburban mom.

The two sisters huddled together, talking intently, careful not to be overheard.

As children only two years apart, they frequently whispered together, especially when their older brother was around. "Well-mannered people don't have secrets," their mother admonished, but with little effect.

A short time later, when they entered the bank, the receptionist recognized them and smiled pleasantly. Two uniformed guards helped carry the sealed boxes to Ellen's Jaguar. The plain cardboard containers filled the back seat as well as the trunk.

They drove out of the parking lot and past the town's sparkling harbor. Neither sister spoke, acutely aware of the close presence of their grandmother's elegant silver pieces, enshrined in white tissue paper and plastic bubbles, resting in the boxes just behind them.

Ellen interrupted the silence. "Have you thought about which of us should have the *epergne*?"

Judy knew the George V *epergne* was a museum piece. "Oh, not really, although I'd like the Georg Jensen flatware—for Helen, of course." Judy watched for a sign of assent, but saw none. "Marrying a Sergeant means that her monogram will be the same as her great-grandmother. And you know the Sergeants." Judy arched her eyebrows and tipped up the end of her nose with a finger.

Ellen reached across and patted Judy's hand. "We'll see."

Judy remembered the organdy gown, and whether she would be able to wear it for the May Day dances at school. The two girls wore almost the same size, so their mother said they should decide. Judy desperately wanted to, but Ellen as the older had first choice, yet she couldn't seem to make up her mind. The very day of the festivities, Ellen acquiesced, exacting Judy's new Perry Como recording of "Moon River" in exchange.

Ellen drove the Jaguar fast, skillfully passing slower cars.

"Peter said he'd join us at the bank and help with the silver, but I told him it wasn't necessary, we'd just meet him at my house." Ellen gave her sister a sideways glance. A moment later, to answer the question in both their minds, she added "There's no need for him to know about the signature cards for the vault."

Judy nodded.

Stomping the accelerator into passing gear, Ellen roared past a Volvo sedan.

"Old Mr. Stevens from Tiffany's came out from the City to appraise the silver" she added.

Moments later a car behind them honked a high-pitched beep. Startled, Ellen angrily jerked the wheel to one side, and Judy reached for the grab bar. A sports car whizzed by, and a man's shirtsleeve arm jauntily waved good-by.

"Bastard!" Ellen shouted through the windshield. Judy settled back into the soft leather seat.

Still ruffled, Ellen said "Anyway, I just got my copy of the appraisal this morning. You should have yours when you get home. Peter called to say he'd gotten his at the office."

Judy knew she'd have to ask if she wanted to find out. "What was the total amount of the appraisal?"

"A lot." Ellen liked knowing things other people didn't.

"I mean, what was the total dollar amount?"

Smiling with satisfaction, Ellen divulged the figure.

"That much, huh? Wow."

For several moments, both were silent. Then, without looking at Ellen, Judy said, "I wonder how Peter will react when we tell him all the silver belongs to us."

"Well, I'm sure he won't like it." Ellen reached into her purse for the packet of Marlboros, shook one out, put it between her lips, and pushed in the lighter. "He thinks, of course, we'll just divide it up among us." The lighter popped out. She lit the cigarette, inhaled, and blew out the smoke with a rush. "Let me deal with him when we get there."

Within minutes they reached Brookview Lane, where Ellen and her husband, Jerry McKenzie, lived. Branches of century-old trees met in a canopy overhead. The Cape Cod house on the circular gravel drive seemed too grand for the forthright New England style.

Peter's black BMW was parked in front, and Ellen pulled in behind. The Portuguese maid opened the front door, and announced that their brother was in the study.

Peter came to the door of the room. Of the three children, he resembled their mother the most. Tall, erect, he had exuberant dark hair and a Mediterranean look. His face was lean, and looked strained, as if he'd just been jogging. Peter Ridgeway worked on Wall Street, in mergers and acquisitions. Greeting their brother, both sisters stepped forward to receive a peck on the cheek.

When they were children, their older brother was someone to look up to but also someone who might take your toys away from you and not give them back. Even worse, he might make fun of you. This grown-up Peter Ridgeway on Wall Street was someone they didn't know, couldn't really imagine, and even someone who didn't especially interest them.

"Hi," Peter said. "Everything okay at the bank?"

"Yes, they're very accommodating." Ellen slipped off her coat.

"Then I'll go out and carry the silver in from your car."

"No, no, that's not necessary. Jerry can help when he gets home." When Peter looked at Ellen curiously, she added, "He should be here any minute."

"Okay, if you'd rather." Peter walked over to a polished walnut table bearing a Lalique decanter filled with dark amber sherry. Six crystal sherry glasses, arranged in a precise oval, circled the decanter. "Can I pour you a sherry?"

Ellen was irked, thought him presumptive. After all, it was her house. She wondered if he did things like that just to get at her.

Peter handed each of them a glass, raised his and said amiably, "Well, here's to Grandma Orthwein".

Ellen and Judy sat down side by side on the large, amply pillowed sofa. Peter relaxed in an upholstered chair close to the fireplace. Flames cozily licked the artificial gas logs.

"How was the drive out?" Ellen asked, her tone cordial.

"Fine, thanks. Enjoyable, actually. The color in the trees this time of year is really spectacular. I envy your living out here. I like being close to the Street, and our apartment is great, of course, but still, I miss Connecticut, especially in the fall."

Judy smiled at her brother. "We used to have fun, didn't we? I mean, living right on the Sound, and all. I can't bear to drive by the old place, now that Mother's gone."

"Peter," Ellen began carefully, "we need to tell you something about the silver."

"Something missing? Damaged?"

"No, not that, it's just that Mother wanted the silver to go to Judy and me." She lit a cigarette, not looking at him. "So we really don't need to divide it up."

"Go on." His tone was neutral.

"Well, Mother felt the silver should remain on the female side of the family. You know, daughters in the family get the silver, table linens, that sort of thing."

"Funny, there wasn't anything in Mother's Will about that. Besides, everything else we've divided up evenly, even our use of the summer house on the Island. Why would the silver be different?"

Ellen abruptly twisted about on the sofa and sat back against the pillow, her body rigid. "Don't make such a big thing out of it," she blurted. "It's done, over with." A wave of her hand dispensed with the issue. "Mother gifted the silver to us three years ago, when she updated her Will."

"Gifted? You mean she gave you the silver outright? She wouldn't have done that without telling me."

"Well, she did, because the silver rightfully belongs to Judy and me."

"Rightfully? I don't know what that means." Peter looked hard at Ellen. "I checked Mother's tax returns each year after Father died. I'd have noticed a gift tax return, and there wasn't one."

Judy glanced quickly at her sister, and Ellen said, "I didn't see the returns. How would I know?"

"I think you'd know." Peter's voice was hard-edged. "Mother's accountants who prepared her tax returns also do yours, Judy's, and mine. Remember? That's to make sure we report our family investments the same."

"Maybe Mother didn't need to tell the IRS," Judy said.

"No, that's not right. There's a federal tax, a big one, on giving valuable assets to your children. It would have been illegal to give you all that silver. Mother knew that."

Peter looked intently at Judy, then at Ellen. "So what's going on with you two?"

Ellen stood up, scattering ashes from her cigarette. "You always were selfish, Peter. You make plenty of money. I read about you in the *Journal*, the big deals you put together. You don't need the silver. Why do you make such a big thing out of it?"

Peter shot back, "Because I expect my share. Nothing less, nothing more." He stared at her. "You really can be a bitch, Ellen."

"Bitch or not, that's the way it's going to be."

"No, it's not." Peter rose to go. "Mother's estate hasn't been settled. I'm co-administrator with the bank, and I won't sign off on the distributions until we divide up the silver." He caught the look Judy gave Ellen. "That, Ellen, is the way it's going to be."

The front door opened and Jerry breezed in, calling out hello.

Peter ignored the greeting, and said, "It's time I head back to the City."

"Can't you stay for a drink?" Jerry asked, bewildered,

Peter shook his head, and walked toward the entrance hall, his sisters glaring. "You two better think this over." He let himself out the door.

That evening, churning with anger, Peter told his wife Martha what had happened. He was incensed that Ellen, whom he knew was the instigator, could be so unfair, so blind.

"And how could Judy go along with her?" he asked. "Why would she turn against me?"

"Sisters can" Martha replied. "And brothers, too, I suppose. Isn't it a question of how honest they are, down deep?" Then Martha remembered. "Peter, a couple of years ago, before your mother died, we received a statement from a Connecticut bank. It was for the rental on a storage vault."

"Yes, but . . ."

"I asked you about it, and you said just go ahead and pay it, the vault was undoubtedly your mother's. You thought the statement had been sent to you by mistake."

"Right. So?"

"Could you find out whose name the vault was in? I mean, whether it really was in your mother's name?"

On Monday, as soon as he reached his office, Peter telephoned the Greenwich bank. A woman looked up the vault authorization card, but then unexpectedly refused to give out any information. Peter patiently explained he was co-administrator with the bank for his mother's estate and that he was looking for some personal property she had in storage. The woman gave in.

"What I'd like to know," Peter said, "is when was the rental on the storage vault taken out, and who has the authorized access."

"The rental began two years ago," she said, and reading from the card, gave the names whose signatures were on it.

Peter thanked her, hung up the phone, and turned slowly in his swivel chair to gaze out the window. So Ellen and Judy had in fact stored the silver in a place out of his reach, surreptitiously putting it in their names only, where he couldn't lawfully get to it. The act was evasive, underhanded. He was furious at their treachery, that they would gang up, would treat him like this.

As he stared out the window, brilliant morning light reflected off the glass towers of the World Trade Center. Beyond, on Lower New York

Harbor, the eastbound and westbound Staten Island ferries, colored a bright orange, met and silently passed each other, trailing wakes of white water that soon dissipated.

Should I forget they're my sisters, he asked himself, just not have any contact with them anymore, except at weddings and funerals?

The phone rang. His secretary said his sister Judy was holding. Peter hesitated, then picked up the phone.

"Hello, Judy."

"Peter, I'm going to be in the City today, and wondered if we could have lunch. Are you free?"

"No, I'm not." His eyes went to the framed photograph on his desk of Martha and the kids, taken years ago, at the house on the Island.

"Could you possibly break away, Peter? I think it's important—important that we talk."

In the snapshot they were sitting on the steps of the wide front porch, the girls in swim suits and terrycloth cover-ups, his sons in tennis whites, racquets in hand, laughing as he snapped the shutter.

"Okay, I guess I could change things around. Where would you like to meet?"

"At the Four Seasons? One o'clock? I'm going to be up at the Met, if it isn't too difficult for you getting there."

"Right. I'll call Jerome and have him reserve a table."

"That will be great," Judy said, and the phone clicked.

Peter took the subway to Grand Central, transferred, got off at East 52nd, and walked over to the Four Seasons. Judy had just stepped up to ask Jerome if he had arrived when Peter got off the elevator. They greeted each other, both on edge. From force of habit, Peter smiled, and Judy returned it. They followed the maitre d' to a table.

The waiter took their orders, and Peter selected a bottle of Muscadet. He asked Judy how she liked the Van Gogh retrospective. Her observations were, as he expected, knowledgeable and very much her own.

"Peter," she began, "I feel badly about what happened at Ellen's house." He remained silent, so she went on. "I can understand your being angry, because you didn't know——."

"So, what do you propose?"

"I know you don't like it, but the silver does belong to Ellen and me. Mother gave it to us."

"Exactly what did Mother say to you, about the silver?"

"Well, I stopped by one day to have lunch with her, and we talked a little about the collection. Mother used the tea service at lunch, even though it was just the two of us. She had asked the housekeeper to polish it, knowing that I was coming, and I told her how beautiful it looked." Judy's face suddenly constricted, and tears filled her eyes. After a moment, she continued.

"Mother talked about Grandmother Orthwein finding the more important pieces in Europe when she went with Grandfather on business trips to England and Belgium. That was in the twenties, when Europe was recovering from the first war. There were lots of pieces on the market, if you had the contacts. Families who'd lost so much during the war were selling heirlooms to raise money. Grandmother Orthwein concentrated on early eighteenth century silver makers, and knew what she was getting."

"I'll bet she did. Still runs in the family, but go on."

Ignoring the dig, Judy said, "Well, Mother hoped that someday her grandchildren would enjoy the silver as much as she did. I didn't tell her that young couples today like pewter and earthenware, and don't have silver."

"That can change. When Martha and I began buying antique furniture, we appreciated the collection more. Mother sometimes loaned us several of the major pieces when we entertained, and we got a kick out of using them. Our guests were impressed," he added with a smile.

"Well, she did the same thing for us," Judy quickly added.

Peter saw in his sister's expression the old rivalry, surfacing momentarily, like something ugly from the deep.

The waiter removed the soup bowls and served the Bay scallops, deftly pouring a glass of wine for each of them.

"So when did Mother put the silver in storage?" Peter asked.

"She was worrying a lot about being alone in the big house, except for the housekeeper at night. She'd fret about where things were, and there'd been some robberies." Accusatory, Judy asked, "Were you aware of that?"

"No, I wasn't. I knew she was getting forgetful, but living in New York, I just didn't see her that often." He was silent for a moment. "I regret that I didn't, but I can't change that now."

"Mother said she'd like to take the silver to the bank, that it'd be safe there. So Ellen and I helped her with the arrangements."

"When you took the silver, did you make it clear that Mother was the owner? Have her sign as the principal depositor?"

"Oh, I'm sure we must have, but I don't remember the details. You know me."

Peter looked hard at his sister, decided now was the time. "That's not what the bank told me this morning."

Judy looked startled.

"I called Greenwich and talked with the bank vault supervisor. The only names on the signature card are yours and Ellen's. Mother's name doesn't appear anywhere."

"Oh, no, I'm sure—"

"Sure what?"

"Well, maybe Mother changed the names when she—"

"Gave you the silver? Was the storage vault in her name originally?"

"Yes, I'm sure it must have been."

"That's not what they told me this morning." He waited for Judy to volunteer information, but she didn't. "The vault was rented two years ago, Judy. You and Ellen rented it. No one else."

"Well, Ellen and I felt it was our responsibility. To look after the silver."

"Why?"

"Because Mother had given it to us."

"When did she do that?"

"Well, maybe not in those words, exactly, but what I mean, Peter, is that Ellen and I think that the silver rightfully belongs to us."

"That word again."

"Well, we're the women in the family."

"But what about the women in my family, Judy? Martha. And my daughters. And my sons' future wives? Don't they count?"

When Judy didn't respond, Peter added, "You and Ellen like having me take on family obligations, look after family business, as your older brother, but when it comes to dividing things up, you always damn well expect your full share, and in this case, a lot more. It's time . . ."

Peter stopped, waiting until the waiter poured coffee and moved away. "You've lied to me, Judy. You and Ellen have been downright deceitful." He looked at her as if seeing her in a new light, but also with a sudden sense of calm. "So what are you going to do about the silver?"

"Let's divide it up, like we did the other things." Her voice was brisk. "Ellen will be difficult, but that's the way it is."

He nodded his head.

Peter signed the check, then reached across and lightly touched his sister's arm, resting on the table. "Think about it, about what I said. About the other women in the family."

Judy acknowledged the admonishment with just the trace of a smile, laid her napkin on the table and gathered up her gloves and purse.

The Board Member

Brad Corrigan drove south on Biscayne Boulevard. In a few minutes he would meet privately with the chairman of United Industries. Apprehension soured his stomach, yet he stiffened his resolve.

Corrigan looked across the water toward the big-ships channel giving access to the ocean. Two tugboats, bows cushioned by blankets of padding, imperceptibly nudged a tanker away from the dock, stern-first, easing the ship from its berth out into the channel. Inexorably the enormous vessel was compelled to proceed in the direction of the energy the tugs applied.

That's exactly how Calvin Phillips operates, Brad said to himself, steering United Industries by absolute force of will, as if he and his family owned *all* the damn stock!

Corrigan visualized Calvin Phillips at the head of the boardroom table, a man of spare build, perched slightly forward in his chair, peering down the length of the table. Lean face impassive, accented by rimless owl-shaped glasses, thinning hair combed meticulously to each side, Phillips held a financial report in pale-white, feline hands. He wore a black silk blazer and brilliant red tie. A paisley handkerchief, bold yellow, embellished the breast pocket. Despite his peculiarity, Calvin Phillips emanated soundless intensity. Corrigan admired the chairman's drive, his corporate triumphs, but intuitively distrusted him.

Brad Corrigan, sixty, was a solid man, square face, dark hair, who carried his sizable bulk erect and moved with unexpected ease. Today, as most days, he wore a conservatively-patterned sport jacket and soft-blue button-down shirt. In the Lincoln's trunk was a large, battered tackle box, a worn canvas bag holding several casting rods in protective slots, a long-handled net, and rubber boots. A little after daybreak tomorrow he and a friend would be in the lower Keys, sitting hunched over in a small boat tautly anchored against rushing channel waters, casting for tarpon or mangrove snapper.

The principal owner of a large insurance agency, Corrigan had accepted an invitation from Calvin Phillips a few years ago to join the board of directors of United Industries. They belonged to some of the same clubs and ran in much the same social crowd. Like Phillips, Brad was the beneficiary of a business founded by his father. Phillips related to that, liked having men on his board from a similar background.

Corrigan turned off the boulevard. A condominium apartment building, pyramid shaped, faced eastward toward the waters of Biscayne Bay. Potted tropical foliage, verdant and entangling, spilled over stair-stepped terraces. Just ahead a row of sparkling office buildings stretched skyward. Dominant among them was a tower of black glass and polished steel, thirty floors of extravagant architecture capped by gleaming aluminum letters proclaiming "UIC", corporate headquarters for United Industries Corporation.

Lush green turf bordered the broad sweep of entrance drive into the grounds. Corrigan swerved to avoid the sudden spray from a wayward sprinkler, and glanced up at the burnished tower. He felt intimidated by this brandishing of the pervasive financial muscle wielded by Calvin Phillips, then instantly angry at himself for permitting that power to bother him. This was a weak prelude to the confrontation with Phillips, and he shrugged it off as best he could.

Wendell Carter, a friend and lawyer in the law firm representing UIC, had alerted him to what he might expect. They ran into each other at a business reception.

Taking him by the elbow, Carter steered Corrigan off to one side. "Brad, what do you know about the stock plan Calvin Phillips is toying with for UIC?"

"I haven't heard anything about it," Brad replied. He finished the scotch and soda, spinning the ice cubes in his empty glass. "But that's typical of how Calvin functions," he added with a grimace. "He waits until he has all the chips in place before he presents any proposal to the board."

"Well, as a friend, I think I should alert you to what's going on." Carter glanced over his shoulder. "I've heard at the office that Calvin might go for an exchange of Class 'B' common stock with super voting rights for the big block of Class 'A' stock he and his family own." He paused. Corrigan did not react. "Do you know what I'm talking about?"

"Not really." Brad looked around, surveying the crowd, his interest not yet fully engaged. He felt disdain for the way people wedged inexplicably close together near the center of the room, ignoring the empty space around them. With arm bent and clutching a glass with one hand, it seemed as if everyone gestured hysterically with their free hand and shouted in order to be heard at faces only inches away.

"The way it works is this", Carter continued methodically, unaware of Brad's discomfort. "The plan would give Phillips ten voting rights with each share of the new Class 'B' stock. That compares with the one vote per share that all other stockholders have for their Class 'A' stock." Wendell Carter dropped his head slightly to peer at Corrigan over his glasses, and spoke deliberately. "Such a plan would make it possible for Calvin Phillips and his family to have absolute control of the company."

Brad stared at Carter. "How could he do that?"

"UIC wouldn't be the first to adopt such a plan. It's been put in place by other corporations to defend against unfriendly takeovers. You know, by corporate raiders or by other companies that might make a pass at buying a targeted company. It's called a 'poison pill'."

Corrigan caught a waiter's attention, and traded his empty glass for a fresh Scotch and soda. "Sounds implausible to me. What about the one share, one vote principal?"

Carter called after the waiter, asking for a Jack Daniels on the rocks. He lit a cigarette. "Out the window, for all practical purposes. And you say 'implausible', but, my friend, it's actually very real." Carter fell into a lawyer-like tone of voice. "Calvin Phillips would have to agree to accept a lower dividend on the new Class 'B' stock. Certain restrictions would be placed on the disposition of his stock. But basically, it makes the company impossible for someone else to acquire, because Phillips would control virtually all the voting rights."

"Sounds suspicious to me. But I'm glad you warned me. Thanks, Wendell, I really appreciate it."

Brad Corrigan winced at the proposed scheme even as he slowed his car to approach the entrance to the underground garage of the UIC Tower. The sun's first rays, just topping the trees, struck him in the eyes. He raised a hand to shield them, then stopped the car at the sentry box where a uniformed guard sat, reading a newspaper.

"Good morning, George!" he called out through the lowered window.

"Morning, Mr. Corrigan!", the guard responded with a grin. "Ain't this a little early for you?"

"No doubt about that!" Corrigan smiled back. The security guard touched a button and the gate arm rose snappily.

"You're the only director here, Mr. Corrigan, so take your choice of stalls." Corrigan nodded and pulled into the garage. The tires of his car squished on the painted concrete surface.

Brad had received a call at home the night before. "This is Cal Phillips," the chairman said when Corrigan's wife answered. She handed her husband the telephone, raising her eyebrows. The chairman never called Brad at home.

"Say, Brad, I was wondering if you could have a bite of breakfast with me tomorrow morning at the Tower. Say 7:15." His voice was smooth as always. "Just the two of us. I've got an idea I'd like to talk with you about." Corrigan wasn't misled by the casual tone. Money and power were forces ever behind Phillips' bland expression. "I'd like your opinion about something I've been considering."

Corrigan said he'd be there, and Phillips concluded with "Real nice of you to do it on such short notice." Corrigan waited for the click of the telephone, then hung up himself.

"So what did he want?" Phyllis asked.

Brad told her. "I wonder what he's up to," she said. "You've had to be careful of him in the past." They sat down together on the sofa, and she tucked her legs beneath her, turning toward him.

"You're right, I have."

"Remember the time Calvin maneuvered to get some import restrictions through Congress? To protect his prices against the Taiwanese, I think it was. You told me about it then, remember?" Brad nodded, and Phyllis continued. "He wanted to get some campaign money into the hands of a U.S. senator who agreed to sponsor a bill that would give Calvin what he wanted. Right?"

Again Brad nodded, and said "I was worried that Calvin's strategy in channeling the corporation's money through the company's political action committee might be found out, might be construed as a pay-off, which of course it was in a way."

"And that if the government found out, or if the money was traced, it would look bad for UIC, isn't that what happened?" she asked.

"That was about it. I talked with Calvin, privately, and told him I was concerned. He listened, and thanked me for my interest."

"And you later found out he'd gone ahead and done it anyway. Isn't that the point?"

"That's about the size of it."

"Why didn't you follow up on it then? Did you ever talk about it with some of the other directors?"

"No, I didn't. I thought about it, but I let it drop."

"Why?"

"Well, I guess I have to admit I didn't have the guts to take Calvin on. I believed it was wrong, but I was new on the board." Brad rubbed his hands over his face. "If we were under fire, I knew the company's lawyers would argue forcefully that it was legal. They usually do. But the news media really worried me. If they'd gotten wind of it, the publicity would have been awful. And formal charges could have been brought. The directors could have been liable, too."

Brad looked at his wife, saw the distress in her face. "I think one or two other outside directors were uneasy about it, when they learned what had happened, but I don't know whether they ever questioned Calvin about it. They probably didn't." He thought a moment. "Looking back, I guess I should have done more about it than I did."

"Do you know what he wants to talk with you about tomorrow?" Phyllis asked matter-of-factly.

"I think so," and he told her about the warning from Wendell Carter.

"But Brad, that's fundamentally unfair! Anyone can see that. I think it's deceiving the stockholders!"

"Yes, I agree with you." Corrigan got up, stretched, took a deep breath, and leaned back on his heels as he slowly exhaled, releasing some of the tension in his back and shoulders. "Would you like a liqueur?" Phyllis nodded, and he poured a Grand Marnier for each of them in small crystal glasses.

Phyllis sipped the sweet, honey-colored liquid and watched her husband as he sank down on the sofa next to her. Brad carefully rested his feet on the edge of the marble coffee table.

"You and I think it's a bad plan," Corrigan continued, "but other directors may not see it that way. A few of them are heads of public companies where they and their families also own big chunks of stock. From their perspective, the plan makes sense. They can hang onto their control." He swallowed the rest of his liqueur. "I think the bottom line is that the plan takes away the rights of the majority of the stockholders. They would still own by far the biggest share of the company, but would have no say when it comes to the performance of management or a sale of the company."

"How many stockholders are there? Do they really care?"

"Oh, there must be about thirty-five hundred. Old Rockland Phillips, Calvin's father, started the company in the 1930s, and raised the initial capital from only a handful of friends. But the business grew, and eventually he was forced to make a public offering, you know, raise capital by selling stock to the public."

Phyllis asked again, "Do the stockholders really care if they end up having no voting rights?"

"Probably not as long as they think the company is well run and they're getting a reasonable dividend with some growth in the value of their stock. But if things don't go right, their only out is to sell their stock." Brad was silent for a moment. "I think knowing stockholders really don't have a vote sends the wrong message to management. What's more, the directors would be abdicating the responsibility we have now to represent the interests of the stockholders."

Phyllis looked worried. "Are you thinking about going against Calvin on this?"

Corrigan considered the question. Since his talk with Wendell Carter, he'd been asking himself what he should do, looking for alternatives. "That's going to be a tough call. I don't like being out there all alone on a major issue of this kind, and I don't know whether he's talked about this with any of the other outside directors."

He looked at Phyllis for her reaction as he said: "My term as a director ends at the annual meeting next March. Whether I'm nominated for another term is up to Calvin. As chairman, he nominates whomever he wants. The board's nominating committee goes along with whatever Calvin proposes. They're all friends of his."

"How important is it to you, to remain on the board?"

Brad smiled wryly. "Well, the quarterly director fees do add up, and when I take the fees in United Industries stock, the company adds one share for each share I buy, so that's worth a lot over time. There's also the prestige." He grinned. "It's a nice package, overall."

Brad lifted his legs off the coffee table, his expression serious. "The most important consideration is that United Industries is a big buyer of property and casualty insurance from our company, as you know. Maybe as much as 40% of our total premium income. I'd hate to lose them as a customer." He added in a flat tone: "I know Calvin would pull the business if I bucked him on something of this magnitude."

They were both silent. Brad then said quietly, "It would make a difference in our lives, at least for a time."

Phyllis reached over and put her arms around him. "Don't worry. If that happens, we'll make it." She gave him a hug. "Do what you think is right."

Brad put his arms around his wife and nuzzled her ear, breathing in the fresh scent of her hair. "Let's sleep over it," he said. "Maybe the old bastard has something else on his mind."

Once parked, Brad Corrigan got out, and locked his car with an electronic key. From the wallet in his jacket he took a plastic security card bearing the magnetic code that would open the sliding doors from the garage into a lower level lobby of the Tower. It would be a half-hour before the building's two thousand employees flooded the building.

He had slept uneasily the night before, wrestling with the dilemma. Opposing Calvin Phillips was not easy. He groped for another way out. Maybe a majority of the outside directors would say no to the plan. He didn't know. His body felt strained, stretched out.

Brad activated the elevator's control panel with the security card and pressed the button for the 30th floor. The elevator rose without feeling of motion, and then stopped gently. A computer-generated female voice softly announced the 30th floor, asked him to watch his step. The doors slid open. Corrigan glanced at his wristwatch: 7:14. He liked being on time.

Across the executive floor lobby Mrs. Henley waited to greet him.

"Good morning, Gladys! It's nice to see you here, but how in the world do you manage things to get in so early?" Corrigan admired her loyalty and sense of duty.

"Good morning, Mr. Corrigan! Oh, there isn't as much traffic this time of day." She smiled warmly. "Mr. Phillips asked if you would go on in to the dining room. Breakfast is being served in the Pissaro Room. He's finishing up a call to our office in London, and won't keep you waiting long."

Corrigan thanked her and walked toward the several dining rooms named after French Impressionists. Calvin Phillips collected Impressionists, so the names were his idea.

Brad entered the dining room and glanced at the Honduran mahogany paneling with Gabon ebony accents. Such extravagance troubled him, but Calvin Phillips always went first-class.

Standing patiently just inside the room was the waiter who usually served at small gatherings.

"Hello, José, how are you?"

"Just fine, thank you, Mr. Corrigan." José turned to the sideboard to pour a cup of coffee.

Calvin Phillips was ebullient when he strode into the room. "Good morning, Brad!" and extended his hand in a quick greeting. "Let's sit down. I'm hungry, and you probably are, too."

Two places were set. Phillips indicated with a gesture the chair Brad was to take. José stepped forward to pour orange juice from a frosted silver pitcher.

"Just to save time, Brad, I've ordered breakfast for us. Hope you don't mind."

"No, not at all, a good idea."

"Business seems to be going well for us abroad. London said our new lines of electronic products are making strong inroads against the European-based competition. I need to get Purchasing to be a little tougher on our suppliers, though, to lower our material costs."

Brad listened attentively, yet he was impatient for Phillips to introduce the real subject of their meeting. Silently, José served a hearty country breakfast on handsome china bearing the Company's logo. He poured fresh cups of coffee, asked if they needed anything else, and withdrew into the adjoining serving area.

Calvin Phillips finished his review of the markets in Europe, then changed the subject.

"Brad, I've been giving serious study to the subject of management succession for our company." His voice was silken. "My health is good, I feel great, and I'd like to run this company for another ten years. You know what we've accomplished. I feel I've still got a lot of pulling power left, but I recognize that my father was only a few years older than I am when he died so unexpectedly . . . .".

Phillips paused, but Corrigan didn't change expression or make the expected comment. He knew that Calvin Phillips was about the same age as was his father, old Rockland Phillips, when the still-vigorous patriarch collapsed in the board room from a massive heart attack and died a few hours later.

"Anyway," Phillips continued, "at the next quarterly Board meeting I'd like to propose that my son Jerry be named President and Chief Operating Officer." Phillips quickly finished the last of his eggs and dabbed at his lips with the napkin. "Jerry's doing a great job, and that would assure the ongoing involvement of our family in the management of the Company." He paused and, inviting a reaction from Corrigan, turned his attention toward buttering a biscuit.

His voice neutral, Corrigan asked: "What about Henry Hollingsworth? He's been in that slot for just about two years and seems to be taking hold pretty well. Henry's not near retirement age."

"I've thought about that. For one thing, Henry never has accumulated much of our stock." The disdain was undisguised. "But he's been with us for a long time, so he's got considerable retirement benefits already built up. I thought we'd just fully vest those rights, and give him a big enough severance package that he'd be willing to walk away. We'll throw in a non-compete clause, of course."

Corrigan kept his counsel.

"Also, our lawyers have warned us that we're vulnerable to an unfriendly takeover. Too much of our stock is owned outside the company. That includes several institutional investors whose only interest is the price of our stock. Those vultures look for a big profit if the company is acquired." He frowned. "The market never has fully reflected the real value of our stock." Corrigan nodded.

Phillips continued. "Well, frankly, I've been worried, too, about the possibility of a takeover. There are a lot of corporate wolves circling out there. They'd like to catch us at a time when our stock has taken a dip and go after our public shareholders with an offer to buy the stock at a price well above market. But whatever they paid they'd still be buying us on the cheap." The chairman looked pained.

"It's no secret," Phillips said, "that my family and I own about 11% of the Company's common stock. The employees stock plan, together with our directors, own another 8% combined, so we control about 19% overall."

Corrigan nodded.

"Unfortunately, 19% of the stock isn't enough to fend off an aggressive corporate raider with a pocketful of cash and big bank loans. Wall Street is plenty anxious, and God-knows greedy enough, to back a strong buyer. The huge fees they make lead to some astonishingly brazen moves."

Phillips scowled. "So we've got two matters to deal with. Who's going to succeed me, and how do we keep the wolves at bay."

Phillips pushed his chair back from the table. "That's what I've been working on, and I think I've got a solution." He lit a cigarette and exhaled the smoke slowly. His eyes had a bright, satisfied look in them as he proceeded to outline the plan that Wendell Carter had explained to Corrigan.

When he finished, Phillips paused and looked at Corrigan expectantly, but Brad, anticipating, dodged the look by raising his cup of coffee to his lips, and said nothing.

Not to be put off, Phillips put it to Corrigan: "How does that program sound to you, Brad?"

Corrigan took a moment to respond, as if weighing the matter for the first time. "Let me be sure I understand what you're describing," he said slowly. "The Phillips family would have ten times more voting rights per share than all the other shareholders. That means your 11% ownership effectively outweighs the votes of all other stockholders."

He paused, looked the chairman in the eye, and said evenly: "For all practical purposes, the majority shareholders would no longer have a voice in the management of the company. They would be giving up that right to the Phillips family. In the final analysis," and he said this more slowly, to indicate that he was thinking about it carefully, "whoever votes the stock held by the Phillips family has the final word, not the Board and not the outside stockholders who actually own the majority interest in the company."

The chairman's face tensed for little more than an instant, but the blank expression quickly resumed its place. "Let's have some more coffee," he said, his voice carefully controlled. He touched the buzzer on the paneled wall. José entered the room carrying a silver coffee pot. Both men remained quiet until he had filled their cups and left.

Brad found himself becoming angry as the full impact of Phillips's strategy sank in, but he let the chairman have his say.

"Let's put it this way, Brad," Phillips continued in a reasonable tone. "No one wants this company to fall into the hands of a bunch of Wall Street bandits. Who knows how our employees might be treated."

Phillips lit another cigarette, and puffed on it thoughtfully for a moment. "Besides, our lawyers say that now is the time to get this done. We could come to work any day and find that some bastard has launched an unfriendly takeover of our company."

Agitated, Phillips rose abruptly from his chair, jostling the table so that coffee slopped out of the cup into the saucer, and walked over to the window. "They'd really have a fight on their hands if that happened!" Quietly, as if to himself, he said: "And they'd be foolish to underestimate me."

Phillips gazed intently out the window for a moment, then returned to stand behind his chair, hands resting on the back. "There's another thing." He lowered his voice. "We understand that Congress is looking into federal legislation that would limit the use of this Class 'B' stock plan. We've got to move before that can happen."

Corrigan struggled to conceal his reaction. He pushed his chair back a little from the table, laid his napkin carefully on the table, and forced himself to sit back in a relaxed manner. "Calvin, let me first comment on your plan for management succession. Unquestionably it's wise to be thinking about that."

The face across from him brightened. "I think your son, Jerry, is a bright, energetic guy. He's still young, but he has a lot of your drive. Given time, he might someday very well make a top-notch C.E.O." Corrigan left unsaid his feelings about the brash, arrogant son of the chairman, and about Jerry's frequent excursions mountain climbing in exotic places around the world.

"Under your guidance, Calvin, Jerry will probably develop into a good corporate executive. But if something happened to you, and you're not around, I have to say that I wouldn't feel comfortable as a director and shareholder with Jerry having absolute control of the company." Corrigan leaned forward slightly. "There would be no way to stop him, if for any reason he went off the deep end."

Phillips's face was no longer impassive, but contorted by anger. "Why do you think Jerry would ever do that?" he cried out. "He's perfectly sound!" Then, masking his momentary loss of control, Phillips rang for José. "How about some more coffee, Brad?"

Brad nodded.

José removed Phillips's cup and saucer, replacing them with clean ones, and poured fresh cups. After José departed, Corrigan continued. "Admittedly, that's highly unlikely, that Jerry would be a loose cannon, but it illustrates my point. There's just no way around it, Calvin. There's good reason for outside shareholders having voting rights. Sure, they almost always go along with management. But if things did go wrong, they would no longer have the right to vote for a change. Their votes would be meaningless."

Phillips remained silent, his face taut. He toyed with the coffee spoon resting in the saucer.

Corrigan decided he had to get it out on the table. "Calvin, another thing about this plan bothers me. Handing over complete control to your family does away with any potential sale of the company down the road. A sale at a fair price would reward longtime shareholders with a handsome return on their investment."

"Is that what you want?" Phillips asked icily, tossing his napkin onto the table. He got up and walked over to close the door into the corridor. Instead of returning to the table, he stood next to the sideboard, leaning slightly against it, arms folded, and looked down at Corrigan. His face was hard. "You want to sell the company?"

"No, not now, but I think it's wrong to take that possibility away from the outside shareholders, with your ten-to-one voting rights."

"Don't you think my family and I would like to make a big profit on the sale of our stock as much as anybody?" Phillips shot back, and moved back to his chair.

"Well, yes and no." Corrigan decided to lay it all on the line. "After all, Calvin, both you and your son draw substantial salaries, bonuses, and stock options from UIC. Not that you don't deserve them, because I'd be the first to say that under your leadership, this company has come a long ways. But if other management was brought in, or if new ownership promoted others within the company to the top executive positions, you and your son would no longer have these benefits, nor would you have the top positions."

Drained, Corrigan was nonetheless compelled to finish. "Calvin, what you're proposing, and what the lawyers have said you should do, doesn't square with what's right and what's wrong. Besides, who's to say that new ownership wouldn't take a responsible attitude toward our employees? It's in their best interest to do so."

Anticipating Phillips's rebuttal, Corrigan added "Sure, the outcome with a corporate raider may be more uncertain. But if the company comes into play, we could seek out the kind of buyer we'd like to have. Everyone would benefit from this: employees, suppliers, and especially our shareholders."

Abhorrence and disbelief twisted Phillips's face. He ground out his unfinished cigarette in the ornate ash tray and seemed ready to explode.

But after a moment, he said evenly: "I think you're wrong about all this, and I'm sorry to see you take this position." He stared at Corrigan. "I thought you would understand what I want to do."

For what seemed like a long time, neither man spoke. Then Phillips said, as if changing the subject, "Brad, I've been thinking there might be substantial savings in costs by consolidating our insurance coverage overseas with our domestic programs. You've got access to those overseas markets, don't you?"

Brad nodded, his mind quickly calculating the kind of premium volumes such additional business would generate.

Phillips said nothing more, his eyes holding Brad's in an expressionless gaze.

Then, his voice skillfully implying another change in the subject, Phillips continued. "You probably don't know this, Brad, but you're the last of the outside directors I've talked to about this matter over the last few days." He changed position in his chair, and looked out the large glass window at the distant ocean, colored a startling blue and speckled with whitecaps.

For a moment he was quiet, then turned back around to face Corrigan. "The outside directors were evenly split on this question," he said coldly, "until I met with you this morning. You tip the scale toward those who oppose the plan. In effect," and he seemed to draw out the words, "you were the swing vote."

Corrigan remained silent. Phillips shifted slightly his position in the chair, watching carefully the expression on the face of the director seated across from him. "You understand what I want to do?" he said again.

Brad, his face coloring slightly from the emotion he was feeling, replied "I understand, Calvin, but I don't agree with you. This is not a step we should take".

"Well, I will not accept that view," Calvin Phillips said flatly. "If I can't persuade you to change your mind, I intend to fight you on this." He stared at his opponent. "You know I can do that, don't you? You *know* what you can lose."

Corrigan returned the look. "Yes, I do, and I'm sorry," he replied, pushing back his chair and standing up to go. "Sorry that I have to oppose you on this, sorry about what it does to our relationship." He looked at Phillips, still seated, who somehow seemed diminished, one thin, pale hand lying flat on the white damask tablecloth. "I had hoped, Calvin, that *you* would understood what *I've* been trying to say."

Calvin Phillips shrugged slightly, his face again impassive. A slender spiral of smoke rose from the cigarette he held between his thumb and forefinger, cupped and unseen in the palm of his hand, the arm hanging motionless to one side.

Corrigan quietly left the room, sensing the force of the chairman's antagonism at his back. He knew that Phillips would not give up, that his own relationships with the chairman and the company were ended by the encounter.

Gladys Henley looked up expectantly from her desk as he crossed the reception area. "Good-bye, Mr. Corrigan. It's always nice to see you. I hope you have a good day."

"Thank you, Gladys." Unexpectedly, he paused, smiled, and reached across the desk to shake her hand. For an instant, she looked startled.

Corrigan stepped into the waiting elevator.

The Late Arrival

A GHOST STORY FOR CHIDREN

The night watchman glanced up at the clock above the Inn's reception desk. He sighed, noting that the time was after one o'clock in the morning. He stretched his hands toward the wood fire burning in the great stone hearth for a last warming before beginning his rounds.

"This is no night for a God-fearing man to be out and about!", he grumbled in a raspy voice, as rough as gravel, with an immigrant's brogue.

The dark windows rattled from the wind, and sudden torrents of rain blew against the steeply slanting roof a full three floors above the open lobby. Enormous cedar logs, shorn of their bark and the color of honey, smooth to the touch, angled upward in a scaffolding of beams and joists to support the roof and the balcony circling the lobby. The building was strongly built to withstand the heavy winter snows, but in the face of such a storm, the Inn clung like a great bird to the rock shelf on the side of the mountain, and seemed to hunker down and turn its back against the force of the wind and the rain.

"I'd best take a look at the bridge over Great Boulder Creek on my next rounds", the watchman muttered. "The water rises real quick in a rainstorm like this one. That old bridge ain't gonna last forever!"

I nodded my head in agreement, and continued my duties as desk clerk, checking off the names of expected guests who had arrived that day and were now safely in their beds. "All here except one", I noted to the watchman, and drew a circle around the name of the distinguished guest who had not yet arrived.

There was a notation from the manager of the Inn attached to the reservation card that the missing guest had telephoned earlier in the evening to say that he was just leaving the train station in the village far below. Despite the nasty weather, he had persuaded someone to drive him from the village up to the Inn, following the twisting road etched out of the mountain's flanks. A tedious trip even in fair weather, he hoped to arrive by midnight, he had told the Inn's manager. I said as much to the watchman, who shook his head in disbelief.

"He'd best have a driver who knows the road up here blindfolded", he grumbled. "You can't see nothing beyond an arm's reach, what with the fog and the driving rain and the blackness!"

As the watchman pushed back his chair to get up, the legs grated against the rough-hewn planked floor of the Inn. Cursing to himself about the ferocious weather, he struggled to put on the stiff, heavy coat, and pulled his hat down hard on his head, so that his ears crumpled under the brim. He gave a last, forlorn look at the leaping flames and soaring sparks rushing up the chimney only to be dissipated by the wind. Before he opened the massive front door of the Inn, he pulled the collar of the coat up close around his neck.

Looking back at me over his shoulder, he called out: "I'll keep an eye out for that man, foolish as he is!" and stepped out into the angry darkness.

I shivered from the chill gust of air tumbling into the room before the watchman could close the door behind him. Stepping out from behind the reception desk, I walked over to the great stone hearth where the cedar logs crackled dryly and spit out tongues of fire. I envied the guests and other employees of the Inn who had finally tired of waiting for our renowned guest and gone to their rooms, content to wait until the new day to greet him. While waiting for the watchman's return, I lay back in the overstuffed chair pulled close to the hearth, propped my feet on the wood bench, yawned, and closed my eyes. I thought about the famous man who was long overdue, and wondered why he was ignoring warnings against traveling the road up to the Inn on such a night.

It was true, the guest who had not as yet arrived on this stormy night was indeed a man of international reputation, a musician and composer of intense energy and perseverance. The story was that he had survived the concentration camps of war-devastated Europe during World War II by posing as an obscure violinist, a man of small talent, who played only in the local Austrian cafes. Thus he had gone unrecognized by his captors and by the prison guards.

When Europe recovered after the war, von Frohnknecht fled to the New World to conduct his mighty In Memorium symphony and other compositions before audiences in major cities. Morose, enigmatic in its composition, the powerful music of Eric von Frohnknecht spoke with a dark fury and unrepentant anger, yet achieved levels of ecstasy evocative of the final choral passages in Beethoven's Ninth Symphony.

I had read that Dr. von Frohnknecht, an Austrian by birth, spent his boyhood among the spectacular mountains of his beloved country. In winter the slopes of the mountains were covered deep in snow, and ragged black peaks glistened in coatings of ice. With several days remaining before his next performance, he had decided to arrange a visit to America's boundless range of coastal mountains that face the Pacific Ocean and, unseen across thousands of miles, alien vistas of the Far East. He deeply longed for the Austrian mountains of his boyhood, and sought replenishment of his spirit among these ancient volcanic peaks in America's Pacific Northwest. Disregarding the storm warnings, Dr. von Frohnknecht appeared to be determined to reach the mountain Inn before the day's end, so that he might rest from the rigors of his concert tour.

The unrelenting storm pummeled the Inn crouching on the ledge of the mountain. Cedar boughs brushed harshly against the windows, like a broom in the hands of a furious witch. A charred log, still glowing with the fire's heat, abruptly fell from the andiron where it had precariously balanced until the tongues of flame, licking at the dry wood, finally toppled it.

Suddenly the wood-and-iron door to the Inn was flung back against the wall. Clouds of fog billowed into the room. Standing in the midst of the swirling white vapor was a strange man wrapped all around in a great black coat. The turned-up collar hid all except his eyes, staring at me as if from a great distance. Water dripped from his coat and from the European-style fur hat he wore low on his head. The wood floor was already stained dark by the water that fell from his clothes.

The door shut with a loud noise, although I did not see him turn to close it. Removing his hat with an impatient gesture, he strode across the lobby toward me. Thick black hair scored with streaks of gray swept back from his forehead and fell over the sides of his head. A burgundy-red scarf was wrapped tightly around his neck. Strong features, a jutting nose, dark eyebrows almost too thin for such a large man, he had the look of a powerful aristocrat, a man of strong convictions, someone intent on getting to where he wanted to go.

Recovering my wits, I stammered "May I help you, sir?", and immediately regretted such an inadequate remark.

Standing directly in front of me, he placed his unexpectedly delicate-looking hands face-down on the registration desk, as if by the weight of his body to fasten it to the spot. He continued staring at me, without saying a word.

Recovering somewhat, I said "Pardon me, sir, but would you be Dr. von Frohnknecht?"

"I am!" he declared forcefully, accenting the second word, without loosening his gaze upon me. And then again, "I am!"

"Welcome, sir, we have been expecting you, sir, and we are delighted that you have arrived, sir!", I gushed breathlessly.

The eyes were strangely vacant, as I looked back at our guest, and his pale face was grayish-white in color, puffy, and of an odd-appearing texture.

"I hope the drive up the mountain was not too uncomfortable for you, sir", I said solicitously. "May I ask you to sign the guest register, and then I will gladly show you to your room. I know you must be weary from your journey."

The great man picked up the pen. Moving stiffly, and holding the pen awkwardly in his right hand, he scrawled ERIC von Frohnknecht, moving the pen in a painfully slow movement across the page, as if his fingers were still quite numbed by the cold. The pen recorded his name in scratchy, short strokes of black ink.

He then dropped, rather than laid down the pen on the reception desk, so that the pen clattered and rolled toward me. Uttering a long sigh, as if from great fatigue, he raised his right hand to brush away the dark hair that had fallen over his forehead as he bent to scrawl his name. It was then that I saw a vivid red gash traced across the forehead, just beneath the hairline. My first instinct was to look away, out of politeness, and so my eyes dropped to the line on the guest register where I had just seen our guest sign his name.

To my astonishment, the line was blank! There was nothing there! The black ink of his signature had disappeared from the page!

Suddenly I felt a gushing in my head, and dizziness, and my legs seemed to have lost their feeling. A deafening sound from a great distance off filled my ears. I heard rock boulders tumbling downward and the roar of water plunging unchecked. I saw a vision of wood planks torn from a bridge to make way for the relentless torrent of water. As the bridge disintegrated from the descending force, the wrenching sound of the bridge being torn apart sounded like screams carried away in the wind. A large dark object that appeared to be an automobile, trapped on the falling bridge, disappeared from view.

A heavy hand on my shoulder caused me to shudder. Distraught, I gazed about me and saw the night watchman looking at me with a puzzled expression on his face. The wood fire was now only bright-red glowing coals. The lobby of the Inn was filled with cold, dark shadows, and the only sound was of steadily falling rain that seemed to have greatly abated in its intensity.

As if to calm my distracted appearance, the night watchman observed in a disinterested tone of voice, "I seen the lights of a car at the head of the valley slowly comin' this way."

He paused, contemplating his next observation. "My guess is that the late arrival and the man bringin' him up probably pulled off to one side of the road, waitin' for the worst of the storm to pass."

I nodded my head, rubbing my hands over my face to get the sleep out of my eyes, and rose to my feet. A shiver ran through my body. Reaching into the woodbin, I drew out several sticks of firewood and laid them onto the smoldering coals. I hoped that the logs, bringing warmth and light into the Inn, would burst into flame by the time our distinguished guest arrived.

Going Back

When John awoke, the train was slowing down as it approached the Seattle outlying areas. He lay still for a moment in his berth, remembering the great summer he had spent at Mount Rainier National Park last year. The General Manager had approved John's application for a job as desk clerk for the new season.

He thought of Jean, the girl he had fallen in love with last summer when he was nineteen, and wondered what it would be like to see her again after almost a year. They had exchanged letters frequently, both writing that they were anxious to see each other again.

John's mother, however, had cautioned him that either one of them might feel differently after such a long separation. She counseled him that he could be disappointed.

John raised the window shade in his berth. The morning sky was quickly brightening. Then the train rounded a curve, and across the great distance of the plains John saw the snowcapped peak of Mount Rainer, more than 12,000 feet above sea level at Seattle.

He thought of the final day of hiking that he and Jean had shared last August, at the end of the season. He had awakened early that morning in his dorm. During the night, gray fog had silently filled the valley and left the mountain hidden from view. Climbing out of his bunk, he put on khakis, hiking boots, and a sweater over his wool shirt. The Inn was at 5500 feet above sea level so early mornings were often chilly.

John headed toward the snack bar in the Lodge. His friend, Bill, who lived in Tacoma, had just opened the door and was preparing for the usual busy day of visitors.

"Morning, Bill. Heck of a day, though, isn't it?"

"Yeah, sure is. How about some coffee? Donuts?"

"I'll take the coffee, but Jean and I are going for a hike, so I'd also like to have two of those sandwiches to take with us, and a couple apples. And two Snicker bars. And two bottles of water."

"You going hiking despite the weather?"

Glancing at his watch, John said, "Yeah, it's our last day off work before the Inn closes next week."

John placed everything in his backpack and, putting his arms through the shoulder straps, hoisted it onto his back. He then headed toward the dorm for women employees located on the second floor of the Guides Center. When he called up the stairs, "Hey, Jean, are you ready?" another girl answered, "She'll be down in just a minute."

When Jean reached the bottom of the stairs, a little breathless, she asked "Are we still going?" Wearing slacks, boots, and a sweater tied at her waist, she was prepared for the hike. Her light-brown hair was tied in a long pony tail. They both had hats for protection against the sun at that altitude.

"Sure, if you want to."

"I do" she replied quickly, and smiled.

John grinned. "Great, let's go!"

Making lame jokes about the fog, they started off for the trail leading toward the Tatoosh Range on the other side of the valley lying below Paradise Inn. Once across the valley, they followed another trail, narrower and steeper, that crisscrosses the slopes of the Tatoosh Range. The fog remained, limiting their distance vision but not hazardous to their climb.

The climbers moved slowly, pausing frequently to catch their breath, and then starting up again. Mount Rainier, still hidden from view, was at their backs, across the valley and beyond Paradise Inn. More than 9,000 feet higher than the elevation of Paradise Inn, the Mountain eons ago had been an active volcano. Now, with its mantel of glaciers and deep snow, it remained an awe inspiring challenge of nature.

They had now climbed for more than an hour, conversing little, and stopping from time to time to regain their breath. The climb was strenuous, but not daunting.

Both were silent as they trudged up the last swing of the trail before it reaches the valley rim. The gray fog, still hovering about them, seemed less dense.

John shifted the burden of the backpack to ease the pressure. He was grateful that he and Jean could have this last hike together. They had become more than friends, and he pushed aside his sadness that the summer was almost over. They must soon part, John to finish college and Jean to begin a program leading to a Registered Nurse degree.

The rim was not far above when, almost as if by magic, the fog dissipated and they stepped into clear air with bright sunlight. Behind them, the fog remained below in the valley.

Jean turned and hugged John and they scrambled up the few remaining steps until they reached the meadow where the air was warm and aglow with the brightness of the sun. It was as if they were alone high above in a world of their own.

John took Jean's hand in his hand and, together, they ran across the meadow sprinkled with colorful alpine flowers. Side by side they ran, dashing across the brow of the open meadow high on the top of the world. Ahead of them was a narrow strip of land near the very tip of the peninsula jutting out like the prow of a ship into the great mountain valley.

Breathless, laughing and happy, John shed his backpack and they collapsed onto the soft blanket of the earth.

* * *

The train slackened speed, and with discordant grinding stopped at the railroad station. Jumping quickly to his feet, John seized his luggage and walked hurriedly toward the front of the car. The flash of the porter's broad smile welcomed him from the station platform. Stepping off the train, John placed a five dollar bill in the porter's hand and strode off toward the gate marked "Exit".

He hailed a taxi for the short ride to where he would board a Rainer National Park Company bus. He knew quite a few of those on the bus. Bob, who had been a desk clerk at the Lodge the summer before, and Don, one of the bus boys, were also on the bus. Don had put on a little weight, and John joked with him about what several weeks of bell hopping would do to his extra pounds. Charley, the dour bus driver who taught in the high school during the winter, told a few jokes as he always did. And the girls who had worked in the dining room as waitresses—Pat, Donna, Irene, Jo, and the others—joined in the fun.

It seemed as if nothing had changed.

As the bus approached the Inn, Charley held the horn down for one long blast. "All out, gang, we're here!"

John pushed with the others toward the door of the bus. Eagerly he looked as best he could through the bus windows for a glimpse of Jean among those crowded around the bus, but did not see her. He spotted the tanned, wind-roughened face of Les, the head mountain guide. Then, there she was, standing a little to one side, her expression serious, searching for him.

She saw him, smiled, and waved. John jumped off the bus, pushing his way through the excited crowd toward her until they were face to face. He dropped his luggage and wrapped his arms around her. They hugged and with one hand Jean wiped away tears from her eyes. She seemed unchanged, except that she had trimmed her brown hair in a smart new style. Then John picked up the heavy suitcase, and with his other arm around Jean, together they walked toward the Inn's quarters for male employees where John would bunk for the season.

Family

Caroline's Story

Most of the wedding guests could not have known, although more than a few might have suspected, that my twin-sister, Vivvy, was furious. After all, her only daughter, Avery, was marrying the unacceptably poor son of an Italian postal worker from a village near Campobasso. That's in Italy, southeast of Rome. (How could we be expected to know?)

Vivvy's honey-sweet smile seemed genuine enough, and her voice was gracious and solicitous as she glided from one cluster of well-dressed guests to another, bestowing her radiance with discrimination so subtle that one seldom noticed. But she was inwardly fuming.

My husband, Jerry, chuckled at what we both knew was Vivvy's discomfort.

"But I have to hand it to her," he said when we were alone for a moment. "She carries it off magnificently. Who else but Vivvy could coax her daughter's about-to-be mother-in-law, who doesn't understand a word of English, up the stairs to the second floor for a much-needed bath before the wedding guests arrived. But Vivvy did it so gracefully!"

Jerry broke into a laugh. "The old woman actually gave Vivvy a big, toothless smile as they climbed the steps together, talking non-stop the whole time!"

I had watched them, too. Mrs. Salino hoisted her bulk one step at a time up the wide, graceful stairway, leaning heavily on Vivvy's slender arm, and grasping in the other hand a stout wood cane that shared the shifting burden. She was dressed all in black, as she had been since they arrived on Thursday, thick graying hair pulled back in a bun. Perspiration darkened the cloth patches beneath her arms, and she smelled of sweat and body powder.

Not long after, when the wedding reception began in the garden on the shady east side of Vivvy's sprawling Tudor house, Mrs. Salino settled into a white vinyl lawn chair from which she never moved, beaming approval and mopping her face with a wadded-up linen handkerchief. Guests drifted by to express their obligatory greetings. She nodded and smiled, agreeably ignoring the fact that neither she nor they understood a word the other said. However, she was not uncomfortable in the situation in which her son's marriage had placed her. The grand house, her delicate hostess, the fashionable, urbane guests, all this she took in stride. Italy had been an ancient civilization. Why should she be intimidated?

Then I saw Avery, shimmering in her long white gown, talking animatedly with several classmates from Wellesley as she stood next to Stephon, her husband of less than an hour. Avery has an elfin figure, light brown hair cut short, profile delicate and precise as if cut with scissors by an artist out of paper. It struck me that Avery suddenly seemed unexpectedly mature, a woman quite in control of her life.

I recognized that Avery had indeed found love in an English-as-second-language class she taught in defiance of her mother at the International Institute in Back Bay. The student she singled out, admittedly because she thought him a curious, even mysterious sort of person, was Stephon Salino. He was very thin, with the sad, wasted look of an Ellis Island immigrant one sees in old photographs of the last century. Large dark eyes in a pale, rather interesting face, black hair falling over his forehead, shoulders slouched, hand cupping a cigarette with the ash about to fall, like a youth from the gutters in a dark Fellini movie. He also had a sexy way about him. Maybe the sum of his being succeeded largely because he knew who he was and liked what he was.

Stephon says he wants to be a poet, or maybe a journalist, or some other occupation only vaguely grasped, but I see wariness in his eyes when he speaks of it. He has a natural subdued insolence, born of innate confidence, I think, as if in the long view not a great deal really matters all that much.

Maybe it was Stephon's vagabond appearance, his roots in a world remote from her own, that caused Avery to fall in love with him. Opposites attract, you know. Avery might not have been desperately in love, you understand, but she was quite willing to flaunt her independence from—well, from her mother, for starters.

At the time Avery met him, Stephon worked as a waiter—sorry, server—in a seafood restaurant on the Harbor, and still does. He appears unfazed by what others might think of his status in life.

In fairness I have to say that my niece, Avery, more typically dressed in tattered jeans with a hole in one knee, a knit halter top, and scruffy hiking boots, usually doesn't look all that different from Stephon. This afternoon, however, her hair beautifully done by Francois, her mother's hairdresser, and gowned in an exquisite satin wedding dress with embroidered sleeves and wearing her mother's perfume from that little shop on Boylston Street, she is quite another person.

In fact, I feel a pang of sadness that Stephon seems completely wrong for my sister's child, and for a moment I better understand what Vivvy must be experiencing. I like Avery, and I think there's more to her than her mother acknowledges. The trouble is that Vivvy expects something quite different. That's a problem with our family.

Looking around, I spotted Patrick, who is Vivvy's son and Avery's older brother, as he moved uneasily among his mother's guests. Abundant hair, dark like his mother's before she began to streak it, hung to his shoulders, parted in the middle above a sallow forehead. Nonetheless, he has his Grandfather Harding's aristocratic features, yet somehow less so, a nose not as strong, but more benign, a chin softly rounded rather than firm.

Patrick stood with hands plunged deep into the pockets of his slacks, his blazer jacket rumpled after having been extracted only an hour ago from the stuff bag Patrick carries as his sole luggage when he travels. He wandered through the crowd like a derelict ship at sea searching uneasily for a safe harbor. He persists in getting around town on a motor bike rather than more conventional transportation. Maybe I inject too much into how Patrick looks, but I know that at age twenty-eight he's a floundering, troubled person, maybe worse.

My brother, Sandy Harding—his given name is Sandifer, my mother's maiden name—is a stockbroker. As usual, he stands a little to one side of the crowd, talking earnestly with a friend who teaches business classes at Harvard. Older than I, Sandy is my parents' second child, actually. They had a daughter, Jennie, who died in an awful accident when she was six and Sandy was three.

Nearby are Sandy's two sons, Eric and Jack, listening to their father discussing investment strategy with his friend. Both sons graduated from

MIT. They're engineers, like their Grandfather Harding. I assume they like it and they appear to be headed upward.

My other brother, Philip, ambled over to where I was surveying the crowd. I think he's less like a Harding than any of us. Phillip does his own thing, which is 17th and 18th century European painting, and I guess he knows as much about it as anyone. He curates at the Boston, and lives with his "significant other" in a nearby condo. We all like him, even though he's a far stretch from the Harding mold. Philip is quite his own person, irritatingly so at times. Maybe it's because he doesn't seem to care about certain things our family takes quite seriously.

"Hi, Caroline. What do you make of the big fiasco?" Phillip smiled wryly, and patted my arm affectionately. I'm just two years younger than Phillip, and we've always gotten along surprisingly well.

"Only Vivvy," I said begrudgingly, giving the devil her due, "could carry this off. Just look around. Three hundred guests on a humid, sweltering August afternoon. Can you imagine?" I shook my head in mock astonishment. "And a formal wedding ceremony in the garden with a sit-down supper on the lawn. She even persuaded the Ritz, who 'doesn't do catering', to cater the damn affair! And there she is, a little damp, maybe, but fresh and sweet. God, is she sweet! . . . and absolutely not wilting, managing the entire event as effortlessly as John Williams conducts the Boston Pops." Phillip laughed, knowing that I was only half serious. I concluded with exasperation, "I really don't see how she does it."

Dabbing his face with a handkerchief, Phillip nodded amiably. He never lets Vivvy ruffle his feelings.

"Still and all", he said, "you know she's putting a brave face on the whole affair. Young Salino is obviously a far cry from the kind of boy she envisioned her only daughter marrying." He finished the now warm champagne left in his glass with a quick up-tilt and handed it to a caterer's server. "Luckily for her, the rest of his family will be returning to Italy next week, back to wherever it is, that little village they come from. She'll figure out something to do with Stephon. She can't have him waiting tables. It's a popular restaurant, and a lot of our friends eat there." Phillip smiled, with just a touch of malice. He's not *that* invulnerable.

Vivvy's antennae must have sensed that we were talking about her because she left the animated group with whom she had been visiting and came sweeping over. The gardenia-colored chiffon gown she wore billowed airily behind her as she crossed the lawn, appropriately accompanied by the sound of baroque music played by a string quartet seated in a half-circle near the fountain. Actually, she doesn't like being called Vivvy any more, except by family, preferring "Vivian".

When she was named chairperson of the Museum's fund-raising festival last year, the *Globe* did an article on her in the Sunday magazine with a full-color photograph and all. She made sure that the chatty journalist used her full name in the column, Mrs. Vivian Harding Dulaney, throughout. Conferring on us her celebrated smile as she walked up, Vivvy kissed Phillip on the cheek and then brushed her cheek against mine.

"Well, it was a very sweet wedding, don't you think?" Her eyes sparkled with feigned enthusiasm. "Stephon's father looked very old-worldly, I thought, standing up as best man for his son. Very soldierly, with his little mustache and all."

Phillip and I smiled, letting well enough alone. Vivvy went on, taking our silence as affirmation. "Bill," that's Vivvy's husband, Bill Dulaney, who's an executive with our father's firm, "Bill thinks that with a little on-the-job training as a draftsman, and speaking Italian, of course, Stephon could be very helpful to the firm overseas. They have a project coming up in Rome, I understand, an expansion of the international airport there".

She spoke as if Stephon's working for the firm were a *fait accompli*, not doubting for a moment that Stephon would obediently go along, nor that there would be a job waiting for him. As she turned to move on, Vivvy added, "We'll see to it that they find a nice little place to live in while they're abroad. A year or two in Italy should be educational for Avery." I wondered what strategy lurked beneath the matter-of-fact comments.

Phillip and I looked at each other, and he winked, but by then Vivvy was gone, enfolded in a foursome of friends who opened up to absorb and then close about her like some underwater flower capturing passing plankton.

"Have you seen Mother and Father?" Phillip asked, looking about.

"They were sitting on the terrace, last time I saw them", I replied.

Taking my arm in a brotherly gesture, he walked over with me to where our parents sat in a cluster of wrought-iron lawn furniture cushioned in striped fabric of cool green and white, smartly matching the window awnings marching across the front of the house. For just that moment, our parents were alone. That seemed odd to me, for some reason, that in the midst of this wedding celebration, my parents sat apart from everyone, perhaps immersed in their own thoughts.

My mother, Frances Sandifer Harding, is seventy-five. I hope that I will look at least a little like she does, when I reach her age. Her carriage is erect, her hair soft silver, her skin clear with only a few irrelevant wrinkles allowed. She has the refined features of her New England ancestors.

Mother has a special way about her. Doormen at restaurants and hotels quickly step forward to help her out of the car and escort her through the door. At the Ritz Carleton, I've seen her place her hand lightly on the doorman's arm when he walks with her up the steps as if she was entirely trusting him to see her safely inside.

My mother, Frances Harding, is also a woman who seldom doubts her own opinions and decisions. An only child, she absorbed generous quantities of love and attention, not doubting her right to their possession. I think she probably always had things rather much her own way. Self-righteousness (yes, that too, sometimes surfaces) can occasionally turn other people away, but Mother's salvation lies in astutely and candidly recognizing these imperfections and skillfully subjugating them beneath a diversionary veneer, whenever it is in her own interest to do so.

At Wellesley she was class president her senior year. Schoolmates who are still close friends recall she was a good organizer, that everyone loved her. She had great energy and graduated with honors. At thirty-two, the year after Vivvy was born, Mother was elected president of the Boston Junior League.

I've seen how she does it, suffusing her natural aggression and ambition with smiles and pats on the back for good work done by others. Mother has always had the political skills of a Boston ward boss, knowing who has power, cannily sensing who is on the way up, which people can do things for her. Our family acknowledges that Mother sets the pace, announces her expectations, and expects to be obeyed.

Edgar Harding, my father, graduated third in his class from MIT. About ten years later, he and a classmate started the engineering firm bearing their names that now operates as far west as Chicago and in Europe as well as the Far East.

Father is seventy-seven, but he keeps fit, tans easily, has a patrician look about him, and with his crisp-cut white hair and confident manner, enjoys the lifestyle he's earned. I loved being seen with him when he came to visit me in college on business trips to North Carolina, because my friends thought he was so elegant and worldly. He is able to be authoritative without alienating people and likeable without being solicitous or ingratiating.

I'm not sure exactly how I know this, but I think Father decided years ago that the best way to cope with Mother's strong will was to let *her* raise the children and set the family's priorities. Generally speaking, I think he usually concurred or at least acquiesced in what she did; and if he ever openly confronted her, it was done out of sight of us as children.

However, my father did set boundaries for his own domain beyond which Vivvy could not trespass. Politics at the engineering firm he implacably excluded from her sphere of influence. The game of polo, where he was team captain in his forties and competitive tennis at the Racquet Club until recent years, remained exclusively his activities. For occasional wild game hunting trips to such places as Canada and South America, Dad never included Mother although a few of his friends took their wives along if accommodations were not arduous. I speculated that it was his way of freeing himself from her for a time.

More than once I knew that Mother resented his independence in such matters, but she remained silent and honored the unspoken bargain they must have struck early in their marriage.

My parents smiled as Phillip and I approached them, and my father quickly rose, gave me a hug and shook hands warmly with Phillip.

"Caroline, dear," my mother said pleasantly, "give me a call tomorrow, preferably by ten, because I have a full schedule the rest of the day." She looked directly at me, holding my eyes for a moment, and I knew she intended me to comply.

Then I heard cheers and cries of excitement as Avery, perched on the front steps in front of Vivvy's backdrop of Tudor grandeur, threw her wedding corsage into the up-stretched arms of squealing bridesmaids. To the sound of applause from family and an acceptable sampling of the three hundred guests gathered round, Mr. and Mrs. Stephon Salino disappeared inside to change their clothes before leaving for their wedding trip to Quebec, generously financed by Vivvy's husband, Bill.

Avery's Story

Stephon and I gazed at the ramparts of the Citadelle, awash with the pink stain of the dying sun. We were standing on a balcony of the Manoir Sainte-Geneviève, our hotel in Quebec. The sunset capped the end of our first week of marriage. I put my arms around my husband, and held him tight, so as to not ever lose him.

The fortress is immense, so overpowering, I wondered how it was possible that the French had lost it to the British and abandoned the city and the harbor, far below on the river. It was a big battle, the guide said, in 1759, on the Plains of Abraham, and it ended French occupation in North America.

Our wedding now seems so long ago. It feels as remote as long-past history, something I imagined rather than experienced. People I had known most of my life played bit parts, dancing in and out of dream-like sequences, while I slowly drifted in the atmosphere like an astronaut outside the spaceship, tethered and weightless. I had been suspended in time, going to one party after another, addressing wedding invitations, acknowledging gifts, getting fitted by the seamstress for my wedding gown, attending bridal showers. At last, all that was over, and Stephon and I could be alone. I felt confident, and I was in love. What more could I ask?

For the first time ever, I feel detached from my family, released from a bond as easily as I had shrugged off my wedding dress and changed into travel clothes. At summer camp, when I was a child, my mother expected me to write letters each week and send at least one postcard to each of my grandparents and to aunts and uncles.

In college, because the campus was not far, Vivvy (she began asking me to call her that, rather than Mother) expected me to spend weekends at home so that I could participate in family activities. When I graduated, she expected me to do things that she could tell her friends about, like volunteering for a charity or interning at some uninteresting job. Well, all that's in the past now. Instead, I got a job teaching English to immigrants, people Mother didn't know or care very much about. That was the beginning. Now it's as if I'd walked through a door that cannot be opened from the other side, away from Vivvy's expectations.

Stephon and I knew each other barely three months before we got married. That really upset my parents. That and the fact that he didn't have any money, and had not been to college. But away from my family, Stephon seems more confident, and more curious about what goes on around him. He still doesn't talk much, but I like being with him. Our sex has been super, and I really like that.

Other things I guess I'll just have to get used to, like the way he eats, the European way, holding his fork upside down and using the knife to push food onto the fork. It seems kind of weird, especially in nice restaurants. But I think he really does love me. Of course, American women are new to him. He thinks we're pushy, that we expect too much, that I'm bossy.

Last night, we went to the rue Ste-Anne, late. It was fabulous. There was a lot of excitement and laughter, and people walking arm in arm along the avenue. Street musicians played flutes and accordions, a violin and saxophone, then passed a hat around for money. Coffee shops and bars were jammed, noise blasting from open doors. The French Canadians are really far out, the way they dress, the way they like a good time and don't seem to worry about things.

We had just turned off into the rue du Trésor, a narrow alley between two main streets, when a street kid who looked a lot younger than us came up out of nowhere and began tagging along next to Stephon. Speaking French in a low voice, he acted as if he was asking Stephon to buy something. Stephon kept shaking his head, but the boy hung on.

I asked Stephon if he knew what the boy wanted, and the boy switched to English, tugging on Stephon's arm, and pulled him off to the side. He showed Stephon something, and Stephon looked around, then took out some money and gave it to him. The boy handed him a folded-over envelope, and Stephon slipped it into his pocket.

I had hoped that Stephon was off that stuff. A little pot is about all I do, and that's not all the time. But I guess I was wrong.

Back at the hotel, we made love, then talked about what we'd do when we went back home. Stephon said he wouldn't work for my grandfather's firm, like Vivvy expects him to do. It would be okay to go back to Italy, he said, if I'd like that, but Stephon says he'll find a job doing something else, even if it doesn't amount to much. That would be okay with me, at least for a while. That'll really burn Vivvy, but she can't do anything about it. I've got the money from the trust my grandfather set up. We can live on that. Things will work out. They always do.

A couple days later we went to see the Basilique. (I like using the French names for places we've seen.) We were standing outside looking at the guidebook when the same boy we'd seen near the rue Ste-Anne came up to us. He and Stephon left together and walked into the public latrine. Stephon was by himself when he walked out, and motioned to me to follow, so I caught up and we walked on down the rue du Tréor. I was pissed at him. First place, it's my money. Second, he's going to get into trouble, doing this. But I didn't say anything.

For lunch we tried a small restaurant near Place de Paris. Tables outside with awnings plastered with Molson beer ads were already filled, so we went inside and were seated next to a huge stone fireplace that isn't used this time of the year, but you could still smell the dank odor of wood smoke.

I was looking at the different quiches on the menu when two men, one dressed in a dark suit, the other in faded shirt and jeans, walked up to the table. The older man spoke French, but quickly switched to English. They were polite, yet Stephon's face tensed.

The man in a suit said that he was Sergeant someone-or-other with the Provincial Police, and would we please show him our identification. He then asked Stephon to step outside the restaurant with him, so they could talk, and told me to stay where I was. Stephon got up, and the man in a suit followed him out. The other man waited nearby, where he could watch me, and lit a cigarette.

When Stephon and the policeman came back into the restaurant, the second man joined them. The man in a suit said, yes, he had it on him, and told us that Stephon would have to go with them for questioning. That really spooked me out. I was scared.

So I called home as soon as I got back to the hotel. Vivvy answered, and my father got on the phone, too. I explained that the police were holding Stephon, and would for several days. I couldn't help it, but I began crying. Dad said he'd fly up as soon as he could get a flight. I said, No, don't do that, we'll handle it on our own. Mother said, but you can't do that. I said we'd find a way. Mother didn't reply, so I said goodbye, and hung up.

Frances' Story

Edgar and I met while I was still at Wellesley. I already knew who he was. That is, I knew who the Hardings were. His great-great-grandfather, Josiah Hamilton Harding, co-founded the Atlantic-Orient Trading Company, one of those giant merchant firms that dominated Boston commerce in the mid-1880s.

The Hardings were like the Cabots, Lodges, Saltonstalls and other old-family names in Back Bay. They mostly married each other—cousins, for example—as much to keep the money in the family as because they often didn't know anyone else who might make an eligible spouse.

I was an exception, as far as the money was concerned, because my great-grandfather Sandifer was still in Ireland long after J. H. Harding began building his empire in America. He was not wealthy. When the Sandifers finally got to America, they were either clergy, educators, or, like my father, a banker who worked for bankers, but didn't own the bank.

I fell in love with Edgar, of course. Who wouldn't, he was so good-looking and already a member of the Bay Colony Club. A classmate of Edgar's, Amanda Cabot, introduced us.

My children don't realize, for the most part, that much of what they benefit from I had to work for. Their father gave them the Harding name, of course, but that was like planting a sapling and then not watering it; after a time, it dies.

Especially after he formed his own engineering firm, Edgar spent so much time building the business that I had to do all the rest. I saw to it that we made new friends and became established socially among the up and coming leaders in Boston. I made sure that the children were accepted into the right independent schools so they could then get into Ivy League colleges.

I managed to become friends with the wives of men who were backers of the Symphony, the Museum, and other important civic institutions whose boards are made up of people who accomplish things. Edgar's firm got the design job for First Bank's huge new tower downtown at least partly because we became friends with the Chandlers, and Harvey Chandler was chairman and a big shareholder in the bank. There were other such times when knowing the right people made opportunities.

Sometime after the fact, I learned that Edgar had had a mistress. It made me furious. I'm not going to tell you her name. The woman lived in Philadelphia where Edgar spent a lot of time over about two years while the office tower his firm designed for an insurance company was being constructed. She was a marketing executive for the building's developer. I never met her, nor would I want to.

I also found out that after the building was completed, she moved to Boston and Edgar found an apartment for her near the Harbor. The affair ended, I was told, when she chose to go back to Philadelphia. She was about ten years younger than Edgar and able to look after herself and her career. I think she concluded that Edgar was not going to divorce me so she might just as well leave him. It wasn't until after she had returned to Philadelphia that I learned about her from an intended slip of the lip by one of Edgar's subordinates who left the firm to go with a competitor.

Caroline Resumes

On Wednesday after the wedding, my husband Jerry and I stopped by Vivvy's and Bill's on our way home from an early tennis game at the Club. By scheduling 8:00 court time for doubles, the heat was bearable.

Vivvy was not yet down, so Bill led us back to the west terrace, sheltered from the morning sun by the shadow of the house and a canopy of oak trees. French doors from the breakfast room opened onto the terrace. Bill's breakfast dishes, still on the glass-topped table, were partly hidden by sections of the *Sunday Globe* strewn about. A stirring of air brushed across the table and caught at the edges of the newspaper, lifting the pages as if in resurrection. Why that word came to mind, I really don't know. Extra coffee cups and a thermos were nearby.

"Help yourself to coffee," Bill said affably. "Orange juice is in the fridge, Caroline, if you'd rather," and nodded toward the kitchen.

Dressed comfortably in khakis, a blue Brooks button-down with sleeves rolled to just below the elbows, and brown loafers without socks, Bill plunked into a lawn chair and stretched out his legs.

"Some bash, wasn't it?" he said, and grinned. "Vivvy's taking her time this morning. Stephon's family left early for church. They'll be flying back to Italy day after tomorrow. I didn't know there's a Catholic church anywhere nearby where the service is given in Italian, but there is, in North Boston."

He paused, thinking about the wedding. "Wasn't Avery a beautiful bride? I got kinda tearful, to be honest about it, before walking her down to the preacher. Never thought I'd get so emotional."

As if a little embarrassed by this revelation, he looked away for a moment. "Well, you know, so many memories. My little girl a married woman now . . . ." He looked at me, squinted in spite of the shade, his face serious.

I like Bill. He's solid, and puts up with a lot. I know he worries about his kids. Avery off to Quebec with her Italian waiter. Patrick groping to find where he fits, and not finding it.

"I wonder what goes wrong?" he mused, as if I had spoken my thoughts.

Jerry looked at me, expecting me to answer. Silent for a moment, I said, "I don't know that it's a matter of things going wrong." Hoping I didn't sound glib, I added, "I think it's more complicated than that."

"How so?

"I may be treading on toes as your sister-in-law, Bill, but have you ever thought about how much Vivvy is like her mother?"

"Sure, both the good and—well, you know, the less attractive traits, too."

I smiled, letting him know I understood. "After all, Bill, I'm also a Harding, and Vivvy and I obviously have the same parents. I was born just a few minutes after her, but she's always considered herself the big sister." I smiled. "Silly, isn't it? But do you realize what that means in our family?" He looked blank. "Vivvy's the torch bearer. She's the oldest child by default. She's the one expected to carry on."

"But what about Sandy?" Jerry asked from the sidelines. "He's the oldest son. He's the older brother of both of you."

"Well, Sandy does fine, as you know. He's worked his way up to be one of the senior managers in Dad's firm. He's got a lot of his own interests, and pretty much leads his own life, but that's a different arena."

"Arena? You make it sound like gladiators," Bill replied.

"I didn't intend to, but it's not a bad analogy. What I meant is that Vivvy presides in a special world constructed for her—and by her, I guess, as I think about it. Mother did the same."

"Oh, come on, Caroline," my husband chided gently.

"No, I mean it. When you think about it, Vivvy lives very much the same kind of life that Mother lived, and still does." Both Jerry and Bill looked skeptical. "She's my twin sister, but I recognize Vivvy's every bit as aggressive and, let's face it, manipulative, as Mother has always been." I moved my chair a little, to avoid the sun's rays now edging past the tree tops.

"As teenagers we used to joke about Mother always knowing who the right people were. She consistently cultivated those who could do things for her such as place her on committees and boards of trustees, people who would invite Dad and her to dinner parties. You know what I mean. All that stuff. Mother could be acidly critical of those very same people when not with them, but all smiles and confidences when she saw them at cocktail parties and fund raisers."

Bill looked uneasy, glancing toward the French doors, closed because of air conditioning. He didn't like this kind of talk, especially about his wife. However, Vivvy had not yet appeared.

"Come on, Caroline," Bill finally said, "your mother's been a leader in the community—well, you know what I mean" His tone admitted how circumscribed 'the community' was. "She's done lots of good work, and helped a lot of people, and people do respect her. All Vivvy has tried to do is to live up to what her mother has accomplished," and he added defensively, "I think Vivvy's been spectacularly successful."

"And so she has," I assured him. "But why, Bill? I mean why does she run from one board meeting to another, and why does she maneuver to get elected president of this and that? More importantly, at what price?"

"Well, I'm not sure I know what you mean. She's got tons of energy. I think she really likes what she does, and besides, she's helping—."

"Helping other people? Sure, there's some of that, too. But Bill, I really think Vivvy leads the life she does for much more complicated reasons."

"Such as?" he asked, like someone not sure they'll like the answer.

I had thought about this question a lot. Being Vivvy's twin-sister brought some privileges, such as getting put up for May Day queen in high school because Vivvy was so popular, but it also meant letting her run the show.

I got up, poured myself a fresh cup, and sat back down. Bill's question hung expectantly in the air, waiting to be brought gently down to earth.

"We had an older sister, you know. Jennifer. Mother and Dad still refer to her as Jenny. Neither Vivvy nor I remember her because we were only three when Jenny died. Remember, she drowned the summer she was six, the year Mother and Dad rented a house for the season on the Vineyard. It was one of those tragic, terrible accidents that should never have happened."

"Yes, I knew about Jenny," Bill acknowledged quietly.

"Mother and Dad were devastated, especially Mother. She'd left Jenny in the care of a babysitter at the beach while she attended a meeting in Edgartown. Something to do with providing job training to underprivileged islanders so they could find jobs on the Island."

I paused, conjuring up an image of the scene. "The beach was crowded. The young babysitter got to talking with her chums from school, and suddenly little Jenny disappeared. It was maybe only a few minutes, but no one noticed. No one saw her headed for the water."

"Vivvi's never told me the details," Bill said

"Anyway, Mother felt she was responsible for Jenny's death. She felt that she should have been there. Who knows, maybe she should have."

"Must have been awful," Jerry said, shaking his head.

"Yeah, I'm sure it was." I moved my chair a little to avoid the sun. "But you know what? Not long after, Mother threw herself into lots of other such activities, as if to be so busy she wouldn't have to think. Almost frantic."

"How do you know that," Bill said. "You were too young to remember."

"Right, but Dad talked a little about it with me a long time ago, when he visited me at school in North Carolina. I'm sure he must have been thinking about Jennie. She would have gone to a school like Duke had she lived. Parents think about such things. His telling me about it was one of those sudden, revealing glimpses into his thoughts and feelings that he doesn't very often allow."

"But can you blame your mother?" Bill asked. "I mean, people find different ways to overcome their grief."

"I guess. Anyway, what happened was that Mother shifted her expectations. Her ambitions went from little Jenny to Vivvy. Sure, not at age three, but eventually. Maybe she was unaware of what she was doing, but Mother began making sure that Vivvy would achieve all that Mother had wanted Jenny to be."

"So in a way, Caroline," Jerry said, "Vivvy has done what was expected of her. What's wrong with that? Most parents . . ."

I saw the door from the breakfast room open. Vivvy stood there for a moment, her hand raised to her face as if the sunlight were too bright, then hesitantly stepped outside, taking care not to stumble on the step. Although she was dressed in slacks and blouse, I could tell that she had been interrupted in dressing because her face had no makeup and she wore no jewelry.

Vivvy walked slowly toward us, across the brick patio. She seemed unsteady.

Bill got up from his chair.

Vivvy stopped.

"It's Patrick," she said. "Patrick. He's been in an accident. On his motor bike." She gasped. "He's dead . . . he's . . . ."

Bill stepped toward quickly, put his arms around her, and held her close, his own eyes brimming with tears.

The Family

Josiah Hamilton Harding
Paternal great-great-grandfather
of Edgar Lawrence Harding

John Phillip Sandifer
Paternal Great-Grandfather of
Francis Sandifer Harding

Frances Sandifer Harding (3rd generation)
and
Edgar Lawrence Harding (4th generation)

Children

(1) Jennifer "Jenny" Harding (deceased)
(2) Sandifer "Sandy" Lawrence Harding
(3) Phillip Jeffrey Harding
(4) Vivian "Vivvy" Harding Dulany,
a twin–Wife of William "Bill" Dulany
Children: Patrick Harding
                  Avery Harding Salino
(5) Caroline Harding Johnson, a twin—
Wife of Gerald "Jerry" Johnson

The Walnut Desk

A Boy's Story

The Woods

Today I watched the moving men carry out the walnut desk I had used as a boy, out through the front door of my house, down the broad steps and along the walk to the enormous cross-country moving van parked at the curb. The men moved briskly up the metal ramp, each grasping an end of the desk, and disappeared inside, where assorted pieces of furniture destined for our older son and his wife stood wrapped in heavy blankets, safeguarded against the long journey to the far-distant city. The twin beds, also built of walnut, had already been loaded.

Within days, the truck will rumble down a strange street, and the same two men, who have stayed with the truck a great distance, will carry the walnut desk and beds into the house where the furniture will begin a new life. The matching bedside table with the drop-down leaves has already found a place in the apartment of my younger son, as yet unmarried, who lives in the same city. He refinished the table several years ago, something he does well, carefully removing the scars of two generations of youthful exuberance.

The story about this furniture is already known in our family. I was about ten years old when my grandfather had the furniture made for me from a walnut log found on his farm. My grandfather was then sixty years old. He was always fifty years older than I. That never changed, not even when he died at almost ninety.

I often went with my grandfather when he drove his car on regular Saturday visits to his farm. My grandmother would send along a lunch she had made for us. Mine was usually a bread-and-butter sandwich, or maybe peanut butter and jelly, since I didn't like meat sandwiches. There were potato chips, sliced tomatoes, and often times deviled eggs, which I have always liked. For me there would be milk in a Mason jar, packed in ice cubes to keep cold, and an apple and cookies for dessert.

Sometimes my grandfather and I just sat in the car, wherever we happened to be on the farm around noontime, eating our lunch. I wasn't much of a talker, and he respected that, so our times together were somewhat contemplative, you might say, each of us wrapped in our own thoughts. In the summertime we'd open the car's front doors to let the breeze in, along with the flies and whatever else was flying around. That was part of being in the country.

I liked it best when my grandfather drove the car into the "bottoms", where the timber grew heavily, some distance back, on both sides of Blackwater Creek. A barbed wire fence with wood posts separated the pastures on the upper slopes from the timbers in the bottoms. When my grandfather stopped the car at the gate, I'd get out of the car without having to say anything, and close the car door behind me. Then I'd unfasten the latch on the gate, which took some doing, and when the gate fell away free from the post, I'd give the gate a shove and jump on the bottom plank and ride the gate as it swung open, as far as it went until the gate came up against the ground and stopped. My grandfather drove the car through the opening, and then waited for me until I shut the gate and got back in on my side of the car.

The cattle wintered in the timber for protection against the cold winds. Early in the Spring, the ground was pockmarked with the round, deep prints of cattle hooves. But by mid-April, the ground softened, underbrush quickly grew back, and trees filled out with green leaves and occasional splashes of white blossoms and the soft lavender of redbud.

We then got out of the car and walked into the timber. I carried the cane basket in which my grandmother had carefully packed our lunch. We looked for a place to sit down, usually a fallen tree, because I was never much for sitting on the bare ground. There were some big trees in the timber in those days, trunks close to three feet thick. Walnut trees were prized for the beauty of the wood. Houses were built with walnut planks, and furniture, too.

I saw a particularly large log, lying on the ground, some of its branches broken off from the fall, others still attached, but twisted against the ground. At that I age I had to climb up onto the log in order to sit down and eat my lunch, but that was part of the fun, climbing up on the big log. I grabbed hold of a branch, bracing my foot against the rough bark, and pulled myself up.

My grandfather spread a red-and-white checked kitchen towel across the top of the log, and laid out the sandwiches, deviled eggs and potato chips. The timber still smelled of winter wetness, although a neighboring breeze, sliding down the green sides of the pastures to the south, brought the warm, fresh scent of alfalfa. Black-feathered crows, so high above we couldn't see them, quarreled among themselves, and circled fretfully beyond the treetops.

My grandfather found great contentment, I think, in being in the timber, and with my presence. Occasionally he would ask me to listen to the staccato sound of an unseen woodpecker, digging for insects behind the bark on a tree, or point to a butterfly, colored gold and black, dancing a ballet in the sunlight nearby.

Well, it was then he got the idea of having that log made into furniture for me, for my room at home. A desk, twin beds, and a side table. I don't think he said anything about it at the time, but I know that's when the idea came to him.

Haystack

I liked to climb the steep, sometimes slippery sides of the haystack in the pasture behind our house on the farm. When I finally reached the top, breathing hard from the climb, I could gaze far out over the fields. I felt as if my head was in the clear blue sky, with white clouds drifting past me.

I could see ever so far across the countryside, even to the tall, dark timber on Blackwater Creek, and to the farmers' houses and big barns to the east and to the west of us. I watched swallows darting about the eves of our barn, and meadowlarks flying to their nests secreted in the knee-high grass of the pasture. Large, cantankerous crows, ever cawing out their displeasure at the world in general, sat black against the sky in a nearby hedgerow. I was alone in my world, and I was happy.

In the very early Spring, what remained of the haystack after feeding the cattle during the winter months held enough moisture way down deep inside that the straw stuck together, stiffly crusted with frost. This meant I could carefully build tunnels through the haystack, channeling out the straw to form a passage, like digging a cave in the ground.

One time, I made a tunnel from the near top of the haystack, burrowing all the way down to a point just above the ground. If you had the nerve, because it was pretty scary, you could enter the tunnel by climbing up the side of the haystack, then slide down through the narrow chute and tumble, unhurt, onto the ground at the bottom of the haystack.

Like many things, though, the tunnel through the haystack didn't last very long. After only a few days the warming sun reached down into the straw, and the frost went away, leaving the inside of the haystack soft and damp.

The Rifle

My grandfather once told me that when he was a boy, he sold magazine subscriptions door-to-door after school and on Saturdays in the small town where his parents lived. The magazine was *Youth's Companion,* a weekly periodical that he himself enjoyed reading. The publisher of the magazine gave prizes for new subscribers, and my grandfather sold magazines to all his relatives and almost everyone in town, it seemed. He sold so many new subscriptions that he won a single-shot .22 caliber rifle as a prize, when he was about thirteen years old.

After doing his own chores at home, my grandfather also earned spending money during summer vacation from school. He picked berries for 2 cents a quart, earning about 50 cents a day. He also sometimes drove a delivery wagon, pulled by a horse, delivering meat for Sam's Meat Market, for which he was paid $15.00 a month. As if that wasn't enough, he worked when needed in a nursery filling orders for trees and shrubs. Understand, he didn't tell me about all those other jobs he did when he wasn't a whole lot older than me. I learned about them years later, when I read an account he wrote, so that his grandchildren would know something about his life after he was gone.

Ammunition for that rifle my grandfather won in the magazine subscription contest cost 15 cents for a box of 50 shells. He bought a lot of ammunition, whenever he had nickels to spend, because he frequently went practice shooting. He also liked hunting rabbits and squirrels.

So I guess that explains why, when I was about twelve years old, my grandfather gave me a .22 caliber rifle that he had bought in later years. He said he thought I should learn how to shoot a gun, and how to handle it safely. By that he meant without accidentally shooting myself or someone else.

I first practiced with the rifle by shooting at tin cans or paper plates as targets. We'd go to Blackwater Creek, in the timber, and find a place where the water was shallow and narrow enough that I could get across to the other side using fallen logs or even jumping across the creek, if it wasn't too wide. I'd then prop up the tin cans we'd brought with us on the far bank, and return to the other side where my grandfather was waiting for me.

The .22 rifle was a pump model. It held maybe 10 shells or cartridges you loaded into the magazine. After firing a shot, you'd pump the wood handle and another cartridge entered the chamber, ready to be fired. There were three different types of shells you could buy for the rifle, determined by how far the lead would travel when the gun was fired. We mostly used Winchester .22 "shorts", which had the least amount of gunpowder in the casings. Sometimes, though, when I learned to hunt rabbits in the fields, I'd use .22 "longs", said to go as far as a mile, but I knew they really didn't. The third type, that would travel the farthest, were called .22 "long rifles", but I don't think I ever saw any of those.

I first learned to shoot from a sitting position, knees pulled up in front of me, arms resting firmly on my upper legs, holding the rifle in both hands. My left hand cradled the rifle barrel, the right hand gripped the rifle, close to the chamber, index finger near the rifle trigger, my cheek against the polished wood stock.

My grandfather taught me how to hold the rifle barrel very still, so the muzzle didn't move, and to put the gun sight on the target, or maybe just a little above, to allow for the falling trajectory of the bullet. I also learned to hold my breath when I was ready to shoot, and to gently *squeeze* the trigger, not to pull it, in order to *squeeze off* a shot. After a lot of practice, I got to be a pretty good shot with the rifle, or at least that's what they told me.

The Rooster

Between the house and the red barn was a fenced-in area with a chicken coup. My grandfather kept about a dozen chickens, so that we would have fresh eggs every day and, quite often, fried chicken for Sunday dinner. It was my responsibility to go out to the chicken coup after breakfast and gather up the eggs laid since the day before. I carried a wicker basket, with a handle, to carry them in.

There has to be a rooster in with the chickens in order for the chickens to lay eggs. That wasn't something I learned about at the time, but I thought you ought to know, if you didn't already. I was a little afraid of that rooster, because he was big and strutted around in a very confident manner. I could also tell he didn't like my coming into his chicken coup, but there was no other way I could collect the eggs that my mother had asked me to.

One day, I had just let myself through the gate and was headed for the chicken coup when I heard a loud shriek behind me. My heart jumped, and I spun around. Coming right at me was that big rooster, racing over the ground, his wings flapping, and screeching at me as loud as he could.

I dropped the basket and fled for the gate, but couldn't get the latch open. I was terrified! My mother heard all the commotion, looked out the window, saw what was happening, and came rushing out the back door of the house. She waved a long-handled broom at the rooster and shouted "Shoo! Shoo! Shoo!"

By then I had gotten the gate open, and I ran into her arms, unable to hold back the tears.

The Hayfork

Our family lived on the farm a month, maybe longer, each summer. My mother "packed up" (that's what she always called moving to the country) and we drove about fifty miles from our house in the city to my grandfather's farm.

The farmhouse was all on one floor except for a wood-floored attic that ran beneath the eves on either side of the house. I really liked playing in the attic when it rained. It was like being in a tent way off somewhere. The outside of the house was painted white, the shutters at each window blue-grass green. The roof was composition shingles. Two great oak trees, visible long before you saw the house from the road, stood nearby. The oldest was off to one side in the front yard, the other at the rear between the corner of the house and the smokehouse. A rope swing with a grain sack filled with straw for a seat hung from a lower branch. By pumping hard, you could go higher in that swing than any swing I ever saw.

The house we lived in was intended for a farmer and his family, but the tenant who worked the farm already occupied a larger two-story house just to the east of us, on what had once been a second farm before my grandfather bought both farms all at one time.

My grandmother sometimes came to the farm with us, to help my mother look after me and my sisters, and my grandfather was also there a part of the time.

My father drove to the farm on Friday evenings and returned to his office in the city on Monday mornings.

An old wood barn, painted a deep red years ago, stood a little way west of our house. On the ground floor of the barn were storage bins stuffed with corn cobs. A row of box stalls for horses backed up against one wall. In a small tack room, bridals and harnesses, the leather moldy and darkened with age, sweat, and grime, dangled from short wood hooks. Along another wall hoes, shovels, hay forks, and other hand tools stood propped upright.

The rough plank ceiling in the barn was low overhead. I think the reason it was so low was to provide more space in the vast hay loft above that went all the way up past the beams to the roof of the barn.

I liked to visit the barn, even though the inside was dark. Strange smells waited for you just past the door, and unknown noises made me wary. After a while I recognized the good animal smell of the horses, and the strong, sharp smell of the manure. Then there was the dusky scent of straw spilling from the hayloft above onto the dirt floor below. The wood planks and beams of the barn, because they'd stood in that place for so many years, had their own smell, stored up and released slowly, like fragrance from a flower. The dry earth floor smelled strange and secretive.

A sturdy wood ladder, nailed to the wall, the rungs far apart, climbed up through a square hole in the floor above into the hayloft. Like the inside of a cathedral, the space was vast, silent, even a little eerie. Sunlight slipped between vertical planks forming the walls of the hayloft, providing filtered blue light from the outdoors. Towering above me were the great mounds of straw, giant billowing cushions, soft and silky. I shouted with glee as I jumped off the mountains of straw and fell tumbling down their sides. Dust particles floated serenely in the slatted sunlight.

In those days, draft horses hauled the farm wagons and pulled the plows and harrows. Tractors cost a lot of money, so not many farmers owned one. Alfalfa, grown to feed the horses and cattle, was cut in late summer and brought from the fields on wagons into the hay barn to be stored for winter.

One day, my grandfather stood in the barnyard watching the farmer and his helper drive up to the barn with a wagon load of alfalfa to be hauled up into the hayloft. Another helper stood in a doorway high in the loft through which they hoisted bundles of hay from the wagon far below. A continuous loop of hemp rope ran from a pulley fastened to a block of wood on the ground to a pulley mounted on a hook above the door into the hayloft, then returned the same way they had come.

Dangling from the rope were iron jaws, like oversized ice tongs, the length of a man's arm. When lowered into the hay-filled wagon, the jaws opened up, seized a bundle of straw, then clamped firmly shut as the rope tightened. The giant-size mouthful of straw rose swiftly up toward the hayloft. The moving rope was powered by a gas motor coupled to the pulley fastened to the ground. A clutch handle mounted on the motor put it in and out of gear.

The farmer got off the wagon and walked over to my grandfather who was standing next to the pulley on the ground. Pushing back his ragged straw hat, he wiped the sweat from his face with a rag. "That old hemp rope is slacker than it should be," the farmer said to my grandfather. "But despite its age," he added with a chuckle, "I expect it'll make it through 'til we're done."

My grandfather nodded, and reached out a hand to test how much slack there was in the rope. I was standing next to my grandfather, and I reached out my hand to grab hold of the rope to test it, too. Being a lot smaller, my hand was well below my grandfather's, and just above the pulley around which the rope was wrapped.

Looking up toward the door into the hayloft, and shielding his eyes from the sun, the farmer placed his other hand, protected by a heavy work glove, on the handle that controlled the clutch. The helper high up in the hayloft waved his arm, giving the signal to start the hoisting. The farmer shouted back, "Here she comes!" and threw the clutch on the motor. The rope jerked and the iron jaws started upwards, loose straw falling earthward.

I screamed, frantically trying to free my hand, caught between the rope and the sun-hot iron of the pulley wheel. The moment he heard me scream and saw what had happened, the farmer quickly threw the clutch into the off position, creating enough slack that my grandfather could gently remove my bleeding hand.

I don't remember very much after that. They rushed me in a car into town, they said, where a white-haired old doctor cleaned the wound, wrapped my hand in bulky white bandages, and gave me a vaccination for tetanus, to protect me against barnyard infections. I'm older now than my grandfather was then, but the vee-shaped scar between my thumb and forefinger, where the rope dug into my small hand, is still there. It always will be.

Chickens

Beyond the backyard of the house we lived in was what was called a back lot. My grandfather kept it mowed, but it was kind of a utility area. A woodpile stood behind the smoke house, now used as a play house for my sisters. The back lot was where my grandfather went to kill a chicken when my mother suggested we have fried chicken for Sunday dinner.

There were two ways he'd kill the chicken. Both were pretty awful, I thought. The first way was to grab the squawking chicken by its legs, position the chicken's head and neck over a chopping block he kept out in the back lot, and with a sharp hatchet, chop off the chicken's head in a single blow. Even without it's head, it took the chicken's body about ten seconds to realize it was dead, and during that ten seconds it ran around the back lot, flapping its wings, and spilling blood on the ground.

The second way my grandfather killed a chicken was even worse, so I'm not going to tell you about it. You just have to remember that my grandfather had grown up on a farm during the first years of his life, and that was the way things were done in those days.

The next step in preparing the chicken for cooking was to dip it into a bucket of boiling water. Since we didn't have electricity or gas for cooking, my mother would put a tea kettle full of water from the cistern on top of the wood-burning stove in the kitchen, and let it heat until the water boiled. My grandfather then poured the boiling water into a bucket and carried it out to the back lot. He'd pick up the headless chicken, holding it in one hand by its feet, and dunk it into the steaming hot water. The feathers smelled terrible, like plastic burning; I can still smell them.

After a few minutes, my grandfather took the chicken out of the bucket and began plucking the feathers. He asked me if I'd like to help, but I didn't like to do this kind of thing. In fact, I didn't even like to watch. Later, after he finished taking off all the feathers, he'd cut up the chicken with a sharp kitchen knife into drum sticks, breast, wings, pieces like that, so my mother could sprinkle them with flour, dip them in batter, then fry them in a heavy, black skillet on the wood stove.

It probably won't surprise you to know that I really didn't like chicken until I became a grown-up. In fact, I still don't like chicken if it's been boiled.

The Outhouse

There was a modern bathroom in our house at the farm, but anyone using it had to first go down into the cellar and pump up pressure by hand on the water supply system. This was because the water in our house came from a cistern. Rainwater falling on the roof of the house collected in gutters and drained off through a pipe into a dug-out cave lined with stone or maybe tile, called a cistern. It was located beneath the floor of the partly-enclosed back porch of our house. An iron pump about four feet high, with a long handle and a curved spout, sat on a concrete slab on the floor of the porch.

Whenever we wanted water for washing or cooking or drinking, we'd pump the water out of the cistern into a bucket or a cooking pot from the kitchen. "City water", that's what my mother called it, would be a long time reaching farmers out in the country.

I think my grandfather decided just not to bother with the inside bathroom because, between my two sisters and me, we would probably be using it all the time. So we were told to use the outhouse. You may not know exactly what an outhouse is, so I'm going to tell you.

To get to the outhouse you walked out the back porch door, down some steps to the backyard, then through a gate to a little area fenced in behind the chicken coop. I didn't like to go to the outhouse after dark, so my mother let my sisters and me use a pan we'd kept in the bathroom and emptied out the next morning. The outhouse was a tiny, one room shed, less than half the size of the smoke house, built of unpainted wood, now weathered gray. A single step went up into it, and once inside, there was room for only one person. There was what looked like a wood shelf, closed in on the sides, with a hole where you sat.

Our outhouse was probably just about like anybody else's outhouse. The smell didn't bother me, at least not after I got kind of used to it, but the wasps DID! My mother said they were mud daubers, not wasps, and wouldn't sting me, and maybe they were, but I still hated them, and frankly, I was scared to death of them. They'd come flying lazily into the outhouse through a crack in the door or through openings between the roof and board-thin walls. Buzzing busily, they'd fly around, looking things over, including me, whatever I was doing. I didn't stay there a minute longer than I had to.

I have lots of good memories of those summers on the farm, but the outhouse sure wasn't one of them.

Jackrabbit

One summer, my biggest ambition was to shoot a jackrabbit, of which there were only one or two on the farm as far as we knew. A jackrabbit is larger than a cottontail rabbit, and its ears are longer. They can run very fast, springing into the air and looking around, and you don't see them for long, if you're lucky enough to see one at all. It seems like I spent most of one summer hunting for jackrabbits, and seldom saw one. But I was determined.

I was out in the fields earlier than usual, carrying my rifle in the crook of my arm, barrel pointed down at the ground in front of me, as I'd been taught. I followed a barbed wire fence along one side of the pasture. The grass grows higher along the fence, because the farmer can't get close to it with his mower. I figured that the tall grass might be a place where the jackrabbit would hide, considering its large size.

That summer there were lots and lots of grasshoppers, a real nuisance. They were about the size of your thumb, even larger, and looked ugly. I hated those grasshoppers, because they'd jump onto your arms from the grass and weeds as you walked along, and you'd have to brush them off quickly with your free hand. They couldn't hurt you, but they felt really icky if they landed on your bare skin. The sun was already hot, and I was sweating, even though I wore some kind of a hat, like my grandfather did when he walked over his farm.

Suddenly something exploded out of the tall grass in front of me, almost at my feet! It was a jackrabbit! He took off along the fence, running away from me, bounding up and down as he ran so he could see over the tall grass, his long ears waggling. I brought the rifle up to my right shoulder, and slipped off the safety catch, ready to fire. But the jackrabbit made a sudden turn to the left, ducking under a low strand of barbed wire, and started off across the field on the other side of the fence. Boy, was he running fast!

My heart was pounding, and I could hardly think, I was so excited. But I knew I had to act quickly, or that jackrabbit would be out of range and gone forever. I ran up to a wood fence post, and placed my left elbow on top of the post, to steady my aim. The jackrabbit made a zigzag, and began running somewhere parallel to me, but still getting farther away. I was breathing hard and felt like I must be trembling.

"I'm going to get you, I'm going to get you," I said to myself. I fought to control my nervousness and did everything I could to steady my aim. I sighted along the gun barrel a good two feet ahead of the jackrabbit, to "lead" the moving target, and gently squeezed the trigger.

The sound of the rifle firing seemed far off, as if it wasn't me who had the fired the shot, but someone far removed from where I was standing.

I saw the jackrabbit abruptly topple to one side, as if a gust of wind had blown him off track, but he righted himself and continued running, more slowly, as if in slow motion, and I felt like I was in a dream.

I again took aim, leading the jackrabbit not quite as far, and squeezed off a second shot. He suddenly stopped, and crumpled on the spot.

Quickly I slid the safety catch on, grasped the rifle in both hands, and ran to where the jackrabbit lay on its side in the open field.

Its front legs were reaching out, as if still running. But it wasn't, of course. Its fur, a light brown and gray in color, riffled slightly in the movement of the wind. The long ears, with touches of white, were motionless. The jackrabbit's eyes were open, flat, staring at nothing.

I gingerly picked up the dead rabbit by its ears, surprised at how heavy he was. Red blood stained the fur on one side as I carried him, my arm stretched away from my body, the muscles soon aching from his weight. It seemed like a long, long way back to the farm house. I had got him, all right, but somehow I didn't feel like I thought I would feel. I quietly laid the jackrabbit on the ground near the kitchen door and went inside to tell my mother.

The Hoe

My grandfather was not a tall man. When I grew up, I was taller than he. His skin was smooth white, and he was bald except for a fringe of white hair at the sides and back. He had a scattering of brown age spots on his head and hands; that's probably why he always wore a hat outdoors. I don't believe he ever sun tanned, even though he played golf in earlier years. He worked in an office during the week, where he owned the business he had started.

My grandfather wore his felt city hat pushed high up on his forehead, well above his eye-glasses. When he wasn't wearing his suit jacket, he often stood with the back of his hands propped against his hips, elbows out to the side. This gave him a relaxed look, and indicated he was listening. He was a good listener, and smiled easily. When my grandfather perspired in the heat, dampening his shirt, there was a pleasant, sweet odor about him.

There were about eight hundred acres in my grandfather's farm, a relatively big farm in those days. Many of the fields were cultivated, planted with corn, soy beans, alfalfa, sometimes wheat. He also fed and grazed cattle for market, white-faced Herefords, large red-brown animals with white markings. I was always a little afraid of the cattle when I walked through the pastures, I guess because they were so much bigger than I was. My grandfather cautioned me never to enter the pasture where the bull grazed, a heavy-bodied animal whose enormous head hung low as he watched me from a distance.

My grandfather hated weeds in his pastures. You wouldn't think that weeds in such large pastures would bother him, but they did. Wherever he went he carried a long-handled hoe. From time to time he sharpened the edge of the hoe with a file stored on a ledge near the back screen door of our house. Walking over the pastures, my grandfather kept a close lookout for any stray weeds. When he found one, he'd walk up and stand over it. Decisively, with a deft, clean movement of the hoe, he chopped the weed out of the ground and turned it over with the hoe so the roots were exposed to the sun.

Dressed in a white business shirt, the sleeves pushed up above the elbows, sometimes wearing a vest to an old suit, left unbuttoned, and light gray trousers, my grandfather certainly did not look like a farmer, but he meted out swift justice to any vagrant weed he encountered. He did not eliminate the weed in anger, but with a sense of considerable satisfaction.

The Lesson

Along the rear of the back lot of our house at the farm ran a barbed wire fence, separating it from a pasture beyond that was used for grazing and feeding livestock. A haystack from which the farmer got hay to feed the animals in the winter months was located a short distance beyond the fence, inside the pasture. My grandfather kept a large wire basket, taller than I, as big around as a barrel, next to the fence. He used it to burn trash from the house. One of my chores was to take the trash out each day, and when the wire basket was filled, to light a rolled-up newspaper page with a match and set the trash on fire.

One morning, before he left to drive into town on some errands, my grandfather reminded me about the trash and cautioned me to keep an eye on the wind, and the directions from which it was coming, before burning the trash. I told him I would.

After lunch, I was sitting on the spring cot where I slept in one corner of the front room, my back against a pillow, absorbed in a book propped up on my knees. I heard my mother call to me from the kitchen, saying it was time to take the trash out. I hated to be interrupted when I was reading, because my mind was on the story, but I put the book down, the pages open on my bed, and did what my mother asked.

The trash from the kitchen filled the remaining space in the wire basket. I took a wood kitchen match out of my pocket, cupped my hands against the wind, struck the head of the match against a metal hoop on the basket, and lit the paper. The flames took hold in no time at all, and I returned to the house. In my hurry to get back to my book, I failed to notice that the wind was catching bits of burning paper, carrying them up into the air and scattering them in the pasture.

I had barely gotten back into my story when my mother ran into the room, shouting that the haystack was on fire, and I'd better come quick. We hurried out the backdoor, across the yard and toward the trash container. Just beyond, the haystack was burning like the Fourth of July, bright red flames reaching upward and white smoke swirling and twisting in the wind. There wasn't anything we could do. The haystack would just have to burn.

I dreaded my grandfather's return from town. When I heard the wheels of his car crunch on the gravel in the driveway, I kept my eyes on the pages in front of me. I heard my mother slip out the back door to meet him, and could imagine their talking together in low voices. I then heard my grandfather's steps on the front porch of the house, outside the window where I lay on my bed pretending to read.

The front screen door opened and he stepped into the room. I turned to look at him, but didn't say anything, my eyes wide with apprehension.

He looked at me for a moment, then asked me to tell him what had happened. It didn't take me very long. After I'd finished, he said, "Well, Buddy," (that was my nickname), "I guess we can find some more feed for the livestock, but the fire could have been a lot worse. The pasture might have caught fire and burned, too." He thought for a moment. "Fortunately, the wind was blowing away from the house."

I nodded my head, not taking my eyes off him.

"I guess you've learned something, haven't you." It really wasn't a question. I again nodded my head.

"It pays to listen, listen carefully, when someone asks you to do something." He looked at me carefully, as he talked. "Well, I guess if you learn that from this experience, it will be worth the cost of the haystack."

I was somewhat relieved, having expected much worse.

"Oh, I almost forgot." My grandfather held up a paper sack in his hand. "I brought some ice cream from town. Let's sit down with your mother and sisters, and eat it before it melts." He smiled a little.

Well, I'm still working on listening carefully to instructions, but I'm a lot better than I used to be.

The Tressenriter Boys

A family named Tressenriter lived on the farm west of us. We could see their house, just down the reddish-gray dirt road, on top of the next hill. They had two sons, Leland and William. Unlike us, they were real farmers.

It was during what turned out to be our last summer on the farm that my grandfather decided it would be nice if I could get to know the Tressenriter boys. He probably thought I was a little lonely, having only sisters to play with, especially since they were so much younger than me. He may also have thought it would broaden my experience to spend some time with real farm boys.

By then I was about thirteen years old. William, the older of the two brothers, was maybe fifteen. At least, he was a good head taller than me, if not more. Slender, dark hair combed to each side, William was very serious about things. I think he took his responsibility heavily, spending some time with me, that is. Leland, on the other hand, liked to joke around and have a good time. He was skinny like me, and maybe just a year older. He was always grinning. I liked Leland the most, but I also respected William.

After supper, when they'd finished their chores at home, they'd walk down the dirt road to our house, and come knocking on the back door to let my mother know they were there. They called her "ma'am", and were dressed in clean overalls, and had their hair slicked down with water or something. I'm sure their mother told them they had to look nice if they were going over to my grandfather's place. Sometimes, when their father said they could, they came over on Saturday, but that wasn't very often.

We had a lot of fun together. They even invited me over to their house once, while they were doing chores, like milking the cows, or spreading grain on the ground for the chickens, or pitching hay for the horses to eat. They did this so I could see what farm boys did on the farm.

Once in a while we went swimming in one of the ponds on my grandfather's farm. The cattle drank out of the ponds, and sometimes waded in to cool off, but we didn't go swimming unless they were off grazing in another part of the pasture. I didn't much like the muddy bottom you had to wade through to get out to where the water was deeper. Besides, the ponds were so muddy you didn't dare open your eyes under water. I worried about what might be swimming around in the water, things I couldn't see, like bugs and frogs, maybe even fish or water snakes, things like that. We didn't wear swimming suits, either, and this was the first time I'd ever done that, but the pond was a long way from the house, so I guess no one could see.

One evening Leland and William invited me to go with them to a 4-H meeting. This is a club for boys and girls who are farmers, and live on a farm. The meeting was being held at the house of a farm family about a mile south of us. My grandfather said he knew the family, and told my mother it was okay for me to go. Leland and William walked by to pick me up, and then we started off across the field on the other side of the road in front of our house. I had a hard time keeping up with their long legs, but they didn't make me feel bad about it, or anything.

When we got to the people's house who were having the meeting, we all went inside. The front room, what they called the parlor, was filled with boys and girls a little older than me. They seemed to know one another, but were kind of shy, and didn't do a lot of talking. I figured that kids on the farm were probably like that.

There was a regular program, led by an older boy, who seemed to be the leader. A couple of the boys and girls who sat on the floor near me got up and made reports on projects they were working on, like how to raise hogs with certain kinds of feed, and how to cultivate a vegetable garden, and what fertilizer worked best. I didn't know much about what they were discussing of course, because I'm a city boy.

At the end of the meeting, everybody ate ice cream and cake. Somebody's mom scooped helpings of peach ice cream out of a large metal container placed inside a wood tub that had a crank with a wooden handle on top of it. William explained that they used rock salt to make ice cream out of real cream and fresh peaches, and that when the salt melted the ice, it froze the ice cream. I'd never heard of anything like that before.

By the time we were ready to start home, it was already dark. Five or six other boys who lived out our direction left with us. There was a lot of fooling around and horseplay as we hiked through the fields. The sky was clear, the moon very bright, and it felt as if we were walking across the top of the world.

Two of the boy's began joking around about taking off someone's pants, and undershorts, too, so they'd have to go home naked except for their shirt and shoes and socks. I began to fee pretty uneasy, scared, in fact, because I was the youngest one there, and I wasn't one of them, if you know what I mean, so I was kind of the logical victim. You didn't have to be a brain to figure that out.

There was one boy, oversize for his age, and fat, who talked loud and showed off a lot. Slowly he edged over toward me and reached out for the belt buckle on my pants. My heart beat so fast that I thought I might explode.

Before I knew what happened, the big, fat boy went sprawling onto the ground, William on top of him. Everybody laughed at the boy, figuring that would teach him, and it did. All the rest of the way home, William walked next to me, and there was no more trouble.

I don't know what happened to "the Tressenriter boys" after that summer. (That's what my grandfather, who liked them, called Leland and William). I remember that Leland wrote me a letter the next winter, in pencil on a piece of paper from a Big Chief tablet, telling me what they were doing in school, and things like that. I wrote back, but after that, we just never saw each other again. I felt sad about that.

Great-Grandmother

My grandfather bought the farm he owned about 1925. That was before I was born. His own mother, my great-grandmother, still lived in the town nearby where my grandfather had grown up. We always drove into town to visit her, after we'd been to the farm.

My great-grandmother lived in a one-story gray stucco bungalow, that sat close to the street, several blocks south of the courthouse square. Steep concrete steps led up to the front porch. The porch was of wood, and had once been painted light gray.

Although not very large, the house was deep, with a living room across the front, and then behind it to one side, a dining room. Beyond that was the kitchen, with a back door and long steps leading down to the back yard filled by a vegetable and flower garden. To the other side of the dining room, down a short hall, were two bedrooms, one for my great-grandmother and the other for her daughter, my grandfather's youngest sister, who had lovely white hair and a tranquil face that smiled easily. She never married, and looked after her mother until her mother died.

Often, when my grandfather and I arrived at the house, his sister would just be coming in from the garden, her strong hands flaked with the rich black soil she had been working with a trowel. She grew corn, tomatoes, asparagus, lettuce, peas, green beans, and other things whose names I don't remember.

Sometimes we stood in the kitchen just talking, while the summer breeze passing through the screen door from the garden brought the unwanted sound of grasshoppers and sweet aroma of clippings freshly-mowed from rye and blue grass along the borders of the garden, left to turn brown under the vivid sun.

My great-grandmother was a tiny, fragile woman with large, pale blue eyes in a gentle face crowned with angelic hair spun of silver. She always seemed glad to see me, and would ask me to tell her about what I'd been doing. When she died at the age of 97, I was 24 years old and my grandfather was 74.

I never met my great-grandfather, because he died before I was born. He was remembered as a fine gentle man. My mother called him "Papa Joe", and I was told she liked him very much.

My grandfather had two sisters, younger than he, living in the town. One was a teacher at the state teachers college, widowed with two young children when still very young. The third sister, energetic and sparkling, worked hard and read books. My grandfather married my grandmother when he was 22, and she 20.

You may wonder how I know all these things, because my grandfather hardly ever talked about himself, and I didn't know enough to ask questions when I could have. Well, you'd be surprised by what you can pick up when you're young, just by watching and listening to grown-ups when they don't think you're paying attention.

My Father

During the humid summer night, it began raining. I awakened, the cotton sheet beneath me wet from perspiration, and shut the window next to my spring cot. It was one of those double-hung windows that depended on a peg fitting into a hole at various levels along the sides of the window frame to prop it open. The window was awkward to close, and I did it carefully, so it wouldn't drop with a bang.

With daylight, the rain continued to fall steadily, not hard, "a right good rain", the farmers would say. It was Friday, and we were expecting my father to arrive before supper, driving down from the city. We wondered whether he would be able to make it over the two miles of mud road, earthy-red in color, from the highway to the farm. The road was one mile north, then one mile west to the farm gate.

We stayed indoors all day, playing Monopoly and other games, waiting. There wasn't a telephone in the house, because without electricity, you can't have a telephone. So my mother wasn't able to talk with my father at his office, to find out whether he was still coming, and of course, he couldn't call her, either.

My mother was uneasy, maybe even apprehensive, about my father driving by himself all the way from the city. Last year, when he had tried to make it after a hard rain, his car slid off the mud road into a ditch alongside, before he had even made the first mile. I don't remember how my father got from his car the rest of the way to the farm. Next day, a farmer down the road hitched up a team of horses, and pulled my father's car out of the ditch.

When supper time came, my mother went ahead and fed my sisters and me. She said she'd wait until my father came. Even though it was summer, and would be daylight for maybe another two hours, the sky was so dark with clouds that it seemed like night had almost come.

From the east window next to my cot, I watched for my father's car. He drove a LaSalle, a large, heavy four-door car. That was the next-best car to a Cadillac. I don't know why I knew that, but I did.

My mother kept busy doing things around the house. I saw her stop frequently, though, to look out the dining room window from which she could see about a quarter of a mile down the road my father would be coming on. My sisters were enough younger than me that I really don't remember what they were doing, but they were not as much help to my mother as I was, because I was older, and I was a boy. I told my mother not to worry, that my father would be okay.

I was the first to see my father's car, edging over the top of a small hill. The car seemed to be barely moving. I called to my mother, and all four of us quickly went out onto the front porch. The rain made it hard to see, and water spilled out of the overloaded gutters on the porch roof.

You could tell that the front of the car was slipping back and forth, a little to each side, as it moved toward us a few feet at a time. It was like an animal following a new trail, swinging its head from side to side, moving cautiously, watching for the unexpected.

I know my father had the car in low gear, because he had showed me once how that worked. I also knew that he was a good driver.

As he got closer, we could hear through the steady beat of the rain the low whine of the car's powerful engine. We couldn't see my father in the car, but I could visualize him sitting behind the wheel, both hands confidently guiding the car along the treacherous road, his foot expertly applying gentle power to the car's wheels at the right moment.

I knew he'd make it.

The End of my Story

Well, like I said, all of that happened a long time ago. The walnut desk I told you about in the very beginning was in my own room through the years I was growing up. I did my homework from school on that desk, and wrote papers my teachers assigned me. Then I went away for the last two years of high school, to a boarding school for boys in Minnesota. That was a long way from home. Someday I'll tell you that story, too.

When I went to college, I often came home on weekends, because it wasn't far. I'd still use the walnut desk in my room for studying, and I slept in one of the walnut beds, made from that log on my grandfather's farm. After I graduated from college, I enlisted in the United States Air Force, where I was a lieutenant, and I lived for a while in Washington, D.C. When my military service was over, I came home again, and it was at that desk I wrote three or four letters a week to a young woman I'd met who lived in another city. I kept that up until Marilyn, your grandmother, MereMere, and I got married in 1957.

So, I'm a little sad, now that my furniture is gone forever from the house where I grew up. Fifty years ago, more than fifty years now, seems like a long, long time. But I'm glad my older son Byron and his family, who still have several of the pieces of the walnut furniture, including the beds Benton and Risa use, and, also my younger son, Collin, who still has and uses the walnut wing-table in the story, know the story about the walnut desk and beds and side table, and will go on to use them, take care of them in their homes, now that they're grown up, and perhaps one day pass them on to their children.

Terror at the Door

Chapter I

Mary Jane heard a horse whinny. From the big barn, the stallion whinnied back, pawing the floor and straining against its tether. A man's muttered curse was followed by the clumping of horses milling about, the jangling of bridles.

Pulling aside the curtain, Mary Jane looked through the distorting pane of window glass. In the yard outside, armed men on horseback moved restlessly back and forth, looking to all sides. Only one rider sat calmly in his saddle, scrutinizing the house. He was dressed in a dark coat, buttoned at the neck, that fell to his knees. A wide-brimmed hat shadowed his face. He held a rifle muzzle-up in his right hand, the reins in his left.

Two of the riders moved deliberately to opposite sides of the yard, like men on guard. Pistol butts protruded from leather belts at their waists. Hats pulled low partly concealed their faces. Where the road to the house snaked out of a wooded patch, another rider, rifle held in the crook of his arm, watched the road behind. Eight riders, Mary Jane counted, all strangers.

"Leah, stay in your room!" Mary Jane shouted up the stairway to her sixteen-year-old daughter, and then took each of the two younger children firmly by hand, hurrying them into the pantry.

"Millie," she whispered to the Negro nursemaid, "try to keep them quiet. Give them something to play with."

Millie, her eyes wide with fear, picked up the youngest and held her close, wrapping her chubby arms around her. The next youngest child, hugging a doll, clung to Millie's dress, her face bewildered.

Mary Jane, a small woman with precise features, black hair pulled back, quickly closed the door. She pressed her trembling hands against her brown patterned full-length dress, and stepped into the front room.

A man's voice rang out, authoritative and brusque, sounding alarmingly close, as if he were already inside the house.

"Mrs. Gill, we don't want to harm you or your children." He paused ominously. "We know your husband's in Westport, and won't be back 'til tomorrow."

Mary Jane gasped. How could he know that Marcus had taken the foreman and her son with him to buy yearlings to pasture?

"We're hungry, ma'am. We'd like you to cook up something for us to eat." When Mary Jane didn't answer, he called out again, "See here, ma'am, open the door. Otherwise we'll have to force our way in. You don't want that, do you. I'll leave my men outside, if that'll make you feel any better."

Her husband's warning before he had left for Westport raced through her mind. Be extra careful, he'd said, and watch out for strangers. Just a few weeks ago, anti-slavery guerrillas from Kansas Territory had raided a farm near Harrisonville. The men terrorized the family and stole horses. Neighbors said that the guerrillas threatened to take the slaves, too, so they could be set free, but gathered up so much loot that they rode off and left the slaves behind.

Mary Jane cracked the door and looked out. The man watching from the saddle of his horse loomed black against the sky. The horse's chest and flanks were flaked with sweat. The ground, vulnerable from a hard rain, was gouged by hoof marks.

"Who are you," Mary Jane asked, struggling to keep her voice steady. "What do you want?"

"Like I said, ma'am, we'd just like some dinner. We've covered a lot of territory since we left home, and haven't eaten since last evening."

As a Southerner, Mary Jane's instinct was to offer hospitality, but these men were not travelers on the road. "Well, I don't know," she said, hoping to put them off. "I'm sorry, but we've just had our breakfast. I don't think . . . ."

"And I don't want to be rude, ma'am," he interrupted, "but we don't plan on looking anywhere else."

He thrust his rifle through a ring fastened to the saddle horn, and slid to the ground. Handing the reins off to one of his men, he approached the house. "I'm coming in, Mrs. Gill. My men will wait outside until you've got dinner ready." Turning to the rider nearest him, he said in a low voice, "Put two men at the door. We don't want any surprises."

With no other choice, Mary Jane opened the door wider, and fell back into the room. Leah, who had slipped down the stairs despite her mother's warning, passed quickly behind her and went to the pantry to help Millie with the younger children.

The stranger removed his hat, ducked his head, and stepped through the door. Middle-aged, long hair and beard the color of slate. Where his hat brim had pressed against his head, the hair was matted. Dirt rings formed by sweat, now dried, circled his throat above the collar of the black scarf knotted above his coat. He smelled of horses, sweat, and wood-smoke.

"Where're your children? Anybody else in the house?" Suspiciously, he turned his head and looked up the stairway, then toward the closed door into the pantry, and beyond that, the opening that led into the kitchen.

"They're in the pantry, with Millie." Her voice was matter-of-fact; they were no threat to him, she said to herself, so there was no cause for him to harm them.

"She can look after them while you fix us up something?"

Mary Jane ignored the question, struggling to keep her face calm.

"You didn't answer my question," he said. "Anybody else in the house?"

Mary Jane shook her head. "No. Just my oldest daughter. She's with my younger children, back there."

"What's her name? Your daughter's name?"

She told him, then quickly added, "She'll be helping me in the kitchen. Since I guess you'll be staying."

"My name's—" He barely hesitated. "Slater, Mrs. Gill." He then strode toward the pantry, dried mud caked on the sides of his boots flaking onto the polished floor. Standing to one side of the door, his hand on the butt of the revolver in his belt, he pushed it open. Satisfied with what he saw, he turned and bounded up the stairway two steps at a time, the revolver now in his hand. The forceful sound of his boots striking the wood boards of the floor as he went from one room to the next were an unnatural, jarring intrusion in the hushed silence.

Returning, Slater went to the open front door of the house, and motioned to a man who had been waiting to come inside.

"But you said—," Mary Jane called out. "You said that your men—."
By then, Slater had disappeared outside.

The man who entered was short and bony, pale, and nearly bald. Twisted teeth yellowed by tobacco juice, a distorted grin. He carried a chicken in each grimy hand, head cleaved from the neck, white carcasses splashed with blood. Holding up the chickens, he said, "Howdy, ma'am. Thought I'd help out with dinner. Caught these two out back while you and him were jawboning. I'll take 'em to the kitchen and clean'em for you, ma'am." He then snickered, taken with his own devilment.

Repulsed and infuriated, Mary Jane turned away, hiding her anger, and led him toward the kitchen.

Minutes later, another man sauntered through the front door. Stocky, hat low over his eyes, with matted yellowish hair to his collar, he was dressed like a farmer. He appeared to be about Brown's age. Looking carefully about the well-furnished room, he saw what he was searching for. He walked over to a large trunk on the floor against one wall. A brocaded decorative cloth in motifs of rich red, gilt yellow, and deep blue, lay across the top. The man took off the cloth, crumpling it in his hands, and watched, fascinated, when the fabric, as if alive, regained its unwrinkled appearance. He chuckled, and stuffed the cloth into a large pocket on the side of his coat.

The trunk now revealed to him was finely made, no ordinary piece, and bearing no sign of abuse incurred when bounced about in a wagon or stagecoach. It was constructed of belting leather, stretched on a sturdy frame of oak. Dyed the color of mahogany, the leather was polished into dark reflective surfaces. Burnished brass clasps embellished the front.

The man reached down, turned the key in each of the locks, undid the clasps, and lifted up the lid. Rummaging through table linens and comforters, he irritably pulled them out and tossed them on the floor. Next came account books, land abstracts, and bulky ledgers in which were recorded by seasons of the year the minutia of farming, such as seed bought and planted, weather, crop yields, calves born, and slaves purchased and sold. He piled all these on a nearby table, to get them out of the way.

Among the remaining items at the bottom of the trunk he saw a substantial-looking box, a small chest. Lacquered-wood surfaces gleamed with light, and leather trimmed the edges. He leaned down into the trunk, grasped the box with both hands, grunted, lifted it up, and because of its weight, set it down carefully on the table next to the ledgers. "Got it," he muttered to himself with obvious satisfaction, and looked as if he would call out to Slater, but didn't. Opening the lid of the chest, he took out a handful of silver tableware. He selected an ornate silver table knife that he held up to the light from a window, admiring the strange filigree-like decoration.

"Put those back!" Leah stood in the door to the pantry, arms stiff at her side, fists tight. "Those aren't yours. You put them right back," she demanded.

Startled, he looked at her, his eyes widening in surprise.

"I mean it," she said. "What do you mean, getting into our things?"

The man shrugged. "Now, now, little lady, no need for you to get all upset," he said, as if calming a small child.

"But they belonged to my grandmother. We brought them with us, from Kentucky. They're very valuable."

Unperturbed, the man dropped the silver pieces into a cloth pouch hanging from a strap at his shoulder. "I know that, ma'am, that's why I'm taking them. And that ain't all you brought with you, is it?" the man added. "You also brung slaves, didn't you? Slaves, human beings you bought. That you own. You shouldn't have done that, bringing slaves here." He took a step toward Leah, his arms rising as if he might shake her by the shoulders. "We don't want slaves in these parts. We don't like slavery. We don't like Southerners, neither."

"Who are you to tell us what we should do?" Leah retorted, not moving, her head up.

He stopped, looked at her hard, started to speak, them shrugged and turned his back. He finished dumping the remainder of the silver into the pouch slung from his shoulder, and went outside, not looking back.

Leah, tears in her eyes, fled to the kitchen.

She had only just left when yet another man came into the room, blinking his eyes in the subdued light, his face smudged with road dust. About twenty, he was thin and hollow-eyed, with straight, coffee-colored hair. Despite several days growth of beard and an untidy look, he wore a fine bleached-linen shirt, a dark-red neckerchief around his neck, a woolen vest trimmed in black, and a narrow felt hat with a purple ribbon wrapped round the crown.

Seeing the pantry door standing open, he sauntered over and looked inside. "Where's the whiskey kept?" he asked. Millie, clutching the Gill's youngest boy, two-year-old Kibbey, kept her eyes downcast. The boy's sisters, playing on the floor, gazed up at the stranger.

Shrugging, the man began noisily opening cabinets along one wall. When he found what he was after, he opened one of the bottles of whiskey, took a long drink, then grasped two other bottles in his left hand. Walking to the front door, he handed the bottles to one of the men standing just outside. "Here you are, boys. Pass it around. Plenty more inside."

With the whiskey bottle hanging from one hand, he sauntered around the room. He picked up a small glass paperweight lying on a table, held it up to his eye, squinted through the glass at other objects in the room, then dropped it into his jacket pocket. A child's walnut rocking chair sat next to a spindle-backed armchair pulled back from a writing table. The intruder stepped over to the child's chair, and with the toe of his boot nudged the edge of the seat, causing the chair to bob back and forth, the hollow clacking of the rockers against the floor planks scarcely audible.

Restlessly, the man wandered over to an upholstered wing chair near the great hearth where unfinished needlepoint in a floral design, left there by Mary Jane the night before, lay on the seat of the chair. He picked up the needlepoint, scrutinized the intricate needlepoint, but not knowing what to make of it, put it back where it had been.

The man then saw a bulky family Bible, the size of three ordinary books, bound in leather and fastened with a metal hasp, lying atop a chest of drawers. Impatient, he opened it and leafed through the first few pages, squinting at handwritten recordings in brown ink of births, deaths, and marriages. He read a few entries, mouthing the words, took another drink of whiskey; then shut the book, and gazed around the rest of the room.

The rich odor of food cooking and sounds of activity came from the kitchen. He went to the open door and leaned against the door jam, watching the three women preparing the meal. The room was warm from the wood fire in the large iron range. Mary Jane stood at the wood stove, turning pieces of chicken frying in an iron pan, a white apron covering the front of her dress. A woman slave, called in by Mary Jane to help out, sat at a table, peeling potatoes. A pot of green beans simmered on the back of the range. A black skillet with dark-brown gravy sat warming near the edge. No one talked.

Leah stood at a table, cutting pies baked earlier that morning, just removed from the oven. Her face was flushed from the heat, her long dark hair pulled back and tied loosely with a bright ribbon. She placed the pie slices on a serving plate, her agile hands moving adeptly as she worked. The light-yellow blouse she wore was open at the neck, the top two buttons unfastened, the sleeves pushed above the elbows. Perspiration beaded her brow, and her slender neck was moist.

The man remained in the doorway, slouching, and stared at Leah. She seemed preoccupied with her task, and did not look back at him, although her body tensed under his scrutiny.

"My name's Ephraim," he said. Leah said nothing, lowering her head slightly, as if concentrating on her work.

"When do you expect you'll be ready so we can eat? I'm mighty hungry."

Without looking up, Mary Jane curtly replied, "We'll come tell you."

Ephriam grunted, and kept his eyes on Leah. She skillfully sliced wedges of dark-red tomatoes on a wood chopping board and arranged them in circles on a platter. "I live on a farm, too," he said. "West of here, quite a ways. Fact is, took most of the night to get here."

His eyes traveled from her long hair, down her youthful figure, and back to the delicate profile of her face. Leah kept her eyes down.

Ignored, Ephriam looked resentful. Petulance crept into the corners of his mouth. Finally, hitching up his trousers, he took another drink of whiskey, shivered in spite of the heat, and turned away. Passing the stairway, he stopped. No one else was in the room. He looked up toward the second floor, and began slowly climbing the stairs, treading softly, muffling the sound of his boots.

In the kitchen, Mary Jane picked up a plate of food scraps and stepped to the back door to throw them out for the cats. Her eyes widened in surprise at what she saw. Three of the strangers were leading a half-dozen horses out of the corral with rope bridles, headed toward the yard in front of the house. Another man was harnessing two of her husband's horses to one of the box wagons that Marcus kept in a covered shed. The wagon had been loaded with saddles, harnesses, farming tools, and large bags of grain from the barn.

Furious, she put down the pan and hurried into the front room. Slater leaned back in a rocking chair, one leg crossed over the other, smoking a cigar. Her husband's humidor, the cover standing open, sat on the table next to him.

"Mr. Slater, you've got to stop your men," she hurled at him. "They're stealing our horses. They're taking things out of the barn that don't belong to them. You have no right to do that."

Slater puffed serenely on the cigar, returning the stare with eyes partly closed against the smoke. "You just go on back to your kitchen, Mrs. Gill. My men are doing what they came to do."

"But we haven't done anything to you. I don't even—."

"Well, I'll tell you, Mrs. Gill," he broke in, suddenly angry, "me and my men just as soon you and your husband and other Southerners like you would pack up and take your slaves with you back to where you came from. We don't like your ways, and we're not going to tolerate slavery. Not in Missouri, not in the Territory, not anywhere." He got up from the chair, his head nearly brushing the ceiling. "People like you bring slaves and settle down right next to us. We do our own farming. We don't buy slaves." Brown's face was taut, his eyes almost closed. "If we need more help, we hire it. We don't go buy ourselves another slave. What you do is disgusting, immoral. It's abominable. In fact, I—."

From the floor above, from Leah's room, they heard a man's voice singing drunkenly, and sounds of commotion. Mary Jane spun around, and hurried up the stairs. Slater followed at a deliberate pace.

When they reached the bedroom door, they saw Ephriam jumping up and down on Leah's bed, her clothes scattered across the bed and on the floor nearby. Leah's room was never cluttered, yet drawers to a dresser now stood open, and one drawer, completely pulled out, lay empty on the floor. The half-empty whiskey bottle was next to it.

When he saw Slater, Ephriam stopped jumping, and sheepishly climbed down off the bed. "Just having a little fun," he said. "Ain't done nobody any harm." He sidled past them, and went down the stairs, stumbling when he got near the bottom.

Leah came out of the kitchen. She saw the expression on her mother's face as she descended the stairs, but when Mary Jane put her finger to her lips, Leah only said, "We're ready to feed them."

Slater, a thin smile on his face, followed Ephriam out the door.

For Mary Jane and Leah, waiting in the kitchen, the meal seemed endless. All the men except Slater behaved as if they were at a tavern. They passed around another bottle of whiskey from the cabinet while they ate hungrily, told stories, laughed, and boasted about the loot outside in the box wagon, the money they'd get for those fine horses. The pale-skinned, almost bald man who had carried in the headless chickens, carried plates of food outside to the men who remained on guard.

Slater was silent, absorbed in his eating. Mary Jane thought him an odd man: dangerous and determined, yet probably educated, principled in his own way. She had never known anyone from New England. The depth of his repulsion at slavery puzzled her. How could someone of apparent moral substance resort to such violence, force his way into her home, rob, intimidate, all in the name of protesting against slavery? The fact that such a man could conduct himself in this way frightened her even more, because she recognized that without boundaries, without restraints, anything could happen.

When the men had finished eating the slices of pie served on a platter in the middle of the table, all except Slater got up and left the house. Slater pushed away from the table, leaned back in his chair, and lighted a second cigar, as relaxed as if he were a guest about to have a pleasant conversation with his hostess.

Mary Jane began carrying dishes out to the kitchen.

"One more thing, Mrs. Gill," Slater said. "Your husband's a wealthy man. He's got to have some cash hidden somewhere. I want you to show me where it is."

Mary Jane stopped, and looked directly at him. "Haven't you stolen enough? Caused us enough trouble?"

Slater chuckled. "Well, now, we'd have taken more, but we figure we've already got about as much as we can carry." He held the cigar between his thumb and forefinger, his elbow resting on the arm of the chair, and stared at her, his face without expression. "Now, then, where's the money hidden."

"I don't know. There isn't any."

Slater gazed at her thoughtfully, puffing on the cigar. "Your daughter Leah's a mighty pretty young woman, Mrs. Gill. Ephriam seems right taken with her." With a finger he tapped the cigar, dropping the ash onto the floor. "We don't have to leave right away, you know. We've got time."

Mary Jane could hardly speak; her voice was a whisper. "How could you dare?"

Slater didn't reply. The cigar smoke, transparent-white, drifted above him.

"Well?" he asked again. "Where's the money?"

"My husband took it with him. They have to pay cash for livestock."

"You don't have any other money in the house?" Slater watched her closely.

"No."

"Are you quite sure, Mrs. Gill? Like I said, we're in no hurry to leave such fine hospitality." Slater narrowed his eyes against the smoke. "I'm sure Ephriam would be willing to leave whatever he's doing right at this moment and come on back inside."

Mary Jane set the dishes back on the table, and went into the front room. Slater followed. She opened the family Bible, and found 1st Corinthians. Compressed flat between the pages of parchment-like paper were several bills of large denomination.

"This is all there is. I put it there myself. For anything unexpected." She handed the money to Slater.

"Thank you, ma'am. That was very wise of you." He tucked the money inside his coat. "We'll be leaving, now." He turned and left the house.

Trembling, one hand clenched at her mouth, Mary Jane stood for a moment at the front window, watching the men ride off. The stolen horses, tethered by ropes to their captors, trotted along, complacent. She turned and gazed about the room. The very air in the room had been polluted by these intruders, she felt. The clotted mud from Slater's boots soiled her floor. She gazed at the ravaged trunk, the empty silver chest, the table linens and comforters dumped on the muddied floor. These men had violated her house, dirtied it with their coarse humor, their greed, the crude threats.

They were nothing more than thieves hiding behind abolitionist views, she decided, not lawful men like her husband. Marcus believed in lawfulness; it was integral to his character. He would never do what they had done, even to maintain slavery. These men didn't care about freeing slaves; instead, they had desecrated her house. Their purpose, she realized, was to steal property to enrich themselves, and to intimidate the women, to frighten them.

The raiders had threatened her family, and might have done much worse. Still terrified from the awful confrontation with Slater, she could not bring herself to think of how Leah might have been brutally harmed had she not divulged where the money was hidden. The rawness of the fear humiliated her, made her feel weak, and the sense of weakness angered her.

Leah's sudden shriek propelled Mary Jane toward the kitchen. Leah and the slaves stood at the open back door, looking toward the wagon shed. Smoke tumbled above the roof, and flames erupted from the wide door and curled about the window frames.

The raiders had set the wagon shed on fire before they rode off.

Chapter II

A few weeks later, in the crisp October air, Marcus Gill rode his quarter horse across fields cut clean of corn stalks. Dry, twisted fragments of stalks and veined leaves lying on the ground spoke back to the horse and rider as they passed.

Marcus was a solid-looking man of medium height, with black hair and beard beginning to gray, although he was not yet fifty. His eyes, steady and light gray in color, had flecks of ice-green. In conversation, he could appear when listening to be standing back, as if watching from a distance, his gaze remote and his face lacking expression. At times, he would tilt his head back slightly, and to one side, as if contemplating the speaker. Yet, when moved by a guileless question from one of his young children, or by an affectionate gesture from Mary Jane, his face opened with warmth, and his eyes momentarily glistened with pleasure.

Marcus sat his horse with the ease gained when a boy in Kentucky. His hands held the reins as lightly as, when a child playing in the barn, he would pick up a swallow's egg from a fallen nest. When Marcus was only three, his father had hoisted him up and placed Marcus bareback, astride a placid mare. His father threaded the boy's fingers around the reins so that he could hold them in his own uncertain hands; then continued talking quietly, as he led the mare slowly around the barn lot, guiding her with the bit. When the boy was five, his father gave permission for Marcus to ride the mare alone, within a small fenced pasture next to the barn. Marcus did not know that his father had instructed Jim, the slave who would saddle the mare, to keep an eye on his son from the barn door as long as the boy rode, and made Jim accountable for the boy's safety.

But now, as his horse loped across the fields, Marcus thought again about Brown and the men who had been with him. He knew it could have been even worse. Other raiders from Kansas Territory, in moments of anger or drunkenness, or if they met even unarmed resistance, had shot and killed farmers and adult sons with no provocation. Wives and daughters were intimidated and terrorized, a part of the strategy to drive slave-owning farmers out of the state.

Why such violence? Stealing of slaves by anti-slavery forces was increasing. Farmers in Kansas territory near Lawrence, even townspeople with abolitionist views, sheltered fleeing slaves until they could be passed along to other sympathizers and finally reach freedom in the north. Raiders hoped that slave-owning farmers in Missouri would feel compelled to flee, taking their families farther south. But why, Marcus thought, should he yield to such threats? Owning slaves was lawful. He had bought them. They were his property.

When Marcus came to Missouri with his family, be assembled a thousand acres of land in Jackson County bordering the Kansas Territory. Virgin land, it had never been cultivated. He was confident that he could transform this land into a richly productive farm of row crops and livestock for which there would be an expanding market.

Magnificent stands of mature trees covered a part of the property. They provided logs and lumber to construct the buildings he would need. A creek for watering livestock ran through the land. Well water, cold and pure, was within reach not far below the surface. The gentler slopes of the rolling land Marcus could cultivate with row crops; the sharper hills would remain in pasture, fenced with wood rail.

His slaves, more than twenty of them brought from Kentucky, were the sinew, the muscle of this transfiguration. They felled the trees with axes, hacking the undergrowth into brush piles set afire to burn. The smoke twisted upward into the sky, the roiling blaze forcing workers to stand back. Slaves broke the sod with teams of mules dragging V-shaped rugged blades, turning the ground, burying the thick prairie grasses that would soon decay under dark waves of earth. Then smaller blades, set close like soldiers in rank, broke up the solid clods, followed by cultivators slicing the soil even finer, so that at last the seed could be planted.

Other slaves cut down and trimmed tree trunks into logs to build the big main house and the slave cabins. Marcus set up a wood mill, powered by water from the creek, flush with spring rains, to make wood boards for the barns, hog sheds, chicken coops, and wagon sheds.

Nearby, the village of New Santa Fe flourished. The hollow sound of hammer blows driving nails into freshly sawed lumber echoed everywhere. On the town's one business street, new settlers passed by with little notice, there were so many. A general store offered essential supplies. At the edge of town, a blacksmith shoed horses and made iron door latches, hinges, nails, and tools. A post office, church, and a stable shared one side of the dusty street, quick to turn into ankle-deep mud when spring rains came. Ten miles to the north, the town of Westport published a weekly newspaper, four folded sheets that left smudges of printer's ink on a reader's hands.

But abolitionists in Kansas Territory, vehemently opposed to slavery, had begun making trouble about 1854, the year Marcus and his family arrived. County sheriffs, who had jurisdiction in upholding slavery laws, lacked enough men to find and prosecute the lawless. The ranks of Federal troops in the county were slim; and worse, they did not intercede.

The countryside was too vast, the raiders too quick, for enforcement of federal and state laws protecting slave owners and other victims of random violence. Marcus knew he was not guilty of any crime, yet those who thought slavery morally wrong repeatedly threatened him and other farmers. He felt that their attackers envied the wealth that slavery engendered, and feared that slavery might move westward, unabated, into Kansas Territory.

Marcus also felt beleaguered. Like criminals, raiders cloaked their identity, hiding behind faces unrecognized and names unknown. Slavery was lawful, yet these men were not. They manipulated a lawful act, the practice of slavery, to justify their crimes.

Marcus looked about him as he rode across the fields. Now that harvest was over, his spirits lightened. He saw grain bins straining under burdens of corn. Shoots of yellow hay stuck out between slats in haylofts stacked to the eves. Meadowlarks whistled from the pastures, and swallows dipped and soared near the roofs of the big barns. The rich soil rested until next spring the plow blades would once again cut crisply, turning the glistening, fecund earth to face the sun.

Riding across his land, Marcus scanned the horizon from time to time for signs of strangers on horseback. The bold sun warming his back masked the apprehension that burdened him, the fear that he avoided discussing openly with Mary Jane. When he began wearing a revolver heavy in the leather holster at his waist, she did not ask why. Away from the house any distance, he also carried a rifle slung across the saddle, or wore it on his back, secured by a strap over his shoulder and across his chest.

Marcus stopped to open a gate, leaning down from his saddle to lift the latch. The mare dropped her head, straining against the reins to graze on pasture grass, still a lush, cool green, saturated with dew. He pulled firmly on the bridle reins to raise her head.

Looking up, he saw against the skyline a solitary figure on horseback approaching the house from the west, from Kansas Territory. He was not expecting a visitor. His son Turner, seventeen, had left earlier that morning for New Santa Fe, to pick up the mail. This rider was coming from the opposite direction, and would reach his house before Marcus could be there.

With a slight pressure of the reins against her neck, Marcus quickly turned the mare and at a gallop followed a narrow cattle path back toward the house. When he reached the corral, he handed the reins to the stable boy, and saw a groom leading Turner's horse into the barn. Near the house, the stranger's mount was already tied at the rail.

His hand on the revolver at his waist, Marcus cautiously stepped inside the house. In the parlor Turner was talking to a man in his early twenties. At the sound of Marcus's boots on the wood planking, they turned toward him. The stranger held loosely in his hands a dark, low-crown felt hat.

"Father, this is Will Quantrill, the schoolteacher I told you about."

Quantrill stepped forward to shake hands. "Pleased to meet you, Colonel Gill."

The man was slender, about the same height as Marcus. He looked agile, Marcus thought, and supple, like a willow branch that springs back when one's grasp is released. Marcus also sensed the hard muscles beneath the slack, open-necked shirt the younger man wore. Quantrill's gaze, curious and confident, met Marcus Gill's.

"Yes, Turner told me about you," Marcus said. "Says you're a right good teacher. Over at Stanton." Marcus took off his coat, laid it across the back of a chair. "But you're from back East, I hear. Where 'bouts?"

"Ohio. Came west two years ago. Went to Utah for a spell in spring of last year."

Marcus gestured toward a chair. "What brought you to Missouri?"

His lean guest had a sunburned, slightly boyish face, unperturbed blue eyes, and hair the color of wheat chaff, slicked down on each side.

"You may know Henry Chiles," Will replied. "Has a place back toward Westport. Hired me as a bullwhacker when he took fifty wagons of freight to Salt Lake for Russell-Majors." He looked carefully at Marcus for a reaction.

In fact, Marcus remembered that one day in town not long ago, Henry Chiles had complained about the man when telling Marcus about the trip to Utah. Chiles, who had been wagon boss on the trip west, was contemptuous of Quantrill's rambunctious behavior, yet grudgingly admitted he was a fine horseman and an excellent shot when hunting game to feed the wagon crew. Chiles also said that one of these days Quantrill would get himself into serious trouble. Daring, disdainful of authority, that kind of man usually did.

Turner spoke eagerly to his father. "You've said that with me leaving soon for the university, you'd like to have another man on the place. Will would be mighty good for you to have around, if there was trouble. He's the best shot I've ever seen."

Marcus thought for a moment. Despite Chiles's criticism, Marcus liked his guest's assurance, his easy composure. "What are your plans, Mr. Quantrill?"

"Well, sir, I'll be teaching school 'til spring."

"Where are you staying?"

"Mr. Bennings offered to put me up. His place is a mite far from school, though, compared to what you are here."

Marcus knew old man Bennings, a farmer in the Kansas Territory. Unlike many, he was friendly toward Missourians, a pro-slavery man. Marcus probed further. "Coming from back east, how do you feel about Kansas Territory going free-state? Barring slavery. There're some who hold firmly to that idea."

"Well, I figure a man's entitled to his property, including slaves. Law says he can own them. Besides, I'm told settlers in the Territory will have a choice whether it'll be free or slave, but I hope they go slave. Just makes sense, Missouri already having slaves."

His expression unchanged, Marcus turned to his son. "Turner, Mr. Quantrill might like a little of that whiskey we brought from Kentucky last trip I made. Fetch some glasses."

Quantrill sat back in his chair, relaxed. "Turner said you were a colonel in the militia in Kentucky, before you came out to Missouri. I suspect you don't think much of those ruffians coming over from Kansas and causing a lot of trouble."

Marcus said nothing.

"Well, sir," Quantrill plunged ahead, "I've seen what those Jayhawkers do, and I can tell you, it just isn't right. They say they're against slavery, but I'm inclined to think they're mostly interested in raising hell and stealing another man's property." He watched closely for any reaction. "Abolitionists, men like Lane and Montgomery, they don't like folks from the South, folks who've got slaves. They've got no tolerance for that."

Turner returned from the pantry, and sat the bottle and glasses down on a table. Marcus poured the whiskey, handed a glass to Quantrill, and raised his glass in the gesture of a salute.

"Thank you, sir." Quantrill downed the liquor, and sat with one leg crossed casually over the other, his slender fingers playing with the empty glass.

Marcus asked, "Have you had a part in any of the fighting? Helping those who try to keep the raiders away from here?"

"Haven't exactly had much of a chance since I got back from Utah, but I've been thinking about maybe giving some of the folks around here a hand, if they need it." Will grinned, then threw out, "Man got in my way, out in Utah, so I had to kill him. I'm not fearful of doing what needs to be done. Fact is, I'm not much afraid of anything."

Marcus didn't like Quantrill's boasting, and guessed he might be lying about the killing, trying to impress. Quantrill struck Marcus as a young man anxious to please. But Marcus also recognized that such a man could be useful, if he hired Quantrill to help protect his family. He decided to take the chance.

"Like I said, Will's a real good shot," Turner offered. "I once saw him put a bullet hole though a big sow's ear from about ten yards. That old sow let out a squeal and ran around the pen a couple times, but didn't hurt her at all." Turner laughed, and his father smiled. Will looked pleased.

Turner soon left for his first year at the university, halfway across the state. A few days later, Will Quantrill moved into a small, bare-floored room with a low ceiling in the attic of Marcus Gill's house. The room contained only a rope bed, wood chair, clothes tree, coal oil lamp, a mid-size trunk for storage, and chamber pot. For room, board, and a little money, he would be another man with a gun, if needed, when night darkened the roads from the west.

Schooldays, Will was up and gone by daybreak, quietly slipping out on horseback to arrive early at the simple frame building near Stanton. Winter came early that year, bringing snow, then two days of melting, followed by cold and more snow. There was but one schoolroom, almost square, with rough-sawn floor, a window on each of two sides, narrow entrance door, and exposed rafters above which the roof quickly peaked. Will would start the wood fire in the hulking iron stove, sweep the floor, and then wait for his students of staggered ages to arrive on horseback or by foot.

At the end of the school day, he liked to linger for a time, reading or planning the next day's lesson. One afternoon, he began a letter to his widowed mother in Ohio.

Stanton, Kansas Terri. Jan. 26th

My dear Mother
I again seat myself down to pen you a few lines, hoping they may cheer you in a measure, and if so, it is all I can do at this time. . . . In my last letter I said we have had quite fine weather here, but I can now look out of the window at my schoolhouse and see every thing clad in snow & ice, which was put on but last night, and now seems to hold every thing in its cold embrace, indeed so sudden has been the change that it seems not only to have caught the forest & prairie napping in the sunshine but the people also, for I feel it myself and seem to shudder when I look out upon the snow covered ground & hear the cold wind whistle around & through the forest . . .

Will laid down his pen, stood up from the desk, and walked over to a window where he stood for a moment, pensive. Cold air breached the glass, chilling his face as he watched the wind churn the dry snow into cone-shaped drifts against the fence posts. He then went back to his writing.

You have undoubtedly heard of the wrongs committed in this territory by the southern people or pro-slavery party, but when one once knows the facts they can easily see that it has been the opposite party that have been the main movers in the troubles & by far the most lawless set of people in the country. They all sympathize for old J. Brown who should have been hung years ago, indeed hanging was too good for him. May I never see a more contemptible people than those who sympathize with him. A murderer and a robber made a martyr of, just think of it . . .

Abruptly, Will angrily tossed his pen onto the desk, and stood up, jarring the small desk. He felt a rush of anger toward all abolitionists, a swelling up of frustration. He longed to strike out, to take action, to be someone.

In the ebbing light of dusk and the silence of nightfall, Will returned to the Marcus Gill farm, cold, hungry, and despondent, and climbed the steps to his room in the attic.

Chapter III

In early December, Marcus accepted an invitation from a friend who worked actively for pro-slavery forces in the Kansas Territory to hear a man named Lincoln, a lawyer from Illinois, speak at Leavenworth, just inside the Kansas Territory. Marcus arranged to spend the night at Mansion House, where Lincoln, visiting the Territory early in his bid for the Republican presidential nomination, was staying.

Abolition of slavery was gaining support, Marcus knew, in the newly formed Republican Party. Newspapers in St. Louis, available three days later in Westport, reported the stories. Marcus was a Democrat, and Democrats in the South were traditionally pro-slavery. He was curious to learn what this man from Illinois, also born in Kentucky, but already known for anti-slavery comments, had to say about the right of slave owners like himself to keep their slaves. In the face of rising public outcries in the north and northeast against slavery, would Lincoln, speaking from a platform on the edge of a slave state, now reassert the right to keep slaves in order to accommodate a more Southern audience?

Newspapers reported that Lincoln might be content just to stem the expansion of slavery into western territories. He had even declared that if voters would agree with him to commit the nation to equality, to the actual practice of freedom for all men, then the institution of slavery could continue in those states where slavery already existed until it eventually died out of its own accord. Marcus favored this solution; it seemed to him a practical and realistic compromise.

On Saturday evening, Marcus and his friend went early to Stockton's Hall, where Lincoln would appear. Gas-flamed light fixtures high on the walls of the room cast a sputtering, raw light. Tobacco smoke hovered above the heads of those already seated. Standing room at the back of the hall was crowded with men jostling for a better view. Those who couldn't get in collected at the doors where they might catch a glimpse of the would-be candidate for president.

Almost without notice, Lincoln entered the back of the hall and started down a side aisle, stopping to shake a stranger's hand or grasp a well-wisher by the shoulder. Marcus was struck by the gaunt angularity of the man. A head taller than most, Lincoln's beardless cheeks were sunken in the sallow face, the black hair disarranged. He looked austere, not at all like a politician, yet took his time, looking full in the eyes each man he greeted.

On the unadorned stage were two spindle-backed chairs. Lincoln mounted the stairs awkwardly and sat down on one of the chairs, noticeably too small for him. He gazed out at the assemblage from deep-set eyes, his knees apart and thrust high by the low seat, legs stiffly vertical like sticks poked in the ground. Marcus thought Lincoln resembled a great grasshopper, sitting there stolidly in the chair, and smiled slightly in amusement.

Less than respectful, the crowd continued talking among themselves until the man who would introduce Lincoln got up and called for order. After an effusive introduction, he gave the floor to Lincoln.

Marcus watched curiously as Lincoln carefully arose and stepped forward. His tall frame diminished the fragile-looking lectern. As he began speaking, Lincoln seemed inelegant and forbidding, but gradually his voice became strong and firm, resonating in an unexpectedly high pitch throughout the room. Marcus listened intently.

Lincoln knew that there were pro-slavery listeners in the audience. Before long he spoke directly to them.

"You are for the Union; and you greatly fear the success of the Republicans would destroy the Union. Why?"

Lincoln paused, and looked about the room. "Your own statement of it is, that if the Republicans elect a president, you won't stand for it. You will break up the Union." Abolishing slavery was a plank in the Republican platform. Because of that, some called the party "the black Republicans". Marcus thought it an apt description.

The audience hushed as Lincoln challenged the upturned faces. "That will be your act, not ours," he admonished. "To justify it you must show that our policy gives you just cause for such desperate action. Can you do that?"

Marcus fully knew, as did the cagey Lincoln, that slave owners were trapped in a dilemma. On one hand, the Constitution of the United States gave the right to own slaves. But outside the South, this fact flew in the face of public opinion growing vigorously against slavery. How can it be said, newspaper editors who opposed slavery strongly argued, that all men are equal, as stated in the Bill of Rights, yet black men, women, and children are still enslaved? How can a nation founded on freedom, they wrote, condone slavery?

But Marcus believed that slaves are property, like horses, mules, and other work animals. He bought them to perform certain tasks, mostly to work in the fields, once the land had been cleared. Women slaves tilled the large garden, others made clothes or worked in the house.

Marcus acknowledged that pro-slavery members of Congress had for years skillfully used the threat of secession to gain legislation reinforcing slavery. He had supported such efforts. Lincoln, who also knew of the maneuverings, now dealt with that threat sternly.

"Do you really think," he said vigorously, "that you are justified to break up the government rather than have it administered by Washington and other good and great men who made it, and first administered it?" Again silence. Marcus felt uneasy, and looked at others around him, to determine their reaction.

"If you do," Lincoln continued, unrelenting, "you are very unreasonable; and men who are more reasonable cannot and will not submit to you."

The blunt statement dismayed Marcus. How, he thought to himself, can he operate his farm without slaves? He'd spent hard cash money for his slaves, as much as fifteen hundred dollars for a field hand. That's more than he'd pay for fifty acres of good land. Who would repay him, he wondered, for the money he'd invested in slaves, if forced to give them their freedom?

Yet, Lincoln the candidate was making it clear that, if elected president, he would not accept slavery. Neither would he tolerate the threat of secession by those who insisted on slavery. Marcus was alarmed. How could the man be so uncompromising?

Lincoln's long black coat hung loosely on his skeletal frame. He took a few steps forward, almost to the edge of the platform. "If we shall constitutionally elect a President," he averred forcefully, "it will be our duty to see that you submit." He paused, adding, "Old John Brown has just been executed for treason against the state."

Murmurs swept through the crowd. They knew about Osawatomie and Harper's Ferry.

"We cannot object to his execution," Lincoln quickly followed, "even though he agreed with us in thinking slavery wrong. That cannot excuse violence, bloodshed, and treason. It could avail him nothing that he might think himself right."

Marcus agreed. Vindictive and ruthless, John Brown had shot down those who owned slaves. He had been a murderer, acting outside the law.

The candidate was unflinching. "So if constitutionally we Republicans elect a President, and therefore you undertake to destroy the Union, it will be our duty to deal with you as Old John Brown has been dealt with."

But what have we done wrong, Marcus wondered. Slavery was legal. He was not threatening the Union by continuing to act legally and in accordance with the Constitution.

Lincoln turned back to the lectern, grasping the edges with both hands as though to steady it. "We shall try to do our duty. We hope and believe that in no section will a majority so act as to render such extreme measures necessary."

Was Lincoln referring to the threat of secession? Other slave owners talked guardedly about the possibility of seceding, if compromise could not be reached.

Border warfare troubles were also on the speaker's mind. "If I might advise my Republican friends here, I would say to them, 'Leave your Missouri neighbors alone. Have nothing whatever to do with the white people, with slave owners, save in a friendly way'."

The speech over, Marcus left the hall deeply troubled. On the long, solitary ride the following day back to his farm, he went over in his mind Lincoln's words, probing for subtleties that might reassure him, an inflection that might permit a more encouraging interpretation of what Lincoln had said.

Could slavery be wrong, even if permitted by law? Marcus felt that people made choices, among them whether to have slaves or not. He chose to have slaves, and he treated them well. If they became sick or died, he lost their productivity. Nothing in his religious beliefs or in his conscience said owning slaves was immoral.

If this man Lincoln received his new party's nomination, and if Lincoln won the election, unlikely as that appeared, Marcus thought, he might very possibly lose his slaves, and thus the means by which he made his many acres of land productive. The implications of such a great financial loss depressed Marcus, and he felt hugely discouraged. He began to feel that the migration with his family to Missouri was about to become a disaster.

Never before had he considered leaving their new home and going elsewhere, because what he had achieved in Missouri exceeded his expectations. But now he realized that he might lose much of what he had gained. If this happened, Marcus felt he could not begin again.

Chapter IV

Each morning, Marcus conferred with Jed about work to be done that day. Born in Kentucky of Virginia stock, Jed had been foreman on the Gill plantation back in Bath County. Lanky, face like a hound-dog, with long, pointed nose, deep-blue patient eyes, ears too large, and scraggly brown hair, Jed was forever taking off his floppy hat, scratching his head as he talked, then easing the hat back on, tugging at the brim so it fit just right. Below his blanched forehead, the face was scarred by weather.

"Been meaning to tell you, Colonel Gill, ol' Jim ain't been doing well lately."

Jim, a slave now well into his seventies, was the field hand who had dutifully kept an eye on Marcus when, as a boy, Marcus rode the mare alone in the pasture. In recent years, Jim helped out in the stable, grooming the horses, carrying water.

"Not well a'tall. He now mostly . . . ." Jed paused, thinking on what he had to say, as was his way. "Just takin' to his bed, seems like." He tugged again at the brim of his hat. "Effie says he ain't eat noth'n but thin soup and a little corn bread." He turned his head to spit tobacco juice, and switched the plug to the other side. "'Spect you all might want to know."

Marcus went to Jim's cabin, at the far end of two facing rows of log huts, east of the big hay barn. A stretch of scrabble ground, punctuated by spare clumps of rough, resilient weed, separated the cabin rows. In fair weather, children rolled iron hoops in the dust, made doll figures out of cornhusks, or sometimes sat silent on the stoops, watching. Now the yard was empty.

The plank door was slightly ajar. Marcus tapped softly. Effie, the old slave's wife, younger by maybe ten years, opened the door wider. Her face was smooth-skinned, with high cheekbones, her gray-black hair pulled back from a pensive face. Effie, her eyes worried, motioned her master in. She wore a thin gray shawl, pulled close around the neck, over a colorless cotton dress reaching to her bare feet.

The room, darkened by coarse cloth hung across the windows, smelled of wood smoke, greens simmering slowly in a pot, and a dank, woodsy odor like the forest after rain. Marcus had not been there before. A table, two chairs pushed under, an old leather trunk, and an iron bed against one wall was all there was. The timbered floor, laid by Jim himself, was scrub-clean, with a lingering smell of linseed oil.

Marcus approached the bed. Jim lay along one side, stretched out on his back, a rough blanket pulled to the collar of his long-johns. Hands clasped loosely on his thin chest, crimped gray hair unexpectedly gone almost white. Marcus was startled by the sight of the shrunken body, collarbones protruding harshly, neck long and thin, charcoal skin slack.

He remembered the strong, laughing man he'd known as a child, patiently showing him how to hold the bowed wood handle of the great scythe. Jim had stood behind him, the slave's huge body enveloping his own, the black, muscular arms, the large hands alongside his as he struggled to hold the curving blade. Take it firmly in both hands, about this far apart, Jim had showed him, and swing the blade easily, back and forth, smooth-like, with one motion of the body, right to left, right to left, and back again. Their bodies had moved together, the child's body guided by the gentle force around him.

Marcus placed his hand lightly on Jim's shoulder. The eyes opened, focused on Marcus, questioned whom it might be, then knew. A gnarled hand left the security of the hands clasped together, and reached out. Marcus took the outstretched hand in both of his and held it, the hand feverish, the skin dry and rough. All strength was gone from the grasp. A strong emotion suddenly swept through him like a gust of wind across a field of wheat, bending the pliant stalks of grain with its sudden force.

Effie sobbed, raised both hands to her face. She pulled out one of the chairs and sank down, feet tucked distractedly beneath her.

Marcus leaned down and whispered a few words into the old man's ear, but the slave gave no sign of having heard. After a moment, the recognition in his eyes faded, then his hand slowly pulled away to rejoin the other resting on his chest.

Eyes moist, Marcus again placed his hand lightly on the old man's shoulder, then turned to go. He looked about the cabin, stark and gray.

Effie stood up, but kept her eyes directed toward the floor. Her arms hung by her side, the hands loose.

Marcus remained unmoving, a brooding, puzzled look on his face. He then gazed at Effie, as if she had unexpectedly entered the room. In a low voice he asked if there was anything she needed.

Effie raised her head, and looked at him. Marcus saw an instant flare of anger. Effie's stare confronted him, unyielding. Then the fire vanished, as if suddenly drenched by water. She shook her head, and looked away.

Marcus left the cabin.

The following evening, after supper, when Marcus sat alone at his desk writing a letter to his son Turner, Mary Jane came to the door of the room. Jed needed to speak to him, she said. Marcus stepped outside, where Jed stood solemnly waiting, holding his shapeless hat in both hands.

Jim was dead. Died about suppertime.

Marcus thanked Jed for coming to tell him. "I want to bury him in the family graveyard here on the farm," Marcus said. "In the morning, I'll show you just where." Jed's eyes questioned, but he said nothing. "I've been thinking about it," Marcus added.

The grave was dug next morning in a plot of ground chosen hurriedly two years ago, when the infant son of Marcus and Mary Jane had not survived a three-day fever. The burial place lay on a rise of ground in a pasture some distance back from the house. The site chosen for the old slave was in a back corner of the cemetery, now enclosed with a waist-high black-iron fence. Marcus and Mary Jane agreed that Effie would someday be laid next to her husband. Back in Kentucky, Negro nursemaids and long-time house servants were sometimes buried in an abbreviated row of graves along the rear of the family cemetery.

A simple burial service was held late in the afternoon. The wind, now abruptly out of the northwest, smelled richly of rain. Oak leaves russet red and dull gold lay packed underfoot, touched with frost. Enormous, cushiony white clouds moved across the sky. Sunlight flooded the ground; then, fleet-footed, hastily fled, leaving the landscape bereft and without shadows.

On the other side of the open grave from Marcus and Mary Jane, the assembled slaves stood motionless, two and three deep around the mound of freshly-dug earth. Women dressed in ragged coats, scant cotton dresses, and shawls about their heads, stood quietly next to their men who wore cast-off bulky dark coats and hats that covered their heads when working in the fields. Effie, weeping, waited near the torn edge of the grave, her thin body supported by two of the younger field hands.

Jed and a work overseer stood apart from the gathering. Sharp-bladed shovels, crusted with mud, lay on the ground behind them, unhidden.

Marcus read a few verses from the New Testament. He had never presided at graveside before, at the death of a slave; he had never thought to do so. Now, he felt some discomfort in the role, yet was oddly compelled to carry out the task.

Concluding with the Lord's Prayer, Marcus spoke the words, his voice barely audible. Mary Jane joined him. The others remained silent.

Marcus bent down, took a handful of the dark soil in his hand, and let it flow from his fingers down into the open grave, on top of the coffin, naked yellow wood discordant against the black earth.

Suddenly, Marcus sensed that he was no longer needed, that he should not be there. He looked across at Effie, whose bare hands were clutched at her breast. Her tear-flooded eyes gazed through and past him, as if fixated on an object beyond, beyond his vision. Marcus studied the expressionless, downturned faces of these creatures whose lives he owned. It was as if they were strangers, newly met. The open grave that lay between them was an abyss that grew far beyond its narrow boundaries, a vastness far beyond anything he had felt or known before.

Quietly, Marcus took Mary Jane's arm, and led her away, down the hill, back toward the house.

They had gone almost halfway when, very faint at first, Marcus heard voices, low and rhythmic, the words muffled. The slaves had begun singing, a chant more than a song, uncertain and tentative. The sound was restrained, mournful.

Marcus and Mary Jane stopped, and looked back. It was as if the gathering of individual slaves had fused into one large, black shadow against the darkening earth, a strange and new presence. Separate faces became lost, cloaked by the mask of rapidly fading light. At that distance, no lips appeared to move, yet sound emanated from the dark mass, a sad, rich flow of music passed down from generations long ago, from a foreign land.

Engrossed, Marcus and Mary Jane listened. The strangeness of what they witnessed unexpectedly disturbed Marcus. It was like an unidentified sound that awakens one suddenly at night from profound sleep, frightening because the source is not known, can only be imagined.

There arose in his mind the somber figure of Lincoln stepping forward on the narrow platform in Leavenworth, defying those who would keep slavery, summoning those who do to confront the moral issue. But how? Marcus asked. How could I free them? He did not have an answer.

After little more than a long moment, the voices in the distance subsided, then ceased. Without speaking, the slaves turned away from the grave, and walked to their cabins in stillness.

Chapter V

Winter nights descended quickly in January, pitching countryside into isolating blackness. Gathered at the supper table, lighted by a coal-oil lamp, Marcus and his wife sat at either end. Will Quantrill sat on one side, Leah and her two younger sisters across from him. Millie had already fed the younger children and put them to bed.

Will talked easily about growing up in Ohio, eldest son of a teacher who later became a school principal. Marcus respected Will's obvious intelligence, and was pleased by his occasional lyrical descriptions. As a Southerner, Marcus enjoyed telling and listening to stories. They brightened the bleak winter evenings like a fire warming the room.

"My father died five years ago, when I was seventeen," Will said. "I decided to get out on my own. So I went to Indiana, learned some Latin and surveying. Then I crossed over to Illinois. Taught school there awhile. Felt good about that."

Leah watched Will as he talked. His soft, persuasive voice drew her into his narration. Will's upper eyelids drooped in such a way that he looked vaguely foreign, even slightly mysterious. His voice was without the Southern inflections of her own family and many of their neighbors, and that made him seem even more different to her. He often looked directly at her while he spoke, holding her eyes as if he were talking only to her, rather than relating incidents of his life to all those around the table. Marcus noted Leah's fascination with their guest, and Will's obvious playing to the young woman. He and Mary Jane exchanged glances tinged with concern.

"Colonel Gill," Will said after a time, courteously turning the conversation away from himself, "I suppose life here in Missouri is considerably different from what it was back in Kentucky. Missouri is as far South as I've ever been, so I can't really imagine what it must have been like where you came from. Did people leave you alone, let you be what you wanted to be?"

Marcus, his fork pausing in mid-air, looked thoughtfully at Will. "Yes, I believe that's true," he said. "I never thought of it quite that way, but I think it's true." He resumed eating. "We'd been there a long time, you understand. My family goes back to the Revolution, maybe farther. My father's grandfather fought in the war, that I know. He was a captain of cavalry. My father still has a big farm, back in Kentucky. You ask if we had more freedom. Well, I—."

"I meant, was it easier for you to do whatever you wanted to do? Without other folks interfering. Not letting you accomplish what you set out to do. I mean, no one thought anything about your owning slaves, I'd guess. And of course, there weren't no Kansans riling things up like they're doing around here now."

"Yes, I expect we did have more freedom, if you put it that way," Marcus said again. "I think the difference is that the way my family lived, we'd been living that way for quite a few generations. Families like ours from Kentucky, from Virginia, often go back a hundred years in the South, sometimes longer. But in Jackson County, and I'd guess other counties in the western part of the state, settlers haven't been here anywhere near that long. And besides—."

Leah broke in. "Of course not, Papa. After all, Missouri became a state less than forty years ago."

"That's right," Marcus said. "Virginia, for example, was first a colony, then a state. It's been a state seventy years, now. Kentucky almost as long. That's maybe two generations before Missouri obtained statehood. So our way of life in the South was established a long time ago. We've had slavery more than two hundred years. It's part of our life, always was. There's some here in Missouri, and certainly west of us, don't understand that."

Leah again spoke up. "You said you felt more free in Kentucky, Papa. I don't understand that. Except for those horrible raiders, I've never thought I was any less free than I was back home. And I was eleven when we came west." She thought a moment. "That's pretty old."

Marcus smiled. "Sometimes it's the differences you feel, more than the differences you can see," he said. "Back home, we generally kept to ourselves. I'd help my neighbors out, if they needed it, and they'd do the same. But not being dependent on others was a part of being free. If you become obligated to someone, then that person can begin to gain control over you, expect things. Someday there'll come a time when they tell you what to do, contrary to what you want.

That's already what's happening with our federal government."

"I'd feel the same way," Will said. "I couldn't sit still for someone else deciding what I should do."

Marcus nodded. "As I said, owning slaves was accepted. Nobody thought much about it. But it's not the same here, even though I'm told that there are large numbers of slaves in Missouri. Many of them are in counties east of here, south of the Missouri River. But some folks can't seem to accept slavery."

Marcus, having finished eating, moved his chair back a little from the table. "Most of the families in Missouri who didn't come from the South, came from the East, from New England. They didn't know much about slavery, because slavery was not common there. I've come to believe they resent anyone who owns slaves." Marcus shook his head as he spoke. "Others have religious attitudes against slavery, even though scripture doesn't say anything against slavery. Fact is, there were many slaves in times of the Bible. I wouldn't mind folks objecting, if they'd just keep it to themselves. But they don't. It's as if they just can't keep speaking out, letting you know they're against it. And they make you feel like you were doing something bad, owning slaves, something morally wrong."

Mary Jane, until now only listening, said, "Colonel Gill was respected back in Kentucky. He'll think I shouldn't say so, because it doesn't sound modest, but he was. Besides, we've always treated our slaves right. And he was known for being a leader in the state militia. Farmers we knew often asked advice from him. The mill he owned was a fine one. Folks depended on it for jobs, and others built their houses and barns with the lumber the mill turned out."

"Well, times are changing," Marcus said. "I know that. I just wish I had some say as to what's happening."

Supper over, the two men went into the parlor. Marcus offered Will a cigar, lit it, then put the flame to his own. "Just last week, I stopped in the bank at Westport to ask about a loan to buy yearlings. I was told to talk to a bank officer I'd never seen before. Said his name was Schilling, that he'd just come over from St. Louis. He said the bank was investing money for eastern investors. I'd think there's enough money in the banks right here, without bringing in that eastern money. Besides, what do they know about farming out west, out in Missouri?"

Marcus drew on his cigar, the smoke hovering around him. "St. Louis is also full of Germans, I hear. I don't know what draws them from back east. Republicans are registering Germans to vote as fast as they can sign them up, to do away with slavery." His tone showed disgust. "What right have they to do that?"

Marcus got up from his chair and stood next to the fire, flicking a long ash from his cigar into the coals. "That banker from St. Louis knew I farmed with slaves, and I could tell he was uneasy talking with me. He'd look at some papers on his desk, or off behind me, as if he was expecting another customer to appear any moment. Fact of the matter is, when he asked me where my farm was located, he didn't know where New Santa

Fe is, and he had no idea how long I've been in Jackson County. Thought I'd just come west."

"What did you do?" Will asked. "When he treated you that way."

"What could I do? It might have been a strain, if I hadn't taken out the loan, although maybe I'd have gotten by without it. But I've always gotten a loan before, to buy yearlings, so I thought I might just as well do it this year, too. Bankers like things to be as they've been before. And I think they like my business, although they don't often let you know that."

"I'd have walked out of the bank if they'd treated me that way," Will said. "And I'd have looked for a chance to get even." His face flushed. "Could you have gone to another bank? Gone someplace else?"

"Yes, I suppose I could have. There are other banks farther north, in the City of Kansas, near the river. Maybe next time I will."

Marcus sat down again, stretching out his legs, and gazed into the fire. "I think what the bankers and the black Republicans are after is to force land owners like me to break up our farms. They want to put us in a position where we have to sell off parcels to small farmers who would own sixty, maybe eighty acres. That way, they can do most of the work themselves, without slaves, and without hiring labor." He looked thoughtful as he drew on his cigar. "But I know that a man can't make much money farming that way. All he can do is struggle to make enough to provide the necessities for his family."

"What would you do, Colonel Gill," Will asked, "if that came to pass? If you had to break up your property?"

Gill took a moment to reply. "Well, if they take my slaves away from me, that's what I'd be forced to do. I don't see any other way. I'd lose all that money I've already invested in slaves, and I'd have no way of working the farm. Hiring field hands is a lot more costly than owning slaves."

Abruptly, Marcus stood up. "But I don't want to break up my farm. The law says I can own slaves. The law says they're my property. The law says I can get them back, if they try to run away. Besides, it took me a lot of years, a big investment, to build up this place. I'm not going to let anyone walk in and take it away."

Sparks leaped upward as Marcus tossed another log on top of the radiant embers. "I'd hate to give in, because I think those Northerners just want for themselves what I've already got." Then, as if to himself, he added, "What hurts the most is they don't have any respect for us. They just don't think we're as good as them." He tossed the cigar butt into the flames. "And I don't like that. I just can't accept that."

Chapter VI

At the schoolhouse near Stanton, Will sat at his desk, writing his mother back in Ohio. The silence was punctuated only by the popping of the iron stove as the surface began to cool from the dying fire.

"When you write let me know all that you have time to write about, for I feel anxious to know something about home and the village of my boyhood more than I have heretofore and I cannot really say why it is so, but I think of it more, and have lately visited it in my dreams, which was quite rare before, it may be because my mind has become more settled, and my mind must be employed in some way, and I suppose that is the most natural. I wish to know all that has happened of note lately, and I would like to be there and think I will be (if I live) in the course of the summer . . . . "

As Will wrote, nostalgia for his boyhood engulfed him. At the same time, impatience and anger welled up, forcing aside the poignant memories of his youth. Restlessness gnawed at his fragile sense of well being. He felt as if events were careening past him, causing his present life to collapse under the guise of its hapless, commonplace events.

On the journey to Utah and Colorado with the Russell-Majors freight wagons, he had confronted the hardships of winter, meager supplies of wild game, and sometimes churlish companions, but had remained in command of himself.

Will now ached for recognition beyond that of a schoolteacher. He saw himself as a leader of men. He prided himself on his skill with firearms, his adroitness on horseback. He knew that, unlike some men, he was able to remain levelheaded when in danger, and to think clearly and boldly.

But now, seated at the schoolhouse desk, Will felt trapped, shunted from his true calling, however unknown. He realized that he had to find a way to break out, to become engaged in a larger destiny. He felt as if events taking place about him were like a rushing, plunging stream, but he was only a bystander, fixed helplessly on the bank of the stream while the current moved swiftly and surely to a place he wished to be. Unless he could wade into that stream, and be carried by it to whatever lay before him, he would never find his place in history. The more he considered his present circumstance, the more determined he became to leap from the river's bank into the torrent of water.

One Sunday, after the noon meal, Leah and Will rode out along the wide swath marking the barrier between Missouri and the Kansas Territory, the trail used by wagons hauled by oxen teams in the Santa Fe trade. Although her mother was watchful of Leah's relationship with Will, they often rode together, talking and laughing, even sometimes disagreeing on political issues. Leah was drawn to Will's untroubled self-confidence, his enthusiasm, but she did not grasp the extent to which he grappled with frustrated ambition. She correctly perceived the deep, unaccountable undercurrents in his nature, often concealed by his eager manner, his appetite for new exploits, yet she found these forces strangely exciting, inexplicably appealing.

His restlessness and dissatisfaction with life disturbed her, however, because she saw that they threatened their relationship. She feared that he would soon leave her family, leave her. She also sensed from the little Will confided to her that he yearned mightily to be admired, that he sought above all else a role that would bring him prominence. With a woman's mysterious premonition, Leah envisioned Will thrust up above the crowd, lifted high on the shoulders of other men. Perhaps that accounted in part for the strong attraction he had for her.

Will was older than Leah by six years. He thought her very beautiful, possessing spirited courage, an audacious mind of her own. The fact that he ascribed these same characteristics to himself had not occurred to him. When she talked with fervor about the issues of slavery and states rights, he listened, but did not consider that as a woman, she could ever act upon such beliefs. To him, action in conflict was the only course.

Through a gate they entered a pasture far removed from the house. Wild coneflowers, pale purple with yellow centers, were splashed across the dark green fields like flower petals on a full-flowing skirt. Stretching to the western horizon, the sweeping grasslands of the Kansas Territory seemed endless. From the direction of Independence, a wagon train, barely visible at that distance, westward-bound for Santa Fe, moved imperceptibly toward them, brown dust suspended motionless in the air above. Teams of oxen, dark heads lowered, great shoulders working in the harnesses, melded with the ground. Teamsters seated atop the wagons looked like stick figures, wielding their long whips languorously, as if imagined in a dream.

Will spurred his mare, colored a deep chestnut, across the open pasture. Leah followed, urging the thoroughbred into a graceful canter along the shadowed edge of the timber. A gift from her father for her sixteenth birthday, the horse had white socks on its forelegs, and flaxen mane and tail that drifted fluidly in the wind.

Then Leah took the lead, and together they raced, the warm, scented breeze rushing past them. Exhilarated, Will whooped and hollered, holding onto his hat with one hand.

Leah leaned into the wind, and bent close to the mare's mane, urging her horse forward. Not breaking the canter, she began to edge ahead of Will. The hooves of the horses drummed a muffled pattern on the taut skin of the earth. Will held his horse in check, letting Leah pull away, and watched her dark hair streaming out behind. Her lithe figure, moving in rhythm, fused gracefully with that of the mount beneath her.

At the far reach of the pasture, the timber turned to the south, following the creek. As they approached the timber, Leah reined in, brought her horse to a halt, and slid out of the saddle, her face flushed with excitement. Laughing softly, Will rode up behind, kicked his boots free from the stirrups, threw one leg over the saddle, and eased himself off the horse. Taking both sets of reins, he led the horses to a tree and looped the reins around a greening branch. Together, arms around each other's waists, they strolled deeper into the woods.

Leah chatted amiably, and Will was silent. He relished the slight swaying of her body, the swishing of her long skirt, as they walked leisurely through the winter-thin timber to the creek's bank. Blackbirds, scolding noisily, fluttered anxiously from one branch to another at the top of the trees. Along the creek, redbuds threw out splashes of lavender against gray branches.

They stopped near the trunk of a great oak. Leah turned toward Will. He brought her close against him, and kissed her, then kissed her again. Leah's arms reached up about his neck, one hand lightly caressing the back of his neck, the other hand drawing him even closer. She kissed him earnestly, while with one hand he explored the familiar curve of her hip, the delicate indentation where her back melded into the fullness below. Without speaking, they sank down onto the cool, thick grass, hidden by the trees and concealing undergrowth.

Sunlight reaching through branches overhead, like trellises in a garden, patterned the ground with splashes of fresh color. A warm current of air finding its way along the sun-drenched, sky-reaching space above the creek channel stirred blades of grass and rustled dry leaves on the ground, yet otherwise passed unnoticed.

Leah sat on a large log, combing her hair with her fingers, then smoothed the wool skirt about her legs, removing bits of leaves and grass. Will sat down next to her, watching the capable movement of her hands, the graceful way she preened herself. Smiling, she grasped his hand and brought it to her lips, kissing it.

Then, her face becoming serious, Leah asked the question that had been on her mind the last few days. "Will, what are you going to do when you finish teaching school? You've only got two more weeks."

Will gazed off into the timber before replying. "I've been thinking about that. You know I want to get into where things are happening," he said. "I just can't stay out of it. I just can't sit by the side of the road, watching. So I've been thinking about joining up with a gang of bushwhackers holed up west of Independence. They've already had some skirmishes with raiders, and gone over into the Territory once or twice themselves, to get back at those devils. I hear they've done well for themselves."

Leah nodded. Her father had said he felt good about the skill and bold attacks of the bushwhackers. He thought they were forcing the Kansas guerrillas to think twice about crossing over to harass and steal from farmers in the County. "But they're just boys, aren't they, Will? Just farm boys? What do they know about fighting?"

"They do real good, all things considered. Farm boys know how to shoot, how to live off the land, and they like a little excitement. Besides, they're tough. All they need is a good leader, someone who's got experience. And a place in the bush to hide out, away from roads, and something to eat when they get hungry."

Will looked around, as if appraising whether this stand of timber might be such a place. "That's what's good about summer. Plenty of cover and wild game. Besides that, lots of folks appreciate what they do, and give them food and supplies, even ammunition and guns. If war comes, there's several good gangs I'd join up with. Heck, I don't think I need to wait 'til there's a war. I could do it right now."

Leah frowned. "But why not, Will? Why not wait? Papa needs you, and there's plenty else you can do."

"But that's just it, Leah, I don't want to be doing anything else. I'm real good with guns, and I don't get scared when there's fighting, and I think I could soon have my own gang, with me as the leader. That's what I'd really like to do. I want to lead a gang."

"You could fight for the South, Will, if there's war. That's what Turner's said he would do. And my brother Enoch, teaching school down in Texas. He wrote home that he's ready to enlist in the army of the South, if fighting begins."

Picking up a stick from the ground, Will took out a sheath knife, and began skinning off the bark.

"I don't think as how I'd like being in the regular army, Leah, taking orders from someone else. If they'd make me a captain, in the cavalry, then maybe I would, but even then, I'd be taking orders from someone higher up, and that's not what I want. Anyway, can you imagine me saluting some officer who's maybe just learned to ride a horse and shoot a gun, and I'm suppose to do whatever he says?"

Leah smiled, and gave Will a playful shove, before becoming serious again. "Papa thinks the whole country will be at war, if Lincoln gets elected by people who don't like slavery. He thinks it's up to Lincoln to find a way for us Southerners to keep our slaves, at least the slaves we already own. He just doesn't see how any president could take away the property we already own, and not compensate us for it."

Will laid the knife and stick on the log, and eased the pistol holster at his waist a little to one side, to relieve the pressure against his hip. "You'd think slave owners weren't rightful citizens, Leah, entitled to their property, to protection, like everyone else." He sharpened the end of the stick into a two-sided point. "If it comes to war, the Colonel figures bushwhackers can keep Union troops off balance by taking them by surprise, killing and wounding enough of them to do some damage, then getting away as fast as they can ride, and hiding out for a time. I think he's right."

Leah gently touched Will's arm. "Well, you've got to do what you think you should. There's no doubt you're a good rider, Will, and I've seen you shoot, you're the best there is." She looked around, taking in the burgeoning beauty of the timber. Unseen, a woodpecker hammered away at a dead tree, a solitary staccato. "Well, guess we'd best be getting back," she said regretfully. "Papa will be wondering why we're not back."

Will put his arm around Leah's shoulders. Walked slowly back to where the tethered horses stood waiting, they pressed close, shoulders and thighs firmly against each other. Leah reached out to stroke the white blaze on her mare's face. The horse nuzzled Leah's shoulder, searching for a carrot tucked in a pocket of her dress.

"I feel I've got something important to do, Leah, and I need to get on with it. Situation's getting more and more serious all the time." Will untied the mare's bridle from the tree branch. "Neighbors who don't own slaves, they think their neighbors who do are just no good. Those who own slaves, they're never sure which neighbor might be giving information to the raiders, helping them out when they come stealing livestock and burning barns. A person can't never know for sure which side another person else might be on. Folks hide what they think, so you can't tell." His voice rose slightly. "But you got to stand up to them, when they turn against you. You just got to do that. A man's got no other choice. Leastwise, not one he can live with."

Leah looked at Will, saw the hard look in his eyes, the tautness at the corners of his mouth. "I love you, Will. I worry about you, and I don't want you to get killed."

Riding back to the house, they did not again talk about the possibility of war, or about when Will might leave.

Chapter VII

One morning, Marcus and Jed went looking for a stray calf. Will had left the day before to ride over to Independence to tend to business of his own, planning to be back the next day. Marcus rode his dapple-gray gelding, a fine thoroughbred with great endurance and a strong gait.

"Jed, let's search the timber this side of the creek. You start up toward the north, I'll go down to the far end. We'll work back to the middle." Jed nodded his head. "Fire your pistol if you find the calf. I'll do the same." Marcus gestured toward the .58 caliber single-shot rifle slung across his back.

In good spirits, Marcus cantered off, feeling the energy of a new planting season flow through his body. Insects droned in the air and tall grass. The sky was spring-water clear, the humid breeze filled with the rich scent of white-flowered clover. Solid split-rail fences, cut from timber on his farm, sundered with an ax and skillfully interlocked, enclosed the pastures where cows with spirited calves browsed the green fields.

Marcus looked across those fields. Summer haze, lying gossamer-like in the folds of the valley, softened the shape of his house, his barns, the clusters of other farm buildings that stood solidly on the flank of the hill.

Faint voices far off, like the buzz of bees drifting in the hot sun from one flower to the next, touched him with their familiar sound. Marcus felt deeply satisfied with what he saw: his land, transformed into richly productive soil, the product of his vision, his ability, and the leavening of his capital.

He reined in the gelding, and left the pasture, entering the cool shade of the timber. Methodically, Marcus worked through the wooded area lying west of the creek, searching for the calf. He stopped frequently, listening for sounds of the young animal thrashing through the underbrush. He heard only the wind stirring the trees, the raucous cries of crows, and the gelding's snorting as he lifted his legs free of the brush.

Marcus decided to ride to the creek so his horse could drink. They passed through a natural clearing, free of brush, and abruptly came to the bank. Creek water, muddy from the spring rains, as deep as the underside of a horse's belly, moved sluggishly.

Five horsemen sat motionless on the other side, no more than sixty feet away, watching him. The men were young, all bearded. They were not in uniform, but were similarly dressed. They wore hats pulled low on their heads, shading their faces, and were heavily armed. Marcus recognized the .44 caliber Colt carbines two of the men held, stock butts resting on their thighs as they watched him; these men were not farmers, nor were they soldiers. The other horsemen carried rifles on slings across their chests, and pistols shoved into wide leather belts at the waist.

No one spoke. Marcus knew they didn't belong on his land. If he turned and ran, they'd shoot him in the back.

"You own this land?" called out the leader, erect in the saddle, scorn in his voice.

"I do."

"What might your name be?"

"Marcus Gill."

Two of the riders looked at their leader, then back at Marcus. Their right hands rested on the handles of pistols in holsters at their side.

Marcus took the initiative. "What brings you here?"

"We've got business in the area."

Marcus paused, his voice offhand. "Where'd you boys come from?"

"West of here." That would be Kansas Territory.

One of the men leaned closer to the leader, said something. The leader nodded, and called across to Marcus: "I want you to ease that rifle off your back and toss it onto the ground."

Marcus looked back, without moving. He listened for sounds of Jed, but heard none. "This is my property. I don't intend to do that. You boys are trespassing. Why don't you just head on back home."

The second man again spoke under his breath to the leader, and yanked his gun from the holster.

Impatient, the leader called out again: "You best do what I say, rebel. We're planning on taking your horse and whatever money you got back at the house, and . . . ."

A rifle shot exploded out of the timber off to one side of the men. The leader's body snapped forward, shot through the chest. His arms hung useless on either side of the horse's neck. The horse shied to one side and the body tumbled to the ground.

The remaining horsemen turned quickly, shouting in confusion, firing their pistols in the direction of the sound, but a second shot struck another man in the back, knocking him out of the saddle. One boot caught in the stirrup, and the man's limp body fell to one side of his mount, dragging on the ground, but was torn loose by the heavy underbrush as the frightened horse bolted through the timber.

Will Quantrill stepped from behind a tree, firing rapidly, a pistol in each hand. Marcus had his rifle at his shoulder in an instant, the .58 caliber sounding like a canon among the trees. The crashing ball of lead swept a third man off his horse as he attempted to flee. The two remaining gunmen, firing frantically, wheeled their horses, but bullets from Will's guns struck the fourth man who slid sideways from his saddle and plunged to the ground. By then the one remaining guerrilla had vanished into the timber.

Gunpowder smoke, cobalt blue and acrid, drifted in the still air, carved into rectangular shafts by sunlight filtering through the trees.

Marcus rapidly reloaded, then rode the gelding through the creek and up the bank. He dismounted, holding his rifle muzzle-up in one hand.

Thrusting the Colt revolvers back into their holsters, Will picked up the rifled musket he had dropped to the ground after killing the gang's leader, reloaded it with a single linen cartridge and primer, and leaned the gun against a nearby tree. He walked up to each of the riderless horses, soothingly quieted the animal with soft-spoken words, stroking its neck, then tied the reins to a tree.

The body of the guerrilla band's leader lay face-up on the ground, eyes astonished, arms outstretched above the head. Will looked at the face. "Jayhawker," he said, and turned the body over with his boot. The other bodies he left alone, uninterested in who they might be.

"I seen them going into th' other side of the timber when I was coming back from Independence," Will said. "Figured they might be up to no good, that they weren't one of us."

Marcus nodded, and said matter-of-factly, "Glad you came along. Thanks, Will."

Will shrugged. "That's what I'm here for, ain't it?" and grinned.

Marcus later sent some field hands to bury the dead raiders in the timber, instructing that brush and dead leaves be placed over the freshly-dug earth to hide them.

Chapter VIII

School over, Will was anxious to move on. He said good-by to the Colonel and his family, and rode off into Kansas Territory, headed for Lawrence, fifty miles to the west. Marcus wondered why Will would go there. Like many Missouri slave owners, Marcus detested Lawrence. It's leadership dominated by abolitionist New Englanders, Lawrence was the spawning-ground of much of the guerrilla activity harassing Missouri farmers. But Will said he had unfinished business in Lawrence, that he had scores to settle.

Later in the summer, Henry Chiles told Marcus that Will had been arrested by the sheriff in Douglas County, where Lawrence was the county seat, for burglary, larceny, and arson. While charges were pending, however, he slipped away and disappeared. Marcus was skeptical of the arrest, knowing that Lawrence was rife with opposing factions. When he told Leah, she scoffed at the charges, but looked worried.

By autumn, under Jed's watchful eye, the slaves had harvested the summer's crops. Once again they filled the cribs with corncobs shucked of husks, the kernels dull yellow and brittle-hard. They scythed the wheat, loading the sheaths into mule-drawn wagons, then lifted fork-fulls of the hay up into the barn lofts for winter feed for the livestock. Other slaves butchered cows, hogs, and sheep, smoking the meat or salting it down to cure, and hung hams, all for the approaching winter.

Mary Jane was pregnant with her seventh child; she would be thirty-eight when she gave birth. The loss of their son born the first year after they arrived in Missouri still grieved Mary Jane, yet she did not confide to Marcus that having another baby worried her, that she didn't know whether she could mother another child.

Her body heavy, Mary Jane oversaw the women slaves who boiled fresh vegetables from the acre-wide garden for canning, or made fruit preserves and jellies, and shelled garden corn, preserving it in salt brine. They scoured the underground fruit cellar and replenished the earthy-smelling woodbins with sweet potatoes, carrots, apples, plums, and other fruit. Laid down in beds of straw, the food would last in the cool darkness.

Events of each day on the farm proceeded with accustomed rhythm, yet violence remained a dark stain on the countryside. Marcus learned that attacks by abolitionists were more frequent, bolder, and more virulent, despite increasing counteraction by Missouri bushwhackers. To his dismay, he found that anti-slavery attitudes smoldered beneath everyday relationships with townspeople, such as at the marketplace on visits into Westport. With slight provocation, resentments burst into angry recriminations, often when most unexpected.

Unlike states farther south, Missouri had persistent ties to the Union, especially in St. Louis, on the eastern edge of the state. Commerce and industry in that city on the Mississippi River fixed its eyes on New England's advanced prosperity, on New England's proficiency and mounds of capital. Marcus knew this, and he chafed under the knowledge, because he felt powerless to counter these eastern influences.

There was no word from Will. Leah thought of him often, longed for the unrevealed relationship they had shared, but she received no letters, nor was any message passed along from him. Meanwhile, Jesse Noland, son of a prominent family near Independence, was courting her. Marcus and Mary Jane knew the Nolands, Southerners like themselves, and favored the match, if that were the outcome. They had hoped she would not fall in love with Will; he was too unsettled, too unpredictable.

In late November, Mary Jane gave birth to a daughter. They named her Louella, a family name on the Gill side. The baby was healthy, and Marcus was grateful. Yet the assaults on slavery, the lurking danger of another raid, the uncertainty of who was a friend and who was not, suffused his mind to the extent that, by the end of some days, he wondered whether he had the strength to maintain a sense of order in his life.

Less than two weeks later, Will set out from Lawrence with five other men. He had cunningly selected those who rode with him, although they didn't know it, and he didn't tell them why. They had met him only recently, and knew him as Charley Hart, an alias he had adopted in the Kansas Territory. They understood he had a reputation as a fierce gunfighter, but found him likable, opposed to slavery, and very confident. Two of the men were Quakers, zealous abolitionists who saw freeing slaves as a religious mission. The others had no firm views on slavery, but sought excitement and the loot they could garner on a raid into Missouri. So, they had accepted Will's proposition that they make a raid into Jackson County to free some slaves and bring back horses to sell in the Lawrence auction.

Will had told them he knew of a wealthy farmer near Blue Springs, a rural hamlet east of Westport. The farmer's name was Morgan Walker, and he owned almost two thousand acres of land, more than twenty slaves, and about a hundred head of horses and mules. Walker would make a fine target for a raid, Will said, especially because the farm was located in a remote section of the county.

The men left the outskirts of Lawrence in late afternoon under a heavy, foreboding sky, and rode eastward, toward the Missouri line. Fording the Wakarusa River a few hours later, their horses broke through thin ice, splashing in the shallows until they clambered up the river's bank on the far side. Kill Creek, the next ford, was almost dry. For the two Quaker farmers, this was their first excursion across the Territorial line; they seemed innocent of the possibility of violence. The other men, older, had been on previous raids into Missouri, targeting farmers who owned slaves. They were eager, self-assured, and boisterous about the success of prior raids.

The men camped at dusk in woods remote from any farmhouse. Trees and brush hid the yellow light of the campfire from the road. The next morning, they started early, resting the horses in late afternoon not far from Blue Springs. Then they followed a lightly traveled road toward the Walker farm.

Crystals of white frost capped wagon ruts and hoof marks frozen in the black soil. The winter sun, blood red, clung to the western sky, but would soon be gone. Scarlet tinged the gray fields and stark trees.

A mile short of their destination, the band of men turned off the road and rode into a grove of trees, where they dismounted. By agreement, Will continued on alone. He told them he'd alert the slaves to their coming, so they could prepare to flee.

Will reined his horse to a walk when he reached the gate to Walker's farm. Barns loomed black against the scarlet sky. Horses stabled nearby moved restlessly in their stalls, and whinnied with the approach of the horseman. Light from oil lamps in the slave cabins flickered from the windows.

As Will approached the house, the door in the main house opened, briefly splashing light onto the covered porch. A man stepped outside and closed the door behind him, standing close to the wall of the house, partly concealed in the shadows. He held a musket, loaded with buckshot, in the crook of his arm, instantly available but not intimidating to a friend.

"Mr. Walker, sir, is that you?" Will called out, just loud enough for the man on the porch to hear him. "My name's William Quantrill. I'm the one who stayed with Marcus Gill last winter. Over near New Santa Fe." Will remained on his horse. "He told me that you and he knew each other."

Silence. Then Morgan Walker said, "I remember the name." He stepped closer to the railing along the front of the porch, but remained indistinct in the dark. "What's Gill's oldest daughter's name?"

"That would be Leah, Mr. Walker."

"Right. Leah. She and my daughter met in Independence last year."

"Leah and I was friends, when I stayed with the family. She's a mighty fine woman."

"What's your business, Mr. Quantrill?"

Dismounting from his horse, Will grasped the bridle's bit in his hand, up close to the horse's muzzle, and walked slowly toward the man standing in the deep shadow at the top of the steps. They conversed for a few minutes in low tones. Satisfied, Will mounted his horse and headed back down the road from which he'd come.

Riding up to the five raiders waiting for him under the trees, he said, "They'll be ready for us. And those slaves sure were glad to hear we're coming to free them. Makes me feel right good about what we're doing."

One of the men asked if anyone saw him. "Don't think so. Lights were on in the house, but there wasn't a sign of anybody outside. Everything looked quiet. I think they must be at supper."

Will pulled the rifle out of the leather ring on his saddle, checked the load, then slipped the weapon back into its ring. "You, Lipsey, and Charlie Ball, when we get there, go with me up to the house. Ed Morrison, I want you to wait outside, in the front yard. Keep an eye on the road." The men nodded. "Albert Southwick, you go to the barn and pick out the horses we'll want to take with us. Johnny Dean, you decide which Negroes we want, and get a wagon ready to haul 'em." Johnny nodded. "If we have to kill the rebels, we can stay the night in their house, start early tomorrow. I'd rather do that, anyway, than head out tonight."

Will turned his horse out onto the road. The men followed, riding bunched together in an easy canter. White breath-clouds whipped away from the horses' nostrils in the sharp air. Will carried two pistols at his waist, Colt Model 1851 revolvers, .36 caliber. A third rested in the leather saddlebag. If there were a lot of shooting, there'd be no time to reload.

Light shone from the windows as they reined the horses to a walk and cautiously approached the house. Will and three of the men dismounted and tied the reins to a tree some distance back. Southwick slid off his horse and led it toward the barn. Johnny Dean rode on in the direction of the slave cabins.

When Will and the two other men mounted the porch steps, Charlie Ball fell back a little, and cupped the rifle in his right arm. Will pulled one of the pistols out of his belt and knocked at the door. Morgan Walker opened it, peered at the strangers, and asked who they were and what they wanted. Brushing him aside, Will entered the house, a pistol now in both hands. Lipsey went next, Charlie Ball behind him.

"We've come to take your slaves with us to Kansas," Will said brazenly. "We also want your horses and mules and what money you got in the house."

Morgan Walker replied firmly. "If my Negroes want to go to Kansas, they are at liberty to do so. But I don't see any reason why those who don't want to go should be forced to leave." Looking hard at Will, he added, "I don't think you should take any of my stock. They won't be worth much by the time you get 'em all the way over into Kansas."

As Walker protested, Will had stepped farther into the room, a little to one side of Lipsey and Charlie Ball, who stood just inside the door. With an eye on the open doors leading into other rooms, he held both guns thrust out before him, ready to fire.

When Walker said, "Besides, I don't have much money here in the house . . . ," Will spun around and fired a single shot at close range into Lipsey's head. Lipsey dropped to the floor, dead. Will immediately turned to fire at Charlie Ball, but an unseen man suddenly stepped through the door of an adjoining room, pistol raised at shoulder height, and fired at Charlie. Turning in reflex at the sound of the first shot to escape toward the open door, Charlie was struck in the shoulder instead of the chest. He fell back against the wall, regained his balance, and ran outside. Clutching his shoulder, he swung his legs over the porch rail and disappeared.

Hearing shots fired from inside, and seeing Charlie leap from the porch, Ed Morrison raced for the horses, a pistol in one hand. From the direction of the road, muzzle blasts nearby shattered the air, but missed him. Morrison grabbed the reins of his horse, and fired back blindly at the unseen gunmen. With access to the road closed off, he jumped onto his horse and made for a stand of woods east of the house. Albert Southwick, waiting in the barn, heard the gunfire and saw Morrison fleeing for the woods. He climbed on his horse and galloped through the open barn door. Johnny Dean leaped onto his horse, tied up near the slave cabins, and rode off, lashing the animal for greater speed. He soon disappeared into a cornfield.

Back at the house, Will walked out onto the porch and into the shadows along one wall, still grasping a pistol in each hand. He peered out into the yard, searching for the source of the gunfire. Seeing two strangers approaching the house from out of the dark, each carrying a rifle, he dodged behind a column and raised his guns.

"Hold up, Quantrill!" Morgan Walker shouted from the door. "Those men are mine. I had them staked out behind the smokehouse."

Walker stepped back into the front room, where gunpowder smoke hung acrid in the air. Calling to his son, Andrew, to give him a hand, they picked up the body of Lipsey by its feet, dragged it through the open door, and laid the body on the wood floor near the far railing where the blood could drain off the edge onto the ground.

Will looked down at the dead man, one of whose arms lay flung to one side. With the toe of his boot, Will pushed the arm up against the man's body. "That should learn you something," he said.

"Andrew," Morgan Walker said, "get this body out to the tool shed, and cover it up. Tomorrow, have some men put it in a wagon and haul it off into the timber, back in that area where the brambles are taking over. Bury it there, so nobody's likely to stumble across it."

Turning to Will, Morgan Walker offered his hand. "We're grateful for what you done, Mr. Quantrill, warning us about the raid. Five men might have been too much for us to handle, not knowing they were coming. Stay the night, and in the morning, as soon as it's light, we'll look for the two that ran off. One of them being wounded, I don't think they'll get far."

Will nodded. "I want to finish what I started. No sense their getting away."

Morgan Walker was up and dressed before daylight. With his son and one of the men he'd staked out the night before, and with Will, they set out on horseback before breakfast to track down the remaining raiders. A Negro field worker told Morgan Walker he'd seen two men go into the woods near the creek. Because Charlie Ball was wounded, Walker doubted the men could move very fast. He was right. The hunters came upon their quarries by mid-morning. They sighted them concealed in the brush, lying flat on the ground alongside a log for cover.

The four men stealthily approached the hiding place. Ed Morrison, awakened from a light sleep by the cracking of a dry stick, rose to his knees, cautiously looking around. As he reached for his pistols, Morgan Walker knocked him to the ground with a blast of buckshot in the chest.

Charlie Ball struggled to rise up on his elbow, peering over the top of the log. His jacket was splotched with blood, and he shivered from the fever that had come on during the night. Shaking, he held a pistol in his good hand, but before he could get off a shot, Andrew fired at close range with a rifle, killing him instantly, the lead doubling Charlie over onto his back. Will stood by, his weapon at the ready, but did not fire a shot.

Morgan Walker sent his son to get some slaves and shovels. Meanwhile, the bodies were stripped of anything that might identify them. Clothes, boots, hats, leather belts were burned. Andrew Walker took a pocket watch and a miniature portrait locket from one of the bodies, to be disposed of elsewhere. If by chance the bodies were someday discovered, Walker wanted nothing that might identify them.

When the slaves arrived, they dug a common grave only yards from where the men had died, and deep enough that animals wouldn't dig at the buried bodies. The dead men were dumped into the cavity, and the earth shoveled in, then spread with debris from the forest floor. In the silence, as the men stood back to look at the camouflaged burial site, it was as if the raiders had never crossed into Missouri.

Morgan Walker urged Will to stay for the noon meal with him and his family. At table, Will related some of his exploits in Kansas, relishing the approval he got from his host. When Walker asked Will who the men from Kansas were, and why he had led them into a trap, Will smiled, and replied only that he held a grudge against them, that he was righting a wrong inflicted on him and his family. Walker did not pursue the question further, respecting the younger man's right to keep such matters to himself.

That same afternoon, Will left the Walker farm astride a fine new horse, and a hundred dollars cash in his pocket, gifts from Morgan Walker.

A week later, Marcus Gill read in *The Independence Democrat* a sympathetic account of the incident at Morgan Walker's farm. Will was not identified by name, nor did the article give the names of the men who had died in the attempted raid. But the journalist also wrote that "One of the party, whom we understand had joined Montgomery's band for the purpose of being revenged upon by the death of his brother who had been killed by them," had set up the plan to warn the Walkers in advance of the raid, thereby setting a trap for the men who rode with him.

Marcus speculated it might have been Will who led the raiders. Once, when Will had asked him about his experiences in the Kentucky militia, Marcus had told Will of a similar episode of which he had knowledge, cautioning Will to avoid joining up with men he didn't know if his life might be dependent on them. Will seemed to take a particular interest in the story, nodding his head in agreement that one needed to be wary.

Marcus also surmised that Montgomery, a known organizer of anti-slavery raids launched from Lawrence, probably had nothing to do with the raid on Walker's farm, but that Will had planted the notion to add excitement to his feat, to make himself appear more of a hero. When Marcus showed the newspaper article to Mary Jane, she asked, "Did Will have a brother? I don't think he ever mentioned it to me."

"He once told me that he'd had a younger brother who also came out with him from Ohio," Marcus said. "He claimed that his brother and another man were camped out one night on the prairie west of Lawrence, looking after some cattle, when a band of Montgomery's raiders surprised them in their sleep and shot them dead."

"Oh, no," Mary Jane exclaimed, "what a horrible thing to have happen."

"I don't know," Marcus said, shaking his head. "I'm not sure it ever did. Will never spoke of his brother again. In fact, another time he lamented the fact that he was the only son his mother ever had, and he worried about how she would get along if he got killed someday."

"That's strange," Mary Jane said, then paused, thinking back to the conversations at the supper table when Will had lived with them. "But Will did seem to have a need to make things into something bigger than they were."

"I know, but I placed a lot of confidence in him. I still do—he undoubtedly saved my life, that day at the creek—and I know that Leah was real taken with him, when he stayed with us last winter. But Will has something deep inside, driving him so strong he won't be able to let go, should he ever have to. Like being on a runaway horse."

Mary Jane nodded. "I'm just glad the Noland boy has taken such an interest in Leah, and she seems to be feeling the same way about him. But I know she sometimes thinks about Will. Now and then she asks whether we've heard anything about him."

"Yes, I thought that was maybe the way things were. Well, we'll just have to wait to see what happens."

Chapter IX

The last week in January 1860, the winds were raw, the ground frozen, skies unchanging in slate-gray overcast. The country continued to struggle with the issue of slavery. Now it might find some resolution. Within days, a national election was to be held to choose the next president of the United States.

There were four candidates, Lincoln among them. Marcus strongly favored John Breckenridge, who was forthright in his defense and support of slavery. Stephen Douglas from Illinois, a candidate who also had support in the South, was more compromising in his views toward slavery. Marcus felt that by being conciliatory, Douglas weakened the pro-slavery position.

John Bell was the fourth candidate. He ran on the Union party platform that offered concessions to both abolitionists and those favoring the expansion of slavery. Again, Marcus believed that slavery could only be weakened by failure to take a non-compromising position on the issue.

Having heard Lincoln speak in Leavenworth, and having thought frequently about what he had said, Marcus conceded that Lincoln was a convincing candidate. He may have appeared awkward, and his voice high-pitched, even disagreeable when he spoke too forcefully, but the man seemed truthful, well meaning, and resolute. As difficult as it was to accept the view, Marcus had come to believe that Lincoln might win the election; and that if he did, he would do all he could as president to carry through on his resolve to end slavery.

Therefore, Marcus determined that he would raise the question after church in New Santa Fe, when some of the men stayed to talk. Every vote in the country was important. There were about a dozen or more that stayed behind. In the preacher's study, they pulled up straight-back wood chairs and a couple of benches, close to the round-bellied iron stove. Despite the cold outside, the room was too warm, the air close.

Not all those present might agree, Marcus realized, that Breckenridge was the man to vote for, but he felt that if anyone wavered on which candidate to choose, he would persuade him to cast a ballot for Breckenridge.

"You know about the election next week," Marcus began. Several heads nodded. "Other candidates are up for election, not just who's going to be president. Those positions are for the Congress and our State legislature in Jefferson City. But who's going to lead the country, that's the most important decision."

Marcus looked around at other faces in the room. They were mostly farmers like him, all slave owners except the preacher, who he knew was personally opposed to slavery, and a lawyer, whose opinion he didn't know. The same was true for several others present; while they didn't own slaves, neither had they made known whether or not they were against slavery.

"Those running on the Republican ballot," Marcus continued in a level voice, "they're against slavery. That's the party Lincoln belongs to. And that includes Republican candidates for the State Legislature and for Congress. The party's only about eight years old, so they haven't been around nearly as long as us Democrats. They think slavery ought to be abolished. They want to set slaves free. Just like I've told some of you I heard Lincoln talking, up in Leavenworth, when he was running for the nomination."

"That'll ruin the country," a man across from Marcus grumbled. "Where do they think all those slaves are going to go? Who's going to feed them, look after them? Where would they live?"

"They're suppose to find jobs, I hear," a farmer said. "But I read in one of the St. Louis newspapers that there might be as many as four million slaves in the country. That doesn't include another half a million Negroes already free, mostly up north or back east."

"I've heard the same thing," Marcus said. "If the slaves are freed, I just can't figure out what they'll do. I wouldn't want to hire my own slaves to work for me in the fields. So where would they go?"

Another man spoke up. "But that's not the only problem. There's a lot of those citizens up north and back east, white like us, who can't accept the way we live. My wife's family are up in Chicago. They think that because I own slaves, I'm just trash compared with them. They think nothing about meddling, always letting my wife feel like I'm beneath them." His voice rose, and his face showed his agitation. "What I can't tolerate is their preaching to us, saying we're going against God, because we have slaves. It shouldn't concern them. We don't preach back to them about their family owning a packinghouse. I'm told that men in packinghouses work twelve-hour days under terrible conditions. Children, too. Who are they to take after me?"

"You're right," an older farmer added. "I come from Massachusetts, and the way they treat Irish immigrants in Boston City back there is hard to believe. Irish aren't even considered citizens, and they work for next to nothing in wages. How can they give me a sermon about owning slaves?"

The preacher, who had sat quietly, said "But slavery, owning another human being as if he was nothing more than a work animal, that's just wrong. It isn't right. Doesn't that have to change?"

A newcomer who owned a mill east of town, on the Blue River, spoke up. "I understand your thinking that, Reverend, but Negroes are just not the same as you and me. I've only got the three slaves I use in my mill, and one in my house, but they're only good for what they're doing for me now. I can't imagine how they'd get along, otherwise, if I didn't own them, or if somebody like me wasn't looking after them all the time."

Henry Chiles spat into the coal bucket. "Heck, I've got cousins in South Carolina. Lots of those folks just ain't going to go along with freeing the slaves. My cousins won't. They'll pull out of the Union, if need be. Seven states has already said they would." No one was surprised. "Lincoln's so all-fired determined to free the Negroes, maybe he ought to send them off to South America, like he once said he'd considered, so they'd have their own way of life. But no one's said he'd pay us for them."

Jesse Johnson, a farmer whom Marcus greatly respected, shook his head. "Secession ain't the answer. If there's a war, we'll get hurt bad." He tugged on his beard. "Besides, I come here from Illinois because land back home had gotten too costly. But I seen the railroads bring some good, back in Illinois. Those tracks they're laying now, on west from Jefferson City, a war would end that. Bring it to a halt. Railroad companies have already threatened to move the roadbed north, into Nebraska, if there's trouble in Missouri and Kansas. The railroads mean markets we're going to need some day. We'll be left out if we don't have them, both railroads and markets."

Marcus thought of the new banker from St. Louis he'd talked to, and the man's poorly concealed disdain because Marcus owned slaves. He shook his head. "Running a railroad through Missouri also means more people moving here from the east. They'll be going on into Kansas, too, settling there, proving up claims for land from the government."

"And that means Kansas will be free-state," Henry Chiles injected, "because those Easterners will see to it that it happens. They'll vote to prohibit slavery. We'll be up against more folks who don't like what we do. What's more, my slaves will know there's people agitating to set them free."

"What does your father think about this?" Marcus asked Henry. "And how's he getting along? I'm sorry to hear he's been sick."

"We've been worried, no doubt about that, because he seems to be losing his strength, but I'll tell him you asked after him," Henry replied. "Well, I don't agree with him, but he says we might just as well get used to the direction affairs are headed. Thinks we'd do better going along with the Republicans, even giving up slavery, if we have to." Everyone was silent; Henry's father was wealthy, and influential in the county. "He says we ought to look at St. Louis, see what a growing economy has done for them. And being on the Mississippi gives them markets as far south as New Orleans. Lots more people with money back in St. Louis, my father says, compared with folks around here. He thinks we can do what they do."

"I just can't accept that, Henry," Marcus said. "Start thinking like a Republican, that is. I've always been a Democrat, and my father before me. Besides, I can't vote for Lincoln when I know he'll take my slaves. What would I do? I'd have to sell most of my land. You know that. Sell it at whatever price I could get, buyers knowing that slavery isn't allowed anymore. The only prospects to buy land would be folks looking for a small place, sixty, maybe eighty acres. And most of those don't have any money."

Henry shrugged, as if only stating a view other than his own. "Father thinks that's what's coming. People will be moving west to find opportunities they no longer have in the east, where it's mighty crowded. They'll be looking for land to raise a family on. Enough land to support themselves, and lay a little money aside. That's what's already attracting them to settle out in the Territory, where they can homestead, get land for free from the government."

Marcus said nothing. He looked around at other faces, some as serious as his own. "Well, maybe. Time will tell. But you got to look at it this way, too. The money I've got tied up in slaves is almost half the amount I've got invested in land. How can Lincoln expect me to just throw that away, if he's elected and frees the slaves? Would that be fair?"

"I agree with you, Marcus," Henry said. "I'm just saying what my father thinks." Others nodded their head. Most of the farmers there faced the same financial loss if the right to own slaves was outlawed.

"Marcus," Jesse Johnson said, "something else I've been thinking about. You're a Kentucky man, like me. You have two sons, like I do, old enough to fight. What are you going to do if it comes to that?"

Marcus leaned back on two legs of his chair, and spoke with deep feeling. "Took me more than six years to build up what I have now. I have a baby boy, named after me, buried on the place." The words formed slowly. "\" Nowadays, going to bed at night, I put a gun on the table and a loaded rifle under the bed. Two of my field hands stay the night in the barn loft, where they can watch the roads to the house, taking turns keeping awake. I put a dinner bell on top of the barn, so they can ring it good and loud, if someone shows up who has no business on my property."

Abruptly, he sat forward, the two front legs of the chair striking the wood floor loud enough to splinter. "I don't want anybody troubling me. I like things the way they are. I'd be willing to stay with the Union, but not if they're going to steal what's mine." Marcus stood up, reaching for his coat and hat. "Lincoln should see that. He should understand that." He shook his head. "I don't know why he doesn't."

Almost a week passed after the election before Marcus knew the details. Jed brought back from Westport a copy of a St. Louis newspaper. The Republican Party had won by a large margin; Union candidates got a big majority. However, Lincoln received less than forty percent of the vote, the remainder divided between the other three candidates. The newspaper said that joyous crowds had taken to the streets in St. Louis, celebrating the victory over slavery. The same was true in big cities back east.

The reporter wrote that even in Virginia, considered the most important Southern State, voters defeated delegates who favored secession rather than accede to ending slavery. Virginia would remain in the Union. State legislatures in Tennessee, Arkansas and North Carolina either defeated secession candidates or later refused to even vote on the issue. Delaware and Maryland stayed in the Union. Marcus was angry that Kentucky, his place of birth, where Lincoln had also been born, refused to secede.

Missouri delegates chosen in the election were strongly pro-Union. Marcus found the news unbelievable. This meant Missouri would side with the northern states. As a slave owner, he felt that his own government was expelling him from Jackson County, from Missouri.

Chapter X

Early April in 1861, two months after the election, Leah married Jesse Noland. The wedding took place in her father's house. She still had heard nothing from Will since he rode off for Lawrence, and had decided she never would. Seventeen, she went to live with her husband and his family in Independence.

Only eight days later, word reached Marcus that Confederate warships in Charleston harbor had fired their canons on Fort Sumter, a Federal defensive garrison astride a small island in the South Carolina harbor. The rebels captured the fort after only two days of siege. Marcus knew that war would now be declared, and felt the world closing in. Like invaders, events beyond his control pounded on his door, assailed his home, forced him to confront the likelihood of further physical assaults on him and his family. Was he a fool to stay, was he risking the lives of his family? He could not decide.

Then Marcus received a letter from his oldest son, Enoch, living in Texas. He had married a girl whose family had been neighbors in Kentucky. Enoch and his new wife had joined his wife's family when they also moved west to Texas. In his letter, Enoch urged his mother and father to leave Missouri and come to Texas. "Regretfully, you are located in the worst possible place," he wrote. "Those merciless raiders in Kansas will not stop. They will steal your property and very possibly harm you. Without doubt, you and Mama are in great peril."

Marcus anguished over what to do. Outwardly, he went about managing the farm with Jed at his side. They both continued carrying firearms whenever they went out into the fields, away from the house. The slaves seemed apprehensive; Marcus felt that they were watching him whenever he rode by or stopped to talk with Jed. Marcus assumed that Millie and the house servants passed along to other slaves any conversation they overheard. The slaves must have had some awareness of unfolding events, but Marcus did not consider it further; he was too absorbed with the safety of his family and the operation of the farm.

One night, shortly before midnight, Mary Jane awakened. The room was cold. She got out of bed and walked over to the open window to close it. The scent of freshly mowed hay in a nearby pasture drifted into the room.

To the east, she saw a red glow low on the horizon. At first it looked as if the sun was edging upward. Then she turned, and shook Marcus. Waking, he instinctively reached for the revolver on a bedside table.

"No," Mary Jane said, "not that. It's a fire. Look, there, toward Blue Springs."

Even at that distance, he could make out tongues of flame, pulsing like fanned coals in a kiln.

"The Walkers?" Mary Jane asked.

"Could be. The raiders have been active in that part of the county."

"What can we do?"

"Nothing, it's too far, and too late to help," Marcus said. "There's no way to stop a fire like that. But I'll ride over after daybreak, and see what they might need." He shivered, and wrapped his arms around his body. "If it's the house, and not one of the barns, they'll need a place to live. Until they can get it rebuilt. Farmers nearby will help out."

Mary Jane went back to bed. Marcus lay down beside her, unable to sleep.

"Marcus, what are we going to do? I mean, what are we going to do about staying here, with the war going on?"

He put his arm around her, and she lay her head against his chest. "I've been thinking about that, most all the time. But I didn't want to worry you anymore than you already were."

"Can we go someplace else? Until the fighting's over?"

"I'd sure hate to walk away and leave the place. Jed could stay here, look after things, but there's very little one man can do to keep up the place like it should be. And if raiders show up, he'd best hide until they're gone. And they probably will come."

"Why do you think that?" Mary Jane asked.

"Word will get around as soon as we're gone that the house is empty, that there's only one man around. When we come back, we could find all the buildings burned to the ground."

"But you've worked so hard to build up the farm."

"And they'd likely as not kill Jed, if they found him alone." Marcus stared up at the ceiling. The walnut planks were barely visible in the darkness, yet he remembered, seven years ago now, watching them being sawed from a great tree felled in the timber near the creek bank, and hauled by a pair of mules to the site of his new house.

"I think that you, or me, or any of us could be shot and killed, Mary Jane. In war, anything can happen. It's not only the raiders who can harm

us. There'll be Union troops. And the State militia. They'll look at us as
the enemy. We're Southerners, and we own slaves."

"Even though you're not in the army? Even though you're not
fighting?"

"Yes, it can happen. A commander can't always control his troops,
especially when they're spread out. Patrols, just six or eight men. They're
on their own, can do what they want."

"So Union soldiers might be just as bad as the guerrillas?"

"That's always a possibility. Like I said, we're the enemy."

"But you're not a soldier," Mary Jane said. "You're not in the
Confederate Army."

"They might not see it that way. And there's the bushwhackers. They're
organized now, itching for a fight whenever they can find guerrillas or
someone they think is abolitionist. That means trouble can explode just
about anywhere."

Mary Jane nodded. "The Nolands told Leah they know of several
gangs in the county. Jesse is pleased. He figures they're out to help people
like us, and they'll give raiders as much trouble as they cause."

"I'm thinking more about military fighting, with troops, and where
it might take place. You never know ahead of time. But there's no reason
why it can't be right here in Jackson County. There could be a battle here
on the farm anywhere, anytime."

Marcus saw in his mind companies of uniformed soldiers advancing
across his fields and pastures, shouting, firing muskets amidst clouds of
gunpowder smoke, and tearing down rail fences to remove obstructions to
their advance. He saw artillery hauled by struggling horses, soldiers setting
up canons to fire, and explosions from opposing artillery demolishing
his house, destroying his barns, erupting like geysers in the fields and
tearing raw holes in the earth. He saw decaying carcasses of livestock,
corpses of soldiers sprawled in his pastures, heard cries of wounded and
dying men, and saw the thrashing of cavalry horses felled by gunfire. As
a boy, his grandfather had told him vivid stories about the Revolutionary
War, where he had fought as a cavalry captain. Those tales had stayed
with him, enhanced by his own experiences.

"There's something else," he said. "The military road south from
Leavenworth is just to the west, not far from us."

"What does that mean?"

"Armies depend on military roads to move troops and artillery and
supplies. Both sides can use them. Depends on who has control at any

one time. Because of their size, armies stretch out to some distance on either side of the road. They also scavenge for food and horses, mules, wagons, whatever they need, wherever they go."

"Then Enoch was right," Mary Jane said. "We're caught in the middle."

"Others are, too. We wouldn't be the only victims. But if we leave, we ought to do it soon. As soon as we can get ready."

"But, Marcus—." Mary Jane stopped, then said, "Is Enoch right? Should we go to Texas? And why don't we have more time? To get ready?"

"Raiders will step up their activities, now that war's been declared. There will be more gangs, like packs of dogs, yelping and fighting anyone they run up against. Wild dogs."

"And Texas? Should we go?"

"It's a long way. Twenty miles a day, about the best we could expect to do. It would take almost a month, maybe longer. The women slaves could ride on top of things loaded in the wagons. Oxen would haul the wagons. They're slow, but they're stronger than mules." Marcus began to visualize how they might do it, if they went. "The male slaves could ride the horses and mules we'd take with us, down through Oklahoma. The longer we wait, the more likely it is there'll be fighting along the way. Federal troops watching the roads. Confederates looking for a fight with the Union."

"But so soon?" Mary Jane asked again.

"True, it takes time for armies to build up their strength, to where they can fight in other parts of the country. States like the Carolinas, Virginia, Georgia, that's where the first battles will be fought. But before long, they'll likely get to Missouri and Arkansas."

"So shouldn't that give us some time?"

"No, because both sides will be angling early on to control the rivers. That's the fastest way to transport men and supplies. The longer we wait, the more chance that we'll be stopped on the way. They'll steal our wagons and everything we have. We might be harmed, too. Anything can happen when there's fighting all around."

Mary Jane was silent. Then she said, "I've been thinking about Leah, Marcus. Jesse told her he's leaving next week to go South, to enlist in the Southern army. Should we take Leah with us?"

"If she can stay with the Nolands, I think that might be best. They'd be glad to have her. Independence is a big enough town, I think she'd be safe. Many of the folks there side with the Union, but Southern families shouldn't be harmed as long as they don't get caught helping Confederates or bushwhackers."

As they talked it out, Marcus began to accept the growing inevitability of their leaving the farm. He thought the war might not last long, that the Federal government would relent when they realized how determined the South was to retain their rights. Economic strength in the Northern states was greater than in the South, he realized, but the resolve of Southerners not to be intimidated was powerful. He and Mary Jane would probably be back home within a year, he figured, maybe sooner. Meanwhile, his family would likely be safer in Texas, away from the pillaging and guns of the Kansas raiders.

"I've been thinking that I should try to get in touch with Will," Marcus said. "I'd feel a lot better with someone like him traveling with us, at least until we got through Oklahoma Territory. We need another man who's good with a gun, knows what to look out for, and knows how to fight."

"Since Leah won't be with us," Mary Jane said, "I think you're right. Will respects you and he just might want to do doing something like that. He likes excitement, and likes being in the midst of things that show how good he is."

"Jesse's family might know where Will could be found. I'll maybe ride on into Independence, after I leave the Walkers, and see what I can find out about him."

For a few moments, neither of them spoke. Then Mary Jane asked "How long will it take for us to get ready to leave?"

"I'll have to buy some wagons. I want to take as much of our furniture, our household things, as we can. With no one living in the house, whatever we leave won't be here when we get back, even if the house isn't burned."

"I can start packing things up right away. What about the slaves? Will we take them with us?"

"Texas is a slave state," Marcus replied, "so we could. Besides, we'll need them when we come home, to put the place back in shape."

"I can't imagine leaving Millie behind," Mary Jane said. "What would she do if we did?"

"I'm not sure. Follow the roads to Lawrence, maybe. Then someplace farther north, after that."

"You need to write Turner, Marcus. To tell him to come home."

"Yes, you're right. I'll do that directly after I get back from the Walkers. And you write Enoch, to tell him we're coming."

Marcus had slept only a short time before Mary Jane awakened him again; it was time to ride to the Walkers' place, to see what he could do to help.

The next evening, after supper, Marcus went alone to the place where his infant son lay buried. It was four years ago that the boy had died. At the gravesite he found a sprig of dogwood, the fragile white flowers already beginning to brown, lying atop the grave. Mary Jane must have placed it there earlier in the day.

His mind flooded with many thoughts, Marcus stood for a time, unmoving. Then he walked over to Jim's grave, in a corner of the small plot, marked by a rough piece of uncut limestone picked up from the creek bed. On one irregular side, the name "Jim" had been scratched, as if with the point of a nail, and the month and year of his death. The letters and numerals were irregular, and already barely discernible in the soft, sand-colored stone.

At that moment, an image of Effie flashed into his mind. She was standing across from him, on the other side of Jim's grave, as she had the day her husband was buried. Marcus saw clearly her anguished face. He saw the tears on her cheeks, and her hands clenched tightly at her breast. Marcus again felt her eyes looking through him and beyond, as if fixed on something she sought, something beyond him from which she was unwilling to turn away.

How, he asked himself, how had he been able to put the old slave out of his mind during those many years since he had been a boy? How could he have forgotten the man who had patiently showed him how to grasp the worn, smooth handle of the great scythe, how to swing it from one side to the other, his whole, young body moving with it? He had not often seen Jim since, and seldom to speak to, Marcus realized. The slave had become only one of many working in the fields, indistinguishable at that distance.

Marcus felt a sudden rush of tenderness for the old man. He was also deeply sad the slave was gone, now dead. Yes, the old man had belonged to him, had been his property. His father had bought Jim, and given Jim to his son, Marcus. No lawful person would have contested his right to use the slave however he wished. But now a nascent feeling stronger than affection altered that logical fact. Marcus could not identify why he felt as he did.

But gradually, he began to understand why the sight of the old man lying in his bed had disturbed him so profoundly. He remembered the slave's wasted body, the hair gone almost white. He remembered that the old man, although only momentarily able to recognize his master, had brightened when he saw his face. Marcus had found himself at that moment thinking of Jim as someone who had been a part of his own early life, someone important to him in those days of childhood, as someone other than property.

So Marcus had not told Mary Jane that he had been thinking about offering his slaves freedom. The more Marcus considered the alternative, the more unsure he became of his judgment. Others would think he had lost his senses. Perhaps he had; the pressures from all sides were great. Yet he continued to weigh the possibility in his mind, as well as to consider the cost, the great financial loss, that giving up his slaves would mean.

Chapter XI

Turner returned from the university as soon as he received the letter from his father asking him to come home. Marcus and Jed then rode into Westport, leaving Turner and the field foreman to watch out for any raiders who might appear.

Marcus bought five wagons, similar to those used by traders who traveled to Santa Fe, laden with goods to sell or exchange for merchandise to sell when the wagons returned to Missouri. These wagons had iron-shod wooden wheels higher than a horse's back, and wagon beds so deep that the head of a tall man standing inside was barely visible over the sides. He also bought forty head of oxen, enough for four pair hitched to each wagon. When loaded with household furnishings, bedding, a month's supply of food and grain, kegs of well water, farming implements, bales of hay, and other possessions, each wagon would weigh more than three tons.

Marcus had paid for his purchases and was about ready to leave the store when he heard a voice say, "Colonel Gill, heard you were looking for me."

Standing in the door was Will, a wide grin on his face. He looked fit, was dressed in new clothes, and wore two revolvers in holsters at his waist. A long feather stuck in his hatband rose jauntily above the crown.

Marcus was glad to see him, and they walked out onto the street together. Will asked about the family, although he seemed to avoid referring to Leah by name. Marcus told him that Leah was newly married, one of the Nolands in Independence. Will said he'd heard that, and wished her well. Marcus searched Will's face for some sign of emotion, of regret, but nothing showed.

Marcus then explained that he was taking his family to Texas, that they would be leaving in just a few days.

"I'd like to hire you to go with us, Will," Marcus said. "You saved my life once. I don't expect to call on you to do that again, but I need you, in case we run into trouble. You're the best I know. I hope you'll agree to go with us. You can come back after we get to Fayette County, if you like. That's west of the town of Houston. Or you'd be welcome to stay on with us. It would be up to you."

Will made up his mind quickly. "I'd like to go with you. Haven't never been to Texas. Fact is, I'd enjoy doing something like that right at this time."

Marcus reached out his hand. Will shook it, and promised he'd be at the farm early in the morning on the day they'd be leaving.

The departure day set, much now needed to be done. The family worked alongside the slaves, preparing to load the huge wagons with all they'd be taking with them. The leather-bound Bible was placed inside the lacquered-wood container that once held Mary Jane's silver place settings, and wrapped in a blanket, bound with twine. Gunnysacks stuffed with straw were used to pack china, the glass globes of coal-oil lamps, and other easily broken possessions. Furniture was protected by bedding not needed until they arrived in Texas, and then hauled up into a wagon. Clothing was carefully folded and laid in leather trunks.

Mary Jane was determined to leave nothing behind that might be vandalized or stolen. The possibility that men like Brown and his raiders could break open the door and ransack her home, perhaps set it afire in anger when they found little left to plunder, drove her to give away to neighbors, or lend for safekeeping, three chests of drawers, a dressing table, the iron range, and other pieces of furniture they decided not to take with them.

Under Jed's instructions, slaves loaded hand tools from the barn into one of the wagons, together with bales of hay to feed the horses and mules they were taking with them, if good forage could not be found along the way. Marcus reasoned that livestock would become more valuable as the war progressed; that he'd get a better price in Texas, if he had to sell his livestock, than he could now at markets in Westport or Independence.

Marcus waited to execute his plan until the next to last day before they would leave. Even Jed did not know the decision he had been contemplating for days. Marcus had discussed it with Mary Jane, but waited until late that afternoon to tell the older children.

After supper, he instructed Jed to assemble the slaves outside their cabins. The April air, unusually warm, already smelled of summer: the heavy scent of verdant pastures, and the pungent odor of hog pens and of cattle, moving restlessly nearby in a corral.

The slaves stood bunched together by families, or stood a little apart from the others, if they were without family. Several women held infants in their arms. Other children stood next to their parents; a few, very small, clung to a hand or a leg. They were silent, even the younger children, as if sensing something of which they should be afraid.

Marcus saw Effie standing to one side, alone. She seemed to have aged the last two years, her hair more gray, her body more bent than he had remembered. She looked at him for a sign, any sign that might indicate what was happening; finding none, she shifted her gaze toward the woods in the distance, as if disdainful of whatever he might do.

The men, who wore their hats from the fields, despite the evening's warmth, stood quietly. No one talked. Marcus sensed the apprehension displayed by the stiff postures, the arms hanging loosely at their sides, the eyes staring at him, or turned downward, waiting, as if afraid to face him.

Marcus knew that what he would say might not be easily apprehended. So he began slowly.

First, he acknowledged that some of them had made the journey with him from Kentucky, to this new land; that others he had bought after he'd arrived in Missouri. He told them that war had begun a few weeks ago; that Southerners like himself were not willing to give up slavery. They were willing to fight to uphold federal and state laws in which they believed. He said that even though Missouri permitted slavery, the State government had decided not to secede, but to stay with the Union, taking sides with those opposed to slavery. He regretted this decision, he told them, because there were many Southerners like himself who had come west to build a new life, and they felt betrayed by their government.

Marcus wondered how much the slaves understood. What did they know about the laws of which he spoke, the government in Washington? Never in the past would he have undertaken to talk to them as he was now doing. But because of what he was about to say, he felt compelled to explain what was happening in their lives as well as his own.

He had decided to take his family to Texas, he told them. They knew this, because they had been helping in preparations to leave. Fighting would possibly take place nearby, even on his own land, he explained, perhaps where they now stood; no one could know before it happened. There would be much danger, if they remained where they were.

Watching their faces, Marcus saw no changes in expressions, no sign that they comprehended what he was telling them. He wasn't sure that they did. After all, until now there had been no decisions for them to make.

His voice becoming firm, Marcus said that he was offering them their freedom. Whoever chose to be free, he would free them before he left for Texas. Those who decided to remain with him he would take with him, where they would remain with his family.

It was as if he had spoken in a strange language whose sounds reached their ears, but whose meaning remained a mystery. The faces before him were either blank or reflected emotions Marcus could not recognize.

More gently, Marcus repeated what he had just said, phrasing the message in simplest terms. In a matter of such great import, who would not have asked that the message be repeated? He added that they would have until daybreak tomorrow morning to decide. Jed would call them together again at that time. Those who chose freedom would be given a letter of manumission. Marcus explained that this was a written statement, signed by him, stating that he had freed the slave whose name was written on the paper.

Where could they go? For a few days, Marcus said, they could stay in their cabins, if they wished. But it would be best for them if they left right away. Slave owners who remained in the county might not honor the freedom he had granted them. Also, there were renegades who might harm them, once they were out of his protection.

They could take with them whatever food they could carry. But soon after he and his family were gone, he said, he urged that they cross over into Kansas Territory and travel the roads northward to Leavenworth, where there was an Army fort. It would be dangerous for them even on the roads north, because actions of the Kansas guerrillas, while declaring that they wanted to free slaves, were unpredictable. He could not assure the slaves of their safety.

When Marcus concluded, he paused for a moment, as if about to say something more, but abruptly turned about and walked toward his house. Looking back over his shoulder, he saw that no one had moved. They stood where he had left them, as if the energy to move their limbs, to walk, had drained out of their bodies, and flowed silently and unseen into the soil.

The next morning, Jed came to the house soon after daybreak. Marcus had not yet finished breakfast, but e had kept an eye out for Jed, and met him at the door.

Only Effie and Millie, Jed told him, and three of the older field hands had chosen to go with the family to Texas. The rest had all said they wanted freedom.

For a moment, Marcus was angry. He had expected more. He had treated his slaves well, he felt. Most had been with him for years. Why so many would choose the hazards, the uncertain future of freedom, he could not understand.

"Well, then, that's the way it'll be," he said. "Give each slave, each family all the food they can carry."

"What about those staying?" Jed asked, tugging at his old hat. "What I mean is, those going with us? To Texas."

"Tell Effie and Millie there'll be space in the wagons for them to take a few things, whatever's important to them. Take a look at what they want to take, and see where it'll best fit. The same for the men, although I doubt that they'll have much. Use your own judgment."

Jed nodded, and turned to leave.

"Come back in an hour," Marcus said. "I'll need you to give me the names of those leaving, so I can write out the releases. Then you can take their papers to them."

When Jed returned, Marcus led him into the parlor and sat down at his desk. Jed, who was unable to read or write, stood to his side. Marcus opened a drawer and took out sheets of blue-tinted writing paper. He folded each sheet over once, then again; and with the blade of a knife, cut the paper into four parts. Each quarter section of the page was all that was needed to write out the words: "I, Marcus Gill, on this 23rd day, April 1861, do hereby release and manumit for all time my slave . . ." and then fill in the slave's given name, the only name the slave was known by.

From memory, Jed spoke the names. In his mind he passed from one cabin to the next, now pushing the brim of his hat a little higher on his forehead, then giving it a tug to pull it back into place, as he said them aloud. One by one, waiting patiently until the Colonel began a new slip of paper, Jed scrupulously accounted for every adult slave, the slave's wife, and each child, even infants. At the end of the simple, declarative sentence Marcus wrote on the tinted paper, he dropped a line and signed his name in flourishing script. When Marcus had finished writing, Jed asked him to say how many names there were. Marcus counted twenty-two, not including the five whom would go with them to Texas. Jed nodded in agreement. The number was right.

That night, the night before they would set out, neither Marcus nor Mary Jane slept more than a few hours. Their bed had already been disassembled and loaded onto a wagon, so he and Mary Jane stretched a blanket on the floor over cotton bags stuffed with straw. They would use the blanket and straw bags again, each night on the trail. The house, although nearly empty of possessions, seemed alive with both strange and accustomed noises, as if bewildered shapes were wandering restlessly about in confusion.

At dawn, a wagon train of formidable size began to assemble on the pasture north of the house. Herders responsible for getting the livestock to Texas separated Marcus's prize horses and Kentucky mules into manageable herds. The animals would follow behind the wagons, because of the dust they'd kick up and the manure droppings. The oxen, at pasture since they had been brought from Westport, were rounded up, preparatory to harnessing them to the wagons. The hogs, sold to other farmers, were gone from their pens, as were the chickens from the coops, now eerily quiet.

Will appeared early that morning, as he had said he would. When he knocked at the door, Mary Jane let him in, and asked if he'd had his breakfast. She was distant in her greeting, unforgiving for his failure to communicate with Leah after he'd left the family and gone to Lawrence.

Will said coffee would be just fine. The younger children, shy at first, were soon tagging after him, until Marcus told them to leave Will alone, that he had to get ready, too. Marcus saw that Will was in high spirits, excited at the prospect of being bound for Texas, and that he enthusiastically took to his role as protector of the family.

By mid-morning, all else was ready. It was time to harness the oxen to the wagons.

Marcus mounted his dapple-gray gelding. The horse, sensing the excitement in the air, gamboled under a tight rein. Sitting erect in the saddle, a broad-brimmed hat on his head, Marcus rode up to the wagon master, astride a roan mare, and spoke quietly to him. The wagon master, hired in Westport to make the journey, was the most experienced Marcus could find. With sunburned face and a broad girth, the wagon master wore a brightly colored shirt, a hat drawn low on his head, neckerchief at the throat, high boots, and a revolver and long knife in his belt. At Marcus's words, he touched the brim of his hat, turned, and with his hands cupped to his mouth, called out: "Yoke up! Yoke up!", and then again, stretching the words into a prolonged cry, "Yo-o-o-ke up! Yo-o-o-ke up!"

The words sang out over the expanse of wagons and oxen, hanging suspended in the air before they were picked up and repeated by the bullwhackers, also hired out of Westport, who were standing ready. "Yoke up! Yoke up!" they shouted, like soldiers going into battle, and fell to the task of moving the placid, waiting oxen into leather harnesses and massive wooden tongues, each fifty feet long, extending from the front of the wagons. The great beasts, prodded by the bullwhackers, ambled into harness as if to feed at a trough. Astonishingly, within a half-hour, the task was done.

On command from the wagon-master, the bullwhacker perched on the high seat of the first wagon raised his arm, paused, and in a practiced motion, flung the tip of the long whip out and over the backs of the oxen, shouting "H-u-u-up! H-u-u-up!"

Like a gathering storm, energy and force rumbled out of the oxen's massive shoulders, their hooves pushed hard at the ground, the leather harnesses groaned, and the wheels of the wagons shuddered as the inertia of the great weight they bore was overcome, and the wheels turned slowly, slowly forward.

Marcus watched the proceedings, the expression on his face changing almost imperceptibly with the thoughts rushing through his head. He watched swallows, undeterred by the commotion, dart and dive near the roofs of the barns, plucking insects out of the warm spring air. Split-rail fences marched evenly across the hills and valleys of his farm. Redbud again threw splashes of color along edges of the timber, beginning to green with the elegant lace of new foliage.

Marcus gazed beyond his house to the cemetery, sketched against the sky, shielded by the black iron fence. A young oak tree, its bare branches only beginning to leaf out, stood like a torn banner in a field of combat. In his mind, Marcus saw the slate headstone for his infant son, and the smaller, rough stone for Jim, side by side from so far.

Marcus sat solidly on his horse and looked out over the fields, and again toward the house and barns. In the pasture between the slave cabins and the road leading north toward Westport, and then across into Kansas Territory, he saw the figures of his former slaves walking slowly, burdened with bundles of clothing and food. Hardly enough food to take them far, he conjectured, but he had done all he could do.

At that distance, he could not recognize any one slave. They looked much alike, indistinguishable because of the worn clothes they wore, and because they faced away from him, toward uncertainty, toward a future they had chosen.

A future they had chosen. The unspoken words resounded in his mind as Marcus pulled hard on the reins, turned his horse about, and rode to catch up with the wagons.

Epilogue

Marcus Gill

Marcus Gill and his wife, Mary Jane, remained in Texas until the Civil War ended. That same year, 1865, they returned to Missouri, driving a small wagon containing whatever personal possessions the wagon would hold. Their two younger children, ages four and six, rode in the wagon behind the seat from which Marcus drove the team of mules. The three older children traveled in a second wagon, probably driven by Susan, seventeen, a younger sister of Leah.

Marcus had invested heavily in bonds issued by the Confederacy; and at the war's end, the bonds were worthless. When they reached the family farm in Jackson County, he found the house still standing, as well as some of the farm buildings, but the fences had been stolen for firewood, and the fields and pastures showed the neglect and ravages of the last four years.

He set about rebuilding, selling off some of the land when he found it was more than he could manage. Marcus and Mary Jane continued to live on the farm and work it until, at age 69, he divided up ownership of the property among their children. All five daughters who lived into adulthood had been married in the house Marcus Gill built, in front of the great stone hearth. Marcus and Mary Jane then moved to a small place near Plattsburg, in Clinton County, Missouri, about thirty miles north of the Missouri River, where they had recourse to the mineral springs located nearby.

Marcus Gill died only three years later, in 1886, at age seventy-two. Mary Jane lived until 1894; she, too, was seventy-two when she died.

They are buried in the Gill family plot in Elmwood Cemetery in Kansas City, Missouri.

About a third of the original farm remained within the family of descendants of Susan Gill McGee, the second oldest daughter of Marcus and Mary Jane, until 1957, one hundred and three years after the Gills came to Jackson County from Kentucky. By 1957, the property was within the city limits of Kansas City, Missouri. At that time, the remaining acreage was sold for residential development, although construction did not begin until twenty years later.

Today, a 13-acre public park with a small lake at 119th Terrace and Pennsylvania Street comprises a part of the original farm. In all directions, houses march in curving symmetry over the hills and valleys of what was once Marcus Gill's thousand acres. A limestone column bearing two bronze plaques recounts the history of the farm and those few events relating to the border conflict. The boundaries of the farm, when viewed today, were from State Line Road to Wornall Road on the east, and from about 116th Street on the north to 121st Street on the south, two blocks north of the street named Santa Fe Trail.

William Clarke Quantrill

Quantrill returned from Texas soon after he arrived there with Marcus Gill and his family. He was restless, and wanted to be back in Missouri, where he knew the action would be.

In August 1863, in the second year of the Civil War, William Clarke Quantrill carried out an act destined to give him lasting notoriety. He led a band of nearly 450 men on a raid of Lawrence, Kansas, seat of the abolitionist movement in Kansas, in which his guerrillas slaughtered 144 civilians, all men and boys, most unarmed. A sense of Southern gallantry kept the Quantrill raiders from harming women or girls. Not a single guerrilla was killed.

The raid was partly in retaliation for the deaths a few days earlier of five women and the severe injuries suffered by other women, none more than twenty years of age. They had been imprisoned by Union soldiers on the second floor of a three-story brick building at 1409 Grand Avenue in Kansas City, Missouri. The young women were suspected of being spies for the Southern cause. A thirteen-year-old girl, who had provoked one of the guards, had been shackled at the ankle to a twelve-pound ball. For reasons still debated, the building trembled and collapsed with only a few moments warning. The girl shackled at the ankle was among those killed as the building disintegrated. At least eight of the women who died or were critically injured were sisters or cousins of men who rode as guerrillas with Quantrill.

General Thomas Ewing, Jr., the district commander of the Union forces, and a man with huge political ambitions, then compounded the anguish of the survivors of the victims killed in the building's collapse. He issued Order No. 10, which authorized the arrest of all men and women who knowingly and of their own volition assist and encourage the Southern guerrillas, and to remove them from their homes and families to a location outside the state of Missouri. Still stunned by the deaths of the young women only four days before, the guerrillas now knew that their family members risked being deported from Missouri with only those possessions they could carry with their hands, and with little money obtainable for their support.

From the viewpoint of Quantrill's raiders and Southern sympathizers, the Lawrence raid was a magnificent victory. They made off with 400 to 500 horses, terrorized all whom they encountered, left many buildings aflame, and stole vast amounts of loot. The raiders must have felt as if they had vindicated the deaths of their loved ones, and had struck a great blow against the Union and the abolitionist cause. Sadly, their foes were only civilians little able to defend themselves, and not uniformed soldiers in the Union Army, not even Lane's or Montgomery's abolitionist raiders.

For the next year, Quantrill continued to stage daring raids and skirmishes. By October 1864, however, the tide began to turn. Confederate Gen. Sterling Price, a Missourian and leader of many excursions into the state against Union forces, was devastatingly defeated at a battle with Union forces under the command of Gen. James G. Blunt. Price's defeat demoralized troops in the Army of Missouri. Many soldiers deserted; they saw Price's defeat as the end of the war for Missouri Confederates.

Quantrill also read the signs. He and his men, about thirty in all, in December 1864 dressed themselves in Union uniforms and left Missouri for eastern Arkansas, then into Mississippi, Tennessee, and finally into southwestern Kentucky. Still disguised, they duped Union loyalists into giving them provisions, and generally raised hell, robbing individuals, stealing horses, looting, and destroying property. Quantrill's ranks were gradually diminished in skirmishes when, their disguise uncovered, they had to shoot their way out and were killed or caught.

Although Robert E. Lee had surrendered almost 28,000 of his troops at Appomattox Courthouse on April 9, 1865, and was followed nine days later by Gen. J. E. Johnston, who surrendered another 31,000 soldiers, it was not until more than six weeks later, May 26, that the last of the rebel troops gave up their arms.

Meanwhile, near the town of Taylorsville, on the Salt River in the southwest corner of Kentucky, a farmer named James H. Wakefield agreed to harbor Quantrill and his guerrillas when they needed a place from time to time to hide out. On May 10, 1865, Quantrill and twenty-one of his men, including several newcomers, arrived at the Wakefield farm.

The horse that Quantrill had ridden through many episodes of fighting, Old Charley, had been injured shortly before while being shoed, and was irredeemably crippled. Quantrill was dismayed, sensing that the loss of the horse which had carried him swiftly and without serious injury to either of them for so long, was a bad sign. Forced to find another mount, Quantrill borrowed a horse from a woman friend. Unfortunately, the animal had never been exposed to gunfire, and therefore not conditioned to battle. That proved to be a tragic flaw.

Apparently unknown to Quantrill, he and his gang were being pursued by a man named Edwin Terrell, a discharged Union soldier. Terrell was considered by many to be very dangerous and a reprehensible renegade. He had been hired in January by the commander of the Union garrison in Louisville, Kentucky, to hunt down Confederate guerrillas. When he wasn't specifically engaged in that pursuit, he and his gang robbed civilians, yet went without being apprehended. In early April 1865, despite such known nefarious activities, Terrell was instructed by the military commander of Kentucky, Gen. John M. Palmer, to apprehend or kill one man: William Clarke Quantrill.

On that May 10 morning, Terrell and his band were only a few miles from Quantrill. A tradesman had spotted Quantrill's gang as they rode past on the way to Wakefield's, and sent Terrell and his men off in the same direction.

When Quantrill reached Wakefield's farm, he and most of his men climbed into the barn hayloft and fell asleep. A few others remained below, playing cards or talking idly.

One of Quantrill's men happened to look up at the pasture slopes nearby. He saw men on horseback, unslinging their rifles, descending on the barn lot. He cried out a warning.

Quantrill and his companions in the loft scurried down, and some leaped onto horses stabled in the barn or tied up outside. As they fled, they fired their pistols at Terrell's men who were now upon them. Most of the Quantrill gang who were on horseback jumped a gate across their path and escaped through the orchard. The other men, whose horses were rearing at the noise and confusion, were unable to mount; so they ran from the barn and plunged into a pond. Submerged low in the water and hidden by rushes, they waited until their pursuers rode by in chase of the others.

Quantrill struggled to mount his new horse, but the animal was so frightened by the gunfire, and was rearing so wildly, that Quantrill was unable to get his boot into a stirrup, and could not haul himself up into the saddle. He decided to escape by foot, and called out for help as he raced toward the orchard. Two of his fleeing men, astride their horses, reined in and waited for Quantrill to reach them, firing all the while at his pursuers. But one of the horses was struck by rifle fire, and became uncontrollable. Quantrill fired his pistol at riders bearing down on him. He then turned toward the second horse, trying to pull himself up behind its rider.

Suddenly a bullet tore into his back, below the left shoulder blade, and descended downward, lodging against his spine. It paralyzed his body below the shoulders, and he dropped face down onto the ground.

A moment later, the two members of his gang who had tried to save him were shot and killed. The pursuers turned around, and came back to the wounded man lying prostrate on the ground. They stripped him of his boots, lifted his pistols out of their holsters, and went through his pockets. Among the articles they found was a picture of a young woman. Her identity was not known.

Quantrill was taken by wagon a few days later to a military prison's hospital in Louisville. A physician told him that his wound was fatal. His back had also been broken. Quantrill could speak, but he remained paralyzed. Reportedly, he made no effort to contact his mother or other family members, to tell them he was dying.

William Clarke Quantrill died in the late afternoon on June 6, 1865. He was 27 years old. Civil conflict, culminating in the four years of Civil War, was at last at an end. The monstrous price paid was the loss of more American lives in battle during those four years than all other battle deaths in subsequent wars through present times.

Leah Gill Noland

After Marcus Gill and Mary Jane fled to Texas in April 1861, their oldest daughter, Leah, returned to the village of New Santa Fe from Independence. She was pregnant with her first child, conceived before her husband, Jesse, left for the South to join the Confederate Army.

In late January of 1862, nine months into the war, Leah became apprehensive about skirmishes being fought near New Santa Fe. Her baby was due within days. Feeling endangered, she realized that she needed the care and support of her husband's family. So she decided to leave New Santa Fe for Independence, sixteen miles away.

Leah chose to make the journey after dark, hoping that she would be able to avoid exposure to any fighting. With the aid of a Negro girl, she hitched a yoke of oxen to a wagon, loaded the few articles she would need, and set out with the girl sharing the wagon seat beside her. It was a wintry night; flames from houses and barns burning in the countryside lighted the way.

Driving the slow-moving oxen throughout the night, and following less-traveled country roads, it was not until early morning that they reached the outskirts of Independence. Suddenly, they were confronted by a patrol of Union soldiers. Looking for known Confederate sympathizers, the armed cavalrymen demanded to know where her father and brothers, and the men in her husband's family, could be found. Leah replied that they were no longer in Jackson County.

Angered, because they felt that she was simply refusing to disclose the actual whereabouts of her family, the soldiers led her to a nearby house where the unit's commander was located. Again Leah was asked to tell them where the men in the family could be found. Stubbornly, she insisted that she did not know. Two of the soldiers, infuriated by her refusal to cooperate, seized her by the arms and dragged her into a nearby room where they locked her up with the Negro girl.

Soon after, Leah began giving birth, possibly a result of the rough, night-long journey on the ox-drawn wagon to Independence. The unit commander sent for a doctor. Leah gave birth to a boy whom she named Jesse Price Noland, after the popular Missouri Confederate leader, General Sterling Price. Several days later, Leah was taken to a jail in Independence, but was soon paroled on the condition that she leave the area. She was handed a pass through the Union lines.

With little money, Leah set out for Texas with her infant son. They went alone, by oxen-drawn wagon, with few provisions. Of necessity, she foraged off the country. Meanwhile, Jesse Noland had surrendered in the fighting at Vicksburg, and set free under the proviso that he not participate in the fighting again; so he himself was on his way to Texas.

It was more than twenty years later that Leah's father, Marcus Gill, divided up ownership of his farm among his eight surviving children. Leah was the only one excluded from the distribution; only speculation can devise a reason. Two years later, Leah divorced her husband, Jesse Noland, with whom she had borne nine children during their twenty-five years of marriage.

The following year, in 1886, Marcus Gill at age 72 addressed a letter to the husband of the oldest of his married daughters, Susan Gill McGee. From his and Mary Jane's new home near Plattsburg, Missouri, Marcus wrote:

"We (received) a letter of Leah. We will send it to you.

Take care of it and send it back after my children read it as I don't think we will answer it. There is no sense in it."

Leah later remarried and relocated to Colorado Springs, Colorado. She lived there for some years, but died in Ogden, Utah, in 1908, at age sixty-four.

Enoch Bruton Gill

Soon after Marcus Gill and Mary Jane arrived in Fayette County, Texas with Turner and their younger children in May 1861, Enoch and Turner enlisted in the fledgling Confederate Army. Enoch was 22 when he enlisted, Turner only 20. Enoch fought in battles in Mississippi, where he was wounded a year later. The injury caused the amputation of one leg, below the knee. Released from military service, he returned to his home in Texas and taught school for the remainder of the war.

In 1866 Enoch and his wife left Texas and settled in Clay County, Missouri, across the Missouri River from Kansas City, where he again taught school. He began the study of law, and was admitted to the Missouri

Bar in 1871, at age 32. For fifteen years, he practiced law; but in 1886, at age 47, he began giving full time to a farm he owned near Olathe in Johnson County, Kansas, where he became known for the fine quality of farm animals he bred and raised.

Enoch died in 1916 at age 76, and is buried in Elmwood Cemetery in Kansas City, Missouri with his second wife, who lived until 1932.

Turner Anderson Gill

Turner Anderson Gill, like Enoch, was also in the midst of the fighting in Mississippi. Promoted to the rank of lieutenant in Company A, 6th Missouri Infantry, he fought at Vicksburg, where he was taken prisoner by Union forces. In the fall of 1863, Turner was included in an exchange of prisoners. He was immediately assigned as adjutant in the 2nd Missouri Cavalry. Not long afterward, at the age of 23, he was promoted by General Jo Shelby "for merit and gallantry under fire" to the rank of captain of the same unit in which he was then serving.

When the war ended, Turner Gill studied law at Kentucky University, graduating with honors in 1868. He was admitted to the Missouri Bar and opened an office in Kansas City. For a time, Turner Gill was a partner in a law firm whose successor firm is today known as Lathrop & Gage, one of the several largest law firms in Kansas City. A photographic portrait of him is displayed in the firm's offices. In 1875 Turner Gill was elected mayor of Kansas City, Missouri, and re-elected for a second term in 1876. When he left office, he later served as City Counselor.

In 1881, at age 40, Turner Gill was appointed a judge of the circuit court; elected to the same position in 1882; and re-elected in 1886. Two years later, in 1888, as the Democratic candidate for judge of the United States Court of Appeals, Western District, he was elected by a wide margin and served in this position for thirteen years, until 1901.

Turner Anderson Gill died in 1919 at age 77 and is buried in the Gill family burial plot he purchased for his family's use in Elmwood Cemetery. His first and second wives are buried on either side of him.

Index of References Used in the Writing of Terror at the Door

Barton, O. S. *Three Years with Quantrill. A True Story Told by His Scout, John McCorkle.* Notes by Albert Castel. Commentary by Herman Hattaway. University of Oklahoma Press. Norman.1992

Brophy, Patrick. *Bushwhackers of the Border—The Civil War Period in Western Missouri.* A Summary and Appraisal. Vernon County Historical Society. Bushwhacker Museum, Nevada, Missouri. 1980/2000.

Castel, Albert. *A Frontier State at War: Kansas 1861-1865.* Lawrence Heritage Press. Lawrence, Kansas.1985. New material copyright by Edward E. Leslie 1992.

Castel, Albert *William Clarke Quantrill—His Life and Times.* The General's Books, Columbus, Ohio with Camp Chase Publishing, Marietta, Ohio.1992.

Christopher, Sue Hargis. *My Mother's Families (Paternal): Gill, Malone, and Duncan.* 1953. Kansas City, Missouri.

Christopher, Sue Hargis. *My Mother's Families (Paternal): Gill, Malone, and Duncan.* Kansas City, Missouri.1953. NOTE: This material designated for my children is located elsewhere.

Connelley, William E. *Quantrill and the Border Wars.* The Torch Press,

Cedar Rapids, Iowa, 1910. New material copyright 1992 by Albert Castel. Kansas

Heritage Press. Ottawa, Kansas. 1992.

Eakin, Joanne Chiles. *Tears and Turmoil, Order #11.* Distributed by Blue and Grey Book Shoppe, Independence, MO. 1996

Eakin, Joanne C. and Hale, Donald, Compiled by. *Branded as Rebels.* A list of Bushwhackers, Guerrillas, Partisan Rangers, Confederates and Southern Sympathizers from Missouri during the War Years. Printed by Wee Print, 3437 S. Noland, Independence, MO 64055. 1993.

Farley, Alan W. "When Lincoln Came to Kansas Territory." Excerpts from an address to the Fort Leavenworth Historical Society, Fort Leavenworth, Kansas, 17 November 1959. *Abraham Lincoln in Kansas Territory: December 1 to 7, 1859.* Pamphlet. Fort Leavenworth, Kansas.

Fellman, Michael. *Inside War: The Guerrilla Conflict in Missouri During the American Civil War.* New York. Oxford University Press. 1989.

Frazier, Harriet C. *Runaway and Freed Slaves and Those Who Helped Them, 1763-1865.* McFarland @ Company, Inc., Publishers. Jefferson, North Carolina, and London.2001

Hale, Donald R. *They Called Him Bloody Bill—The Missouri Badman Who Taught Jesse James Outlawry.* The Printery, Clinton, MO. 1992.

Gerlach, Russel L. *Settlement Patterns in Missouri: A Study of Population Origins, with a Wall Map.* University of Missouri Press. Columbia, Missouri. 1986.

Gill, Thos F. *History of the Gill Family.* Standard Printing Co.1893. Hannibal, Missouri. (This small book is presently located in the fireproof vault in the basement of the Byron C. Shutz residence.)

Gilmore, Donald L. *Civil War on the Missouri-Kansas Border.* Pelican Publishing Company, Inc. Gretna, Louisiana. 2006.

Hale, Donald R. *We Rode with Quantrill: Quantrill and the Guerrilla War as Told by the Men and Women Who Were With Him, with a True Sketch of Quantrill's Life.* 1974. Reprinted (privately). 1992. Lees Summit, Missouri.

Leslie, Edward E. *The Devil Knows How to Ride: The True Story of William Clarke Quantrill and His Confederate Raiders.* Random House. 1996. New York.

McCorkle, John. *Three Years with Quantrill: A True Story Told by His Scout.* Originally published Armstrong, MO. Armstrong Herald Press. 1914. Written by

O. S. Barton. Notes by Albert Castel. Commentary by Herman Hattaway. University of Oklahoma Press. Norman and London. 1992.

Nelson, Earl J. "Missouri Slavery: 1861-1865." *Missouri Historical Review,* Volume XXVIII No. 4 July 1934. State Historical Society of Missouri. Columbia, Missouri.

Paludan, Philip Shaw. "The Meaning of the Civil War." Lecture. May 28, 1993. University of Kansas. Lawrence, Kansas.

Paludan, Phillip Shaw. *The Presidency of Abraham Lincoln.* University Press of Kansas. 1994.

Paludan, Phillip Shaw. *Victims. A True Story of the Civil War.* The University of Tennessee Press, Knoxville.

Petersen, Paul R. *Quantrill of Missouri—The Makings of a Warrior; The Man, the Myth, and the Soldier.* Cumberland House, Nashville, Tennessee. 2003.

"Quantrill Letters." Kansas Collection, Kenneth L. Spencer Memorial Library. The University of Kansas. Lawrence, Kansas.

Rollins, Laura Hickman. *A Diary of a Missouri Girl of the 1860s.* Edited by Laura Rollins Hockaday, her great-granddaughter. 1973.

Sheridan, Richard. "Victims and Consequences." Lecture. May 27, 1993. University of Kansas. Lawrence, Kansas.

Sheridan, Richard B., Editor and Compiler. *Freedom's Crucible: The Underground Railroad in Lawrence and Douglas County, Kansas, 1854-1865: A Reader.* Division of Continuing Education, The University of Kansas. 1998.

Stuewe, Paul K. Editor, *Kansas Revisited: Historical Images and Perspectives.* Division of Continuing Education, The University of Kansas. 1990. Castel, Albert. "The Bloodiest Man in American History", reprinted with permission from *American Heritage.* American Heritage Volume II, Number 6, 1960.

Willoughby, Robert J. *"I'll Wade in Missouri Blood":* Daggs v. Frazier: A Case of Missouri Runaway Slaves. *Missouri Historical Review, The State Historical Society of Missouri, Columbia.* Volume XCIX, Number 2, January 2005., page 115.

Author's Notes

Pungo River Passage

The village in this story was inspired by a small town located on one of the many rivers of North Carolina. The author and his wife often visited such villages during the years they piloted a series of pleasure crafts they owned along the east coast of the United States from as far north as Maine to the Florida Keys.

The Quarter Mile

For this story the author drew on his experiences as a student the last two years of high school at a college preparatory school for boys in Minnesota. His own experiences there were very positive, despite the travails encountered by his main character in the story. He did attempt, however, to recreate some of the atmosphere that can exist in such schools.

The Writing Workshop

After retirement from active business, the author resumed an interest in writing short fiction that he had enjoyed as a student early in his life at the University of Kansas. He enrolled in a short fiction writing class at the University of Missouri-Kansas City where he received encouragement. He also participated in a group writing program in the evenings and attended a one-week Advanced Short Fiction writing class at the University of Iowa.

Siblings

This is one of the author's early stories. He worked on it off and on over the next year or two until he became satisfied with it.

The Board Member

Another story that draws to some degree on the author's experiences as a businessman. However, the plot and characters are entirely a product of his imagination.

The Late Arrival—A Ghost Story for Children

The author wrote this early short story while an undergraduate at the University of Kansas, drawing on the experiences he had as a desk clerk at the Paradise Inn in the Mount Rainier National Park the summer he was nineteen years old.

Going Back

This story also relates to the author's experiences the summer of 1947 when he had a job as desk clerk at a hotel in one of the national parks in the Pacific Northwest.

Family

The author began this story about 1995 and worked on it periodically. In some respects, it is one of his favorites.

The Walnut Desk

This story was written for the author's grandchildren. As a boy, he was fortunate in being able to live a part of the summer for several years with his family on the farm owned by his maternal grandfather.

Terror at the Door

First published in 2001 by The Patrice Press in Tucson, Arizona, the author has included the novella in this collection because he is still pleased with it.

Byron Shutz
Kansas City, Missouri—2010

Edwards Brothers,Inc!
Thorofare, NJ 08086
25 August, 2010
BA2010237